Very engaging ... I was drawn in and could easily identify with Ms. Crovo's characters as they experienced life's delights as well as bittersweet moments. Emotionally powerful!

—Mary Anne Trollo, educator

I am sorry for a wonderful read to end. This is a very satisfying first novel peopled with beautifully developed characters and life lessons readers can identify with.

—Suzanne Teel, avid reader

MORE THAN
GOOD-BYE

To Janet —
May you enjoy
and find joy is
reading it

D. Carol Gross

MORE THAN
GOOD-BYE

As one journey ends, another begins.

S. CAROL CROVO

Tate Publishing & Enterprises

Published by Tate Publishing & Enterprises, LLC
127 E. Trade Center Terrace | Mustang, Oklahoma 73064 USA
1.888.361.9473 | www.tatepublishing.com

Tate Publishing is committed to excellence in the publishing industry. The company reflects the philosophy established by the founders, based on Psalm 68:11,
"The Lord gave the word and great was the company of those who published it."

Book design copyright © 2010 by Tate Publishing, LLC. All rights reserved.
Cover design by Kandi Evans
Interior design by Stefanie Rooney

Published in the United States of America

ISBN: 978-1-61566-981-3
1. Fiction, Family Life
2. Fiction, Afterlife
10.03.01

DEDICATION

To my husband, Joe, who believed in my vision, supported me in the process, and fortified me through my frustrations. The words are mine, but the book is ours.

ACKNOWLEDGMENTS

With thanks and love to my husband, Joe, and my daughters, Jenna and Rebecca, for their love and support and for allowing me time aside from my chores to write. Couldn't resist. Haha.

With thanks and love …

To my mom, Teel, who persevered through life's challenges and taught me to do the same. Will we ever know who got the talent from whom?

To my grandmother Frome, who gave unconditional love and left me with wonderful memories and who was also a great storyteller.

To my uncle Albert, the great storyteller, the inspiration for my aspiration as that is what every writer aspires to be, a great storyteller. To my aunt Inez for keeping my uncle Albert off of the hill and very happy.

To my great in-laws, Joe, Sue, Betty, and Myron, for their support and enthusiasm.

To my two dogs, Casey and Maggy, and my seven cats, Buster, Samantha, Neko, Melanie, Barney, Ashley, and Rhubarb, for being my devoted four-legged companions!

To Bonnie and Jeff for editing, proofreading, photographing, supporting, and for being the best neighbors and friends.

To Larry and Lynette and the entire staff of the Market Basket for giving me my own little table in the corner to write at and the *best* cup of coffee and town.

And …

To *God*, from whom to each a gift is given. Not one is left lacking. Let each nourish the seed that is within, and may this book, in its own small way, be a testament to the potential that lies in wait in each of us.

CHAPTER 1

Images flashed like a home movie that had lost control. Each frame was a memory moving faster and faster. School days, birthdays, weddings, babies born, loved ones passing: she recognized them all. Memories, her memories, and when the last image revealed itself, all that was left was light, an all-consuming, warm, white burst of illumination.

The train station where Jane found herself was actually quite pleasant. Sitting on a slatted wooden bench, she was surrounded by trees with branches in bloom hanging over her as cathedral arches. The ornate Victorian station would have normally been a place for pleasant repose and anticipation of an upcoming journey if not for one momentous problem; where she now sat was not here a mere moment before. The last place that Jane could remember being was seated next to her husband in a car, so how was she now seated on a bench at a train station? She felt all right, not ill or injured in any manner that she could detect. In fact, she felt keenly aware of everything that surrounded her. Rising from the bench, she took a few steps and then, stopping, looked around. People scurried about on the brick paved walkway that bordered the train track. Everything seemed so normal just like any other train station, but it wasn't. It couldn't be. Shaking her head, she still could not believe what her eyes were seeing. This could not be right. Not one person looked familiar to her, and there was something else. It was the end of November. Jane certainly was not sitting at a train station in her home state of Maine, which at this time was under an early foot and a half of snow. How on earth did she get here, and a more important question was, where on Earth was here?

Standing in this strange place, she should have felt terrified and frantic, yet without knowing why, she felt peaceful and safe. Her surroundings were a comfort to her. Jane had always loved traveling by train. She and David had traveled by train to the Pocono Mountains for their honeymoon. The architecture of the station itself reminded her of the rambling Victorian that she and David had raised their children in and still called home, but this place was definitely not home. Another strange thing: there were two trains waiting in the station, and they were waiting in the opposite direction on the same track. Jane almost laughed at the comical sight of the two cabooses parked snuggly up against each other while the rest of their respective cars seemed to be in a huff and just waiting to pull away. And still the people scurried by, boarding one train or the other, and still no one looked the least bit familiar. Jane began to pace, looking for someone of authority to ask where she was. She tried to make eye contact, but people just smiled without saying a word, not delaying a single step in their stride. Even when Jane stopped and asked someone, he only paused briefly, smiled pleasantly, and then, without a word in answer, continued walking. Everyone else may have been smiling, but Jane was beginning to get angry. Finally, she stood amidst all of these smiling, scurrying people and yelled.

"Can anybody tell me where I am?"

No one seemed to have noticed or to even have minded at all that some strange, middle-aged woman was standing in the middle of the walkway yelling that she did not know where she was; they just kept walking and boarding. "I know," Jane said. "Somehow I have lost my mind and I have gone crazy or I'm hallucinating or maybe it was something that I ate. Oh why did this have to happen now? We had such a nice evening...David..." she yelled skyward, "kids...get help...I'm here...Get Sylvia...I need a pill or something to fix this." There was no response.

She smiled a little at the thought of her family: David, their children, and their grandchildren. Her eyes closed tightly as the thoughts caused tears to seep through the vision. Such feelings of loneliness and isolation enveloped Jane that she preferred the darkness of her closed eyes to the chilling view of these unknown, smiling strangers. Quietly, someone took her hand and, cupping it gently, began patting the top of her hand subtly. Jane's eyes remained closed as the consoling gesture connected as one that she had experienced so many times before. It was a soothing rhythm, as a tonic to a child's heart when at rest in the calm and security of a parent's embrace.

"Jane," said a man's voice.

Jane opened her eyes and saw a young man, in his early twenties, standing before her, his hand holding hers. He was tall, nearly six feet, with gentle yet strong brown eyes and unkempt brown hair touched with flecks of gold. She should have felt intimidated, as Jane only stood on tiptoe at five foot four, but she wasn't.

"How do you know my name?" Jane asked. "I must apologize if I am supposed to know who you are, but right about now I am so confused that I am not even sure of who I am.

Although I did respond to my name, so I must not be totally out of my mind."

The young man laughed. "You are not lost at all. You are, in fact, exactly where you are supposed to be. Let's have a seat over here so that we can talk."

They walked over to the same bench where Jane had first found herself. He gently assisted her as she sat down, and then he sat down beside her, once again cupping her hand within his and patting it gently. A breeze stirred and brought with it the fresh scent of lilac.

"I love the fragrance of lilac." Jane inhaled deeply. "It is always a reminder that spring really does come, even after the mounds and mounds of winter snow." She paused but then was jolted back to her present situation. "Could you please tell me where I am?"

He smiled. "Jane, there are times when what we have to say is difficult and there is just no easy or right way of saying what we have to say. This is one of those times."

Jane looked at him quizzically. Once he told her where she was, she was going to make sure to remember it, because these people were nothing short of strange and she was never coming back here! She knew that she had a piece of paper and a pen somewhere; she was going to write the name of this place down. Now, where did she leave her purse?

He gently reached for her hands and stopped her search for her purse, redirecting her gaze into his eyes. "You will not find your purse, Jane." He was trying to be as delicate with his words as he possibly could. "You have passed, Jane, and that is why nothing is familiar to you and nothing is now as it was."

In that moment she almost laughed; she was not the crazy one to be sure. "That is a pleasant way of putting it. Passed, that means dead, right?"

He kept her hand firmly in his. "In plain language, yes, you are dead. I am your chosen guider, and I am here to show you the path, the path of your life that continues beyond what you have known and enlightens that which has yet to be seen."

She jerked her hand from his and stood up, taking a large step back. This whole place was crazy, and he was crazy too! She was only fifty-six years old! She had many wonderful years ahead of her. She had a husband that adored her! She had strong grown sons that were all married, thank God, and grandchildren! She was in the best physical condition of her life. She walked every day and gave up almost every food that tasted really good because so called experts said they were not healthy. Did this smiling, smug simpleton actually think that she would accept that she had given up chocolate only to have some person that she had never seen before tell her that she died anyway! She was not about to believe it!

"Look, golden boy"—she glared at him furiously—"I do not know who you are, and I do not care. You are probably some druggie that slipped me some mind-altering substance. God only knows that I've seen it happen enough times. I do know one thing though: I am getting away from you, away from here, and I am going home."

Jane looked around for a car or a taxi, but there were none, so she started walking as quickly as she could. She glanced briefly behind her and saw him sitting in the same spot, watching. There was no sense of time. She just kept walking, but things started to look familiar. The green grass gave way to snow-covered hills, and the trees, once adorned with blossoms, were now dressed in white. How could her location have changed so quickly? It did not matter; she knew that she was just about home.

Sure enough, there was her street: Lilac Lane. That was another reason why she liked lilacs. There was her house at the top of the hill, a rambling Victorian wrapped in clapboards with a collection of odd-shaped windows, wooden gingerbread at the eaves, and two huge, welcoming oak front doors.

She stopped. It looked like the finest castle in her eyes. It had the best view of the ocean in town, she was proud to say. The wraparound porches, she always thought, were like arms that wrapped around the people that she loved. The stately turret stood guarding the left corner of the house. Her kids, when they were little, were sure that on just the right day they could see all of the way to England from its windows. She laughed. So many happy memories, so much laughter, and so much love. Jane could not wait to get home.

"David, I'm home!" she yelled as she burst through the door. There was no reply. "I have never heard such quiet, and—good Lord—it smells like a florist shop in here." She looked around and noticed that all of the downstairs rooms were filled with flowers. The living room, the dining room, the library, and the play nook, aptly named by her grandchildren as it usually overflowed with toys and books, were now over-flowing with flowers. The kitchen was not only full of flowers but full of food as well! Suddenly, like a shooting pain in her stomach, it struck her.

"Oh no," she gasped out loud. "Someone must have died." Pausing a moment, she flashed back to her most recent unpleasant experience but discarded the possibility, immediately unwilling to consider the absurdity. Jane's practical nature took control. "Who could it have been?" she asked herself out loud. "Mom, Sylvia, or… oh this is maddening! I have to know who… I have to help. Where is everyone?" she yelled to ears that could not hear and to lips that would not answer. A voice did finally answer, but it was not one that she expected.

"It is not your mom or Sylvia or anybody else that is dead, Jane. I am afraid that you are."

The voice came from behind her, and she spun around. There he was again, the young man from the train station. How dare he follow her home! How dare he continue with these outrageous lies! Somebody was dead. That much was probably true, but it was certainly not her.

"Look, you ... " she hissed.

"I believe that you called me Golden Boy," he responded good-heartedly.

"Fine." She was exasperated. "Look, Golden Boy, I am not in a joking mood. This is my house, and you are in my house, uninvited and unwelcome. It looks as if someone has died, and if you cannot tell me who, with honesty, then get out of here before I call the police!"

The young man looked kindly at Jane. "Can I ask you some questions that may help you answer your own question?" She nodded her head with a wary yes. "Jane, how did you get from the train station to your home?"

"Well, I walked," she responded, though a little uncomfortable with her simplistic explanation.

"And, how did you, a fifty-six-year-old woman, walk from a warm climate with blossoms and green grass to a cold climate with snow on the ground? How did you know which direction to take? Were there road signs? How did your house suddenly appear from seemingly nowhere?"

"Well," she said, feeling even more uncomfortable, "as I mentioned before, you probably gave me some mind-altering drug, and I have probably been home all along. The drug just wore off, and here I am," she said a little too brightly.

"How do you explain all of the flowers?" he questioned her gently.

"Well, it is obvious that someone has died," she shot back impatiently, "and I do not see how any of your questions have helped to answer my question. My family needs me, and I need some answers so that I can help them."

"Perhaps," the young man said, "you should read some of the cards that are with the flowers. What is written on the cards may answer your question."

Jane chided herself for not having thought of reading the cards in the first place. She grabbed one of the cards from one of the arrangements that was closest to her but paused before reading it. The mysterious young man stood before her waiting, and distrust filled her thoughts, or was it fear that made her pause? She pushed her thoughts aside and began to read:

Dearest Bell Family,

Words cannot express our shock and sorrow at the sudden loss of Jane. She was a guiding light in our community. Our thoughts and our prayers are with you all. She was so loved, and she will be dearly missed.

Pastor Beale & the Beacon Lutheran Church

The card slipped from Jane's hand, and as the young man stretched toward her, she brushed him aside and rushed to another floral arrangement and reached for the card. She read it and, once again, let the card slip to the floor. Panic set in as Jane went from arrangement to arrangement and as each card slipped to the floor; the message did not change. Finally, she came to a simple collection of dried wildflowers, lovingly and carefully arranged by hand and placed in a well-used old blue canning jar. The message was simple:

Dear Grandmom,

We know that you are in heaven, but we will miss you and we love you.

Love,
Stephen, Ryan, and Olivia

Holding the small, handwritten card to her heart, Jane fell to the floor and sobbed. How could it be true? How could she be dead? She tried not to believe it, but what about all of the cards and the flowers? The tears continued to pour from her eyes, not for the loss of her life, but for the loss of the people that she loved. Just the thought of not seeing David, her children, and her grandchildren again was unbearable; she did not even have the chance to say good-bye or tell them how much that she loved them.

Time passed; how much time, Jane did not know. The tears slowed, and resignation began to inch its way into Jane's mind along with some hesitant curiosity. Lifting her head from the palms of her hands, she gazed around at the still-familiar room. If she was dead, what was she still doing here? She was not alone, for sitting in her husband's favorite chair was the young man, Golden Boy. Her ire began to rise in her again but then quickly subsided. He had such kind, concerned, and caring eyes that she could not be angry with him again; besides, Jane still had a lot of questions.

"Okay," Jane began, exhausted but still unconvinced, "if I am dead, and I do mean *if,* how did it happen? How did I die?"

The young man rose and walked over to Jane. He gently helped her to her feet, then guided her by her arm to the sofa. He took the seat beside her and faced her, taking her hand into his.

"You just went through a very tough time, Jane," he said, patting her hand. "It gets a little better from this point forward, and you will understand a lot more."

"If I am dead, it can't get any worse," she said then suddenly started. "Unless I am going to hell! I am not going to hell, am I?"

The young man could not help himself; he had to laugh.

"No, you are not going to hell! Hell really is not what it has been made out to be, but we are not ready to talk about that yet. Not that you are going to hell anyway, mind you. Now, let's get back to your first question: how did you die? Tell me what you remember. What are your most recent memories?"

"Well…" Jane thought back and then smiled. "Last night, I mean I think that it was last night. We were at my son Michael's house. They gave us a thirty-fifth wedding anniversary party. It was wonderful! Our whole family was there and some of our friends. The house was decorated for Christmas. David and I were married on Thanksgiving Day, so it is our family tradition that in honor of our anniversary, our house is always decorated for Christmas by Thanksgiving, and our kids have continued the tradition. Oh, it was just the most wonderful evening! Then David and I left, and then we got into the car..." Her voice faded. "The car," she continued. "Did something happen in the car? Did I become ill? Did I have a heart attack? Or was there..." Panic rose in her voice. "An accident?"

The young man continued to pat her hand gently. "You and David were driving home from the party. Can you remember anything else?"

Jane nodded. "Yes, David and I were in the car. We were talking and laughing and reminiscing about the party. We were driving, driving... It was dark, and I remember seeing a few houses with Christmas lights, and I remember looking at David's face, and I remember touching his hand, and I remember..." Her voice grew louder as her mind raced faster to think, to see what had happened.

"You won't remember the accident, Jane," he said to her softly. "Your mind protects you from such traumatic memories. It is there but not in a place that is available to you."

"How do you expect me to believe that I am dead from an accident that I cannot even remember?" she said, pulling her hand from his. "How can you expect me to accept my future and my fate from the words of a stranger... *you?* How can you expect me to accept that the only life that I have ever known is over and I cannot even remember how it happened or why? How can I ever believe..." Her voice trailed away into whispers.

"Jane," he said to her gently, "do you remember getting home after the party?" Jane's eyes snapped to attention at his question. "Do you remember the champagne toast that you and David were supposed to have when you got home that night? Do you remember sleeping in your bed that night? Do you remember the conversation that you always have with your mom the day after any family event?"

Jane felt as if she were frozen. Though her mind scattered frantically through her thoughts to find the answers to his questions, she physically could not move. She finally turned to him as she realized that she had no memory past the drive home that night with David. Nothing; there was just nothing. The only thing that she could remember was the drive, the car, and David, nothing after that. Continuing to stare at her companion blankly, for an instant her expression brightened as she imagined the toast, a good night's sleep in her own bed, and even a lively conversation with her mother as it should have happened and as it would have happened if she could only remember. But her imagination quickly failed her as reality replaced fantasy and drew stark reminder to the moments that had never been and never would be. The darkness resumed, and with it, the emptiness of thought that appeared boundless and infinite. In that horrifying awareness, she knew it to be true; she was dead.

"You and David were driving home after the party. A car went through a red light and hit the car that you and David were driving in. The collision impacted your side of the car; you died instantly."

"David!" Jane cried out. "What about David?"

"David is okay," he said soothingly. "His right arm is broken, and he is a little bruised, but overall physically he is okay. Mentally and emotionally is where he is hurting the most. He loves you very deeply. It will take time."

Jane was too shocked to cry. David. She wanted so much to comfort him and wrap her arms around him and hold him tight. He was a strong man and he had their children and their grandchildren to help him through this, but they had always been their strongest when they were together. The loneliness that he must be feeling overwhelmed even her own feelings of isolation, and her need to console him and to embrace him was unbearable.

"Where are they now?" she asked

"They are at the funeral home," he replied. "You can see them if it would be helpful. You need to understand that they cannot see you or hear you. You can even touch them, and they will not feel your physical presence. It is thought that once we pass, we are no longer felt by those left behind in a physical sense, but it is debated by many of us that we can still be felt in a spiritual sense, especially when there is great need."

"What do you think?" Jane asked, looking intently at his face.

"Well…" A solemn expression bordering on sadness crossed his face. "It has been many years since I have passed, but the times that I have touched those that I have loved in their time of need, I have seen an expression of comfort lighten their face, if only for a few moments. To give that comfort, if only for an instant, is the closest that I can ever come to touching them and sharing in their lives and their love as I once did. This has been my experience, but it is not accepted as fact." He regained his easy expression and placed his arm on Jane's shoulder. "We never stop choosing our own paths to follow, no matter the journey. You now find yourself on a new journey, and you still have many paths to choose; you must choose one now. Use your compass, your heart. It seldom leads us in the wrong direction."

"I want to see them," Jane stated with conviction.

"Okay," the young man said. "Remember what I said before about it getting a little better from this point forward?"

"Yes," Jane responded hesitantly.

"I may have been a bit hasty in my judgment," he added, putting his hand on her shoulder.

Often, the most beautiful building in town is the funeral home. The funeral home in Jane's town was no exception. It stood, a stately brick federal structure with candle lights in every window, on a tree-lined street just off of the main thoroughfare in town. Jane must have passed the J.H. Edwards Funeral Home almost every day, and she had always admired its beautiful architecture, without having thought too much about its purpose. As she approached the brick edifice now, she was keenly and uncomfortably aware of its role. She grabbed the young man's hand as they walked up the steps together, trying to gather as much strength as possible to be able to withstand what was to come.

They entered the foyer, and the first thing that hit Jane was the smell—a putrid combination of flowers and formaldehyde. She had smelled it before, as she was no stranger to funeral homes, yet the smell always repulsed her. No matter the graceful brass chandelier, the seemingly comfy overstuffed benches, or the serene paintings that graced the walls, nothing could disguise the smell of death or its connected feelings of doom in a funeral home. She wanted to leave, but she could not.

"I wish that they had buried me in the backyard or, better yet, buried me at sea. At least the fish would have been fed," she whispered. The young man patted her arm. "I hate funeral homes," Jane added, "and I cannot stand old man Edwards. He looks as if he died twenty years earlier and is now just a walking zombie with some cadaver's smile attached to his face. That smile never changes."

They walked down the hall and came to a room with the door closed. The pedestal stand next to the door displayed Jane's name. She caught her breath when she read her own name.

"Why are the doors closed?" she asked.

"Well, it is still rather early, and this is a private time for the family. Are you ready to go in?" he asked. Jane nodded.

The first thing that struck her was the flowers. They lined the walls, rested on tables, and were even nestled on the few windowsills in the room. There was a kaleidoscope of color everywhere, and the fragrance almost made her forget the formaldehyde. This vision was momentary as her eyes focused on the front of the room. There they stood—her husband, David, surrounded by their family in front of her coffin encircled by a bower of blossoms. Jane could not move. It was too beautiful and to horrible to be real. There they stood—the people that she loved most in the world, grieving, and she was helpless to comfort them.

"Jane," the young man's voice called to her, "go to them."

Jane walked forward and stood behind them. She listened to their whispered words. She watched them reach for each other's hands. She looked as tears streamed down their faces. She knelt beside them as they knelt, and she gently stroked their arms as they each, one by one, reached forward to touch the coffin, to touch her. Then, without understanding why, yet knowing that she should, she stood before each member of her family, and she wrapped her arms around them. Their pain and their anguish struck her first, which only made her hold on tighter. When the pain and the anguish subsided, she felt warmth, as if she were melting into their spirit and into their soul. Love was there. Laughter was there. Hope was there. Conviction was there. Joy was there. She was there. Everything that she had given of herself to them was alive in them and would always be alive in them. She felt so peaceful, and at that moment when she looked into their faces, she could see a calm pass over them. It was only for a moment, but at that moment she knew what Golden Boy had meant. She had touched them. She had touched what was already inside of them, the purest part of her, which was her love for each of them. This is what she had seen cross their faces. She was with them, and she would always be with them; they would be okay.

She stepped away and walked to the back of the room and just stared. It was a portrait she wanted to preserve in her mind. Even in this moment of sadness, it was enough just to be with them and to be near them and to see them. How could she ever turn her eyes away? How could she ever turn her back and walk away? Although the experience of joining in their spirits had warmed her, it was not enough to sustain her. Jane took a seat and stared, willing to spend all of eternity with this vision of her family rather than live all of eternity without them. It was a cruel irony, the shock from the realization of her own death and the pain from her separation from her loved ones felt as if it were killing her, and she was already dead. Golden Boy walked forward and took the seat next to her.

"Jane," he said, "your family will be leaving soon."

"I will follow them," she stated flatly.

"You can't," he said gently. "This life is for those that live in it. We live too but in a different place than they do. Each of us has a responsibility to fulfill our place in the phases of life. You are no longer a part of this place, this phase. You must move on, and you will come to know it and to understand it."

As his words ended, Jane's family turned from the casket and began to move toward the door in the back of the room. Jane reached for each of them as they passed as if to hold them back. She did not want them to leave. They were the only life that she had ever known, and a life without them meant no life at all. They passed without responding to her touch and when they were gone the room was empty except for Jane, Golden Boy, and the casket. Jane dissolved into sobs, and the young man waited patiently for the tears to subside. Her tears slowed, and finally she sat in numb exhaustion.

"What do I do now?" she asked mundanely.

"Now"—the young man motioned—"we take a walk."

CHAPTER 2

They left the funeral home and walked in silence. Jane did not know where she was, nor did she care. She did not notice as they walked, the trees began to lose their snowy cover and blossom. The air swirled with fragrance, and Jane drew a great breath into her lungs. The birds sang cheerfully, and the gloom that had so enshrouded Jane faded slightly. The world was still alive, and she, in her own way, was too. She began to think that it was time to look at what was ahead of her rather than long for what was behind her. As long as she could still think and feel, something of what was her still remained. Many questions began to enter her thoughts. Jane stopped and sat on a fallen log under the shade of a tree.

"Golden Boy, what was the purpose of what I just went through? It seemed like a cruel process unworthy of the heavenly kindness that is promised in the afterlife. Why wasn't I just shown the light, you know, the light at the end of the tunnel? If that was heaven's welcome, it needs some work."

The young man sat next to her on the log. He smiled while he thought, trying to carefully choose his words.

"Just as life is a process, death is a process," he said. "Death does not engender sudden and complete enlightenment. It is truly an awakening, an awakening that is slow and progressive. As much as death is perceived as an end to life, it is really a transition. This transition guides us into transformation, a rebirth of sorts. Just as we were born before, we are born again, and we need to grow and understand as if we were children once more. The first thing that we must understand is our passing from one phase of life into another; to understand it is to first be able to acknowledge our own death. This is one thing that life does not prepare us for, our own death. Think about it. We mourn and acknowledge the death of others, but do we ever really acknowledge and accept our own mortality? Yes, we understand in the back of our minds that someday we are going to die, but we will fight to the end for our last breath, for our life. It is human nature, the will to survive, which is a good thing, but it does not prepare us for the arrival of the inevitable. So, Jane, you have achieved the first stage of your transformation, the acceptance of your own passing from the life that you had known. And now or eventually you will come to believe that death is not the end of life regardless of the fear associated with it. Death is merely a period at the end of one sentence that allows a new sentence and a new paragraph to begin."

"Well." Jane let out a breath of heavy resignation. "I do not know that your explanation makes me feel any better, but it does explain things. You certainly present a good argument." She added wryly. "You must have been a lawyer in your previous life."

Golden Boy laughed. He liked Jane Wilma Krysochowski

Bell. He liked her sense of humor even in the face of the most difficult situation that she had probably ever experienced. This was his first experience as a guider. It was not easy; however, it had been rewarding so far. He looked at Jane. She had a kind yet no-nonsense face with a fair share of laugh lines. She seemed much taller than her actual height; there was strength and confidence to her carriage. Her brown hair with its hints of gray framed her face and her warm brown eyes, and her mouth, though strained, he knew was more accustomed to smiling. Yes, he liked Jane. He was proud of how she had handled herself so far, and he was glad he could be there to help her with what was to come.

They stood up and continued walking and before long were back at the quaint train station. Jane could not believe that she was back at the wacky train station again! The station was no longer bustling with people, yet the two trains remained parked, caboose to caboose, on the same track. Steam from the two trains erupted into the air, seemingly exuding impatience. *What are they in a hurry about?* Jane thought. It did not seem as if a clock had a place in eternity. Golden Boy and Jane walked over to what was becoming Jane's familiar bench and took a seat. There was quiet: no conversation, only the sound of the hissing trains communicated their intent. This gave Jane some time to think. It was obvious that there was a reason for their return to the train station, but what was the reason? She glanced at her young companion sitting next to her. He certainly did not seem as if he were in a hurry. This sense of timelessness was beginning to wear on Jane. There had to be more to this new life than sitting around watching nothing go by. Jane cleared her throat.

"Excuse me," she asked, "what are we doing at this train station again? I will admit that it is a lovely train station and I love traveling by train, but why are we here?"

He turned toward her and looked at her very seriously and

intently. The words he was about to use must be chosen carefully, as the offer he was about to make was certain to be a bit overwhelming. She could handle it, he was sure, but which offer would she choose? It was important that he be candid; it was vital to her decision.

"Jane," he said in a serious tone, "do you remember when I talked about how life does not prepare you for death?"

"Yes." Jane was taken aback a little by the seriousness in his voice.

"When people die suddenly and seemingly before their time, as you did, it is often very difficult to accept and to journey into the next phase of life without having had the opportunity of saying good-bye to the life they knew."

What was this all about? How could she say good-bye to those she had loved when she was dead in their life and they were not alive in hers? What had been somewhat clear was now becoming confusing again. Maybe she should just listen to what he had to say. Maybe there was a chance that there had been a mistake. Maybe this was her second chance. She was brought out of her thoughts by his voice.

"You see two trains before you," the young man stated. "The train on your right will take you on the journey into the next phase of your life. As I said before, it is a journey, and all will not become clear to you immediately. At some point you must and you will want to take this train. It is a journey that we all ultimately take, and to deny its undertaking is to deny life itself and the reason for our very existence. You will know when you are ready, and you may be ready right now."

He paused, and Jane became even more intrigued by the train on her left. Where could this train possibly be headed?

"The train on your left is offered to everyone that dies, and it can be especially important to those who die suddenly and without warning. It is understandable the torment that is faced when the only life that was ever known is taken away.

This is the chance that every person is offered to say good-bye to the life and the loves that they have known. Jane, you have the chance to live your life again, not to change it, only to live it and to see those you have loved and to say good-bye."

Jane was shocked. She stood up and just walked away a few steps. Her hands flew to her head, as if to steady it from disbelief. Her eyes took in the two trains. They seemed almost surreal taking on mystical qualities quite different from their original ordinary appearance. She could say good-bye? She could see her family again? She could hug them and feel them again? She was terrified and elated at the same time. She needed to know more. She turned from where she stood and faced him.

"You are saying"—she gulped—"that I can live my life again? How is this possible? What age will I be? Will my family know me? Will they be able to see me and to feel me? How long will it last? Do I just hug them, tell them that I love them, and then say good-bye? Will anything in my life change?"

"Let's try to answer your questions one at a time," he said calmly. "Yes, you can live your life over again in its entirety, or you can live just parts of it over again. You can be any age that you want to be. You can be a baby if you want, or you can be the age that you are right now."

Jane had to giggle at the thought of being a baby again. A baby; no, she had no desire to be in diapers again!

"How is this possible?" he continued. "When you were young, you believed that anything was possible. Life seemed limitless. Age and attitude changed your ability to believe, but the belief itself, that all things are possible, remained unchanged. It is possible because all things are possible; you need only believe to begin to transform possibility into actuality."

Somehow this young man, Golden Boy as she called him, did not seem so young anymore. She felt suddenly as if she were the child and that she had a lot to learn. When was the last time she had truly believed that anything was possible? She was no cynic to be sure, but being an adult certainly brought with it reality and responsibility. Just the thought of seeing her family again, to see them, to talk to them, and to hold them, brought warmth and hope back into her heart that had vanished. It was almost unbelievable, but belief was what this chance was all about, and she was ready to believe!

"No matter what age you choose to be," he added, "your life and the way that your life was lived, and is lived again, will be unchanged. Your family will know you, see you, and respond to you. You cannot make a mistake, because nothing can be changed through anything that you say or any action that you take. Instead of watching a home movie, you will be living a home movie with all of the happiness and the pain. The sad parts of your life can be skipped but cannot be eliminated. You may find that you do not want to skip anything because everything that you have experienced has made you the person that you are."

Jane pondered his words. She wanted this chance; there was no question in her mind. But how could she be a fifty-six-year-old woman in the body of perhaps a ten-year-old version of herself? It seemed almost silly and unrealistic. Maybe this was the adult in her talking. Maybe she should listen to the little nagging voice in her that seemed to be growing stronger and louder; to be ten years old again, what a wild, crazy, and wonderful thought! She knew the exact day on which she wanted to begin her journey. It still seemed crazy, but there was nothing to risk and everything to gain.

"Okay," she said in a tentative tone, though her body was almost bursting with excitement. "I want to be ten years old again. I want to see my mom, my dad, my sister, my grand-mom, and all of my friends, and I do not want to skip a thing!" Jane was becoming really excited. A weight had been lifted off of her heart. She knew that what she was about to experience would not last forever; she did not need forever! All that she needed was a chance, one last chance to love them again and to feel that love in return.

The young man stood and looked at her with a warm smile on his face without showing the least hint of disappointment. It pleased him to see her so happy; he had done his job, at least the first part of his job. His job was not to force her into something that she did not want to do; his job was to guide her into understanding what she should do, and this was only the first step in that process.

"Jane," his voice jolted her back into focus. "There are a few things that I want you to understand. When you return to being ten years old, your mind will no longer be the mind of a fifty-six-year-old woman. You will not be conscious of what has passed between us. You will only be aware of it when I am with you when I come to check in on you, which I will do on occasion. Your actions will be reflexive and will unfold naturally, not in a forced or a faked manner. Everything that has happened before will only cause you to appreciate more the experiences that you will revisit. It will feel as if you have been gone for a while and have suddenly returned and are happy to be home without any knowledge of ever having left. What has been in the past will once again be in the present accompanied by an increased sensitivity and enjoyment. As I have said, I will visit with you periodically to make sure that you are not having any problems. Again, it is only on these visits that you will be very aware of what is happening, but we will face that time when we come to it. Are you ready?" Jane nodded her head in a vehement yes. "Okay, on which date would you like to start? You said that you had a specific date in mind."

Her smile seemed to spread beyond the width of her face. "The date is July the twenty-first, my sister Ann's birthday, and it was the summer that I was ten years old. I am not really sure of the year; I still have the memory of a fifty-six-year-old woman, I am afraid. I hope that you can help me with that." He grinned and nodded. They turned to face the train, where it still stood patiently waiting. It had lost its foreboding façade and now seemed to be more welcoming. It stood alone as the other train had somehow left without her noticing. The steam from the remaining train still swirled, creating a light fog that gave just the tiniest hint that perhaps, once lifted, it might reveal sights unseen before or maybe just the sights of scenes forgotten. The young man motioned Jane toward the metal stairway, and without a band playing or the mournful shouts of good-bye, they both boarded the train.

They were the only two people on the train, which really was not surprising. It was an old train car; vintage Victorian it appeared to be and just the way that Jane liked them! *How odd a train,* she thought. Why had it not been a boat, a car, or a plane? Why did they need a train at all? There had to be a better and a more efficient means of travel given that she was now in the next, and hopefully more advanced, state of existence. She just had to ask. Her situation had not dampened her curious personality.

"I have to ask," she started, "why are we going by train? I mean we could have traveled by many different means; we could have just walked as we did before."

"What is your favorite way to travel?" he questioned.

She had chosen traveling by a train over a plane whenever possible; she guessed that, like her dad, she preferred that her feet remain on the ground. "You know," she added, "you ask even better questions than I do."

"It was still a fair question," he countered. "This is my first time as a guider, but I have heard a lot of stories from the guiders before me. One of the guiders had an astronaut, and they had to travel back in a spaceship. The poor fellow wound up with motion sickness. I am definitely with you; traveling by train is a much nicer way to get where you want to go."

"Motion sickness in the afterlife?" Jane quipped. "I thought that we would not have to deal with any of that unpleasantness. If you tell me that we still have problems with our weight, I am staying on this train no matter what you say!"

"There is no such thing as perfection, but there is progression and many more important meters for judging enlightenment other than the elimination of motion sickness. I can tell you with confidence, however, that scales are no longer needed."

Jane chuckled loudly and inwardly said amen. The train still had not moved, and when she glanced out of the window, the scene was still the same. Yes, it was a delightful vision. The train station was lovely, and the blossoming trees only enhanced its beauty, but she was anxious to see a scene that was more familiar to her. She began to shift in her seat and to fidget with her hands. A shrill whistle from the train interrupted her impatience. Steam began to billow from the train, as it prepared to leave, to such excess that it started to roll into the car through the open windows. Jane coughed, and in moments found herself wrapped in a wet and blinding steam that seemed to dissolve her surroundings. She felt the train jerk forward and then stop in what felt like only the passage of a second. The steam slowly cleared, and as it did Jane no longer felt a seat beneath her but rather the feel of soft earth covered in grass. Looking up, she saw the branches of a knotty oak tree, and how familiar it looked! She was home!

CHAPTER 3

How often she had sat beneath her favorite shade tree to enjoy its cooling canopy when the blazing breath of summer blew. Jane stood up, and as she did, a book slipped from her lap. Picking it up quickly, Jane read the title *Theodore Roosevelt, Fighting Patriot* by Clara Ingram Judson. She was one of her favorite authors! Jane loved to read biographies, and they were Judson's specialties. Placing the book gently under her arm, Jane turned slowly where she stood, taking in the scene that surrounded her. It was all there, the fields covered with ripening corn, the small apple orchard, the barn with the horses quietly grazing in the pasture, Mom's special barn and its accompanying field, the pig pen, and the house. She rubbed her eyes as if she had awakened from a dream, still a little unsure that what she was seeing was real. Although a question rested unsettled in the back of her mind, Jane cast the shapeless cloud aside and filled her mind instead with the glory of the sights that surrounded her. What joy she felt as she took it all in, inhaling it as a delicious scent; she just wanted to run and jump! A visit to Dad's horses would be her first destination, but as she started to run, the sound of a loud bell and an even louder voice stopped her bolting strides.

"Jane!" a woman's voice shouted, accompanied by the clanging sound of a bell. "Get home!"

That voice was definitely familiar, and that tone meant to get home quick! She changed the direction of her flight and bolted for the house. Slightly out of breath, she reached the covered side porch with the hefty bell attached to its post and burst through the screen door. Once inside, she stopped and once again looked around in wonder. The dining room where she stood looked crowded with its heavy wooden furniture and the large dish hutch spread across one entire wall of the room. To her right was the large living room with its big comfortable overstuffed furniture and the two needlepoint-covered rockers that rested in front of the fireplace. Family pictures lovingly crowded the walls, and all of the walls were painted a robin's egg blue, much like the color of the sky on a sunny day. The color was so reminiscent of the outdoors that it felt as if the floor should be spread with a plaid blanket and covered with picnic fare. It was seldom cloudy in this house. A door suddenly swung open, and into the dining room a woman entered.

It was Wilma, Jane's mom, and Jane could not help herself as she ran to hug her. She held on tight, and her mom returned her firm hold. Wilma was not a tall woman. She was only about five feet three inches, but she was a strong woman. She was dressed in her usual attire of long cotton pants, a plaid cotton button-down shirt with the sleeves rolled up above the elbows, and tennis shoes. Lightly curled brown hair fashioned in a crop cut framed her wide face. Her mouth seemed as if it could do battle with the best, and her eyes twinkled in jest.

The scent of apple blossoms and axle grease, Mom's signature fragrance, filled Jane's senses.

"Jane," said the stern yet quickly softening voice, "where have you been? You know that today is your sister's birthday and you are supposed to be helping Grandmom in the kitchen with the cooking."

"Babcia Grand," called a controlled and firm voice from the kitchen.

"Babcia Grand, sorry!" Mom yelled back and then in a lower voice continued, "you know how she gets when I am with her in the kitchen. She has already had her prayer beads out three times, and the only thing that I have done is boil water. I swear there is not a thing that I can do in the kitchen that pleases Grand Babcia." She finished with an exaggerated sweep of her arms. Wilma considered herself a domestic innovator as she once served a cake raw with the icing on the side, correctly observing that children like the batter better anyway. Her innovation was not welcomed by Babcia Grand, but Wilma's resignation from all cooking tasks was. Though a disastrous homemaker, Wilma was a master at fixing anything with gears or belts, feeling more at home in the barn than in the kitchen.

"Wilma Eugenia," a cold voice called out from the kitchen, "the stove boiled the water, and it is Babcia Grand."

"Jane," she continued in a kinder tone, "could you please help me in the kitchen?"

Wilma raised her arms in mock exasperation, but, welcoming any excuse to escape from the kitchen, she happily handed her apron to Jane and left the house. Jane was not about to wait for a second request from Babcia Grand as she quickly entered the kitchen.

Babcia Grand was leaning over the birthday cake, intently finishing the final row of rosettes as Jane entered the room. What a glorious cake it was with its four moist chocolate layers topped with butter cream frosting and decorated in a rainbow of colors. The blood of a four-star chef ran through her veins, and her family was the welcome benefactor of her talent. Straightening to turn her attention to Jane, Babcia Grand unexpectedly found herself embraced by her oldest granddaughter.

Nestling into her grandmother's embrace, Jane found familiar comfort. Alena Kaleen Krysochowski, or Babcia Grand as she was called by her grandchildren, had always lived with them even before the death of her husband. The farm was a family farm first owned by Alena and Aurek and in Aurek's passing, handed down to their son Filip. Well loved, respected, and looked to often for her commonsense, Alena was dressed, at all times, in a high collar pinned with a family heirloom cameo accompanied by prayer beads in her pocket; the perfect picture of propriety from an era that had passed.

Gently pulling herself from Jane's embrace, Alena smiled at her granddaughter. "Jane," she said with a smile in her steady voice, "I have missed your help today. I am a little disappointed that you were not here as you know that your mother has a few difficulties in the kitchen." Wilma's head suddenly appeared in one of the kitchen windows.

"Are you sure that I cannot help?" Wilma asked innocently.

"Well," Alena responded with just the slightest hint of sarcasm in her voice, "I would let you ice the cake, but it has already been baked." Wilma laughed.

"Oh Babcia Grand! I don't care what anybody says, you have a mean sense of humor. Already baked... I love it..." Her voice trailed away.

They worked away in the kitchen until the meal was just about prepared. It was now time to set the table as they would be enjoying their meal outside under the shade of the trees. Jane scurried to get the tablecloths. They were not ordinary tablecloths. Quilted with bold colors and patterns, they were made by Wilma, an age-old craft taught by Alena but given a new twist by Wilma. Alena was quite proud of her daughter-in-law's handiwork and their mutual toil was shared and enjoyed. Jane grabbed two of the tablecloths and was headed outside but instead found her exit blocked.

Filip Aurek Krysochowski, Jane's dad, stood in the doorway; in fact, he filled the doorway! He was a large man with an even larger heart, and despite his intimidating appearance, he was never afraid to show his love for his family. When he saw Jane, he took her into his arms and held her in a hug that almost made her disappear. Jane felt warm and protected, and she inhaled the scent of the earth and of growing and living things that were as intrinsic to his existence as the air that he breathed. Filip gently pulled his daughter from him so that he could take a look at her.

"Jane," he prodded, "why aren't you dressed for your sister's party? The company will be here shortly, and I know that you do not want to miss anything."

"Well," Jane responded a little breathlessly, "I was helping Babcia Grand in the kitchen, and we just finished, and now I have to put the tablecloths outside on the tables, and then I have to put the Baron in his pen so that he doesn't eat the cake like he did last year and then ... "

Filip put his hand up to quiet his daughter's overture of preparty activities. "Your mom is outside, and I am sure that she can place the cloths on the tables, and I can put the Baron in his pen so that you can get ready for the party. Don't forget to get what you need for the pig feed tonight," he said with a wink and then went on his way.

Jane's hands flew to her head. The pig feed, how could she forget? She flew up the stairs and into her room, and just as she was about to reach into the closet to grab for her clothes, she sensed someone in the room with her. He was standing there as she turned around—the young man, Golden Boy. The sight of him startled Jane at first, but then, the strange feelings that hid quietly in the back of her mind came forward. The memory of who he was and why she was here returned.

"I did not expect to see you so soon," Jane commented, and then having said it, she quickly grabbed her throat. Her voice seemed so strange, and, looking at the young man, she thought he seemed much taller than she had remembered. Suddenly she ran to the mirror and looked at her reflection, initially with shock and then with total amazement. She was ten again! No wrinkles, no gray hair, no budding arthritis, and no padding around the middle. A loud laugh escaped from her lips. She felt wonderfully possessed; a fifty-six-year-old mind in a ten-year-old's body! At least it was her own mind in her own body. The lightness and the agility felt so wonderful that she just could not help herself; she did a cart wheel right in the middle of the room and then with a loud thud collapsed into laughter.

"Jane!" called Babcia Grand from downstairs. "What are you doing up there that is making such a noise?"

Oh no, Jane knew that voice and that tone. She then made the kind of a mistake that a fifty-six-year-old would make; she told the truth.

"I'm sorry, Babcia Grand. I was just so excited about the party that I did a cartwheel in my room."

"Young ladies do not act in a rough and playful fashion inside of the house. Such behavior should take place outside, and even then it is not completely appropriate for a young..." Her voice was interrupted as Wilma issued her own opinion.

"Nonsense. It is important to stay well practiced in the art of indoor cartwheeling lest a sudden rain storm require a cartwheeling competition be moved indoors." Jane could well imagine her grandmother's look of exasperation at her mother's viewpoint. Looking at them both now from a fifty-six-year-old's perspective, Jane remembered and realized how much her mom's occasional silliness had lightened Babcia Grand's stalwart heart and how much Babcia Grand's steadiness had given her mom's spirit a firm foundation from which to fly. They were bound by their love for their family and their respect for each other, even though they did not always agree.

Jane turned her attention once more to the young man who was sitting very comfortably in her favorite reading chair. He looked to be in such a relaxed and peaceful state that he was almost ghostlike, an apparition. Maybe they were all just apparitions. This had a sobering effect on Jane but only temporarily. No matter what this actually was, she only acknowledged what she felt, and she felt wonderful!

"How are you doing?" he began with sincere concern in his voice. "This initial introduction can be a bit overwhelming, and I just wanted to check in with you to make sure that you were all right." Jane could not help herself as she ran to him and gave him a hug. "I would take this to mean that you are doing very well." He laughed. She sat at his feet and looked up at him.

"I understand the purpose of what I am experiencing, but what am I experiencing? Everything seems so real and just the same as it has always been, so how can it be again?" Jane asked.

"If your shadow is behind you, does it mirror where you stood before? If your shadow is in front of you, does it mirror where you have yet to stand? Either is possible as life extends behind and beyond where we stand, Jane. The only factor that determines where we are within that which is unending is the spot or the moment in which we are standing. Time was a limitation created to establish a beginning and an end where none has ever existed. How could what has been be again? Because what was still is. The only thing that begins and ends is us in this form, in this space. We exist in the moment in which we stand, where we have stood, and where we will stand in the future if it is in our past and in our future to exist in those moments. We need only to slow down or speed up to catch up with what was or what will be. The moment in which you now find yourself is July 21, 1957; it is exactly as it was and still is.

The reason that everything is so real is because you are real; you lived in this moment. We can experience any moment, but we can only truly live and exist in a moment in which we have lived or have yet to live. We can move through life in this way as you are doing, but we cannot shift or change that which has been. Life, in all of its forms and phases, continues on with or without us."

Jane pondered his words and promptly found herself even more confused. "So I am dead, some of those closest to me are dead, yet I now find myself alive at ten years of age, along with those who are now alive, who passed even before I did, and you tell me that all of this is real and that it really is July 21, 1957, just as it was when I was ten years of age, only that was forty-six years ago."

"Well, it is a bit more complicated than that," he added a little hesitantly.

"That is impossible, because I do not even understand what I just said," Jane countered.

"Remember what I said before, Jane: all things will not be clear to you immediately; it will take time and maturity. I know that it sounds funny discussing maturity with a woman who has lived a life of fifty-six years, and I am not trying to demean you, but you have entered into a new phase of life, and you have the understanding of a child in that life. There is a lot to learn. Right now I want to ask you a question. Were you alive on July 21, 1957, as well as all of the other individuals that you have come in contact with so far?" Jane nodded. "Then you need only understand that you have moved through life and you now stand and are living in the moment of July 21, 1957. That is enough to understand for now."

Jane was not sure that she understood it, but she could accept it, as her eyes and her mind were witnesses to what she saw and experienced. Everything seemed and felt real and alive, so why should she question? This was certainly better than her perceived notion of death, of lying rotting in some coffin lined in putrid silk. Her body could still be lying rotting somewhere, but at least she was not aware of it. The only thing that she was aware of was this moment. Maybe she was beginning to understand, if only a little bit. She did however, have one question.

"If we can only truly exist in our own life, then why have people seen the ghosts or spirits of people from the past? Why are they not just living in the moment that they existed before rather than in a moment where they do not belong?"

The young man's eyes widened. "Your question leads me to believe that you are starting to understand some of what I am telling you; I am impressed. A ghost is not a shadow or a spirit. Ghosts, as they are called, are not ghosts at all; they are individuals, just like you and me. Unfortunately, they are individuals that have often died tragically, and they are in search of revenge or they are in search of change. They take the opportunity to journey back into their lives, just as you have taken, not to say good-bye, but for the chance to right a wrong or to change an outcome. They are impossible tasks as a life once lived cannot be changed. They travel back into their own life and try to change what cannot be changed, and they travel forward to try to live in a life where they never existed. This is where you see them; they are translucent as they are unable to embody a moment in which they have never lived. It is a very sad situation, one that the individual and their guider can sometimes grapple with for centuries."

Jane felt as if her head was about to burst. She had had enough of past, present, future, lived, not lived, and who was alive and who was haunting who. It was not her wish to appear shallow or uninterested, but if she was on a journey of enlightenment, she did not want to suffer burnout on her first day. The aroma of tasty food and the sweet anticipation of birthday cake began to fill her senses and thoughts, and suddenly whatever had been on her mind before vanished. Whatever it was could wait until later. She sprung up off the floor, placed her book on the empty seat of her favorite reading chair, and headed for the closet. Dressing quickly for the party, she grabbed her extra clothes and headed down the stairs. Ann, her sister and the honored birthday girl, was, at the same time, headed up the steps and did not appear to be in the jolliest of moods.

Jane sat down on a step midway down and motioned for her stormy-faced sister to do the same. "What is that face of yours all about?" Jane asked and was promptly answered with a quickly protruded tongue. Jane gave her younger sister a nudge, which was returned with an even firmer nudge, which turned into a nudging match followed by laughter.

"Oh, Janie" Ann said, using her nickname for Jane, "Babcia Grand expects me to wear that d—" Ann's hand flew to her mouth, and her eyes scanned about suspiciously. Any slip of profanity heard in the house met with a litany of condemnation that bordered on eternal damnation from Babcia Grand. Worse still, she had the most acute hearing. "Janie," Ann continued in a hushed tone, "she wants me to wear—oh I can barely say the word—that dress that she gave me as an early birthday present. You remember? She got all misty eyed when she gave it to me and said how pleased she would be to see her granddaughter dressed as a young lady. Mom, can you imagine, sided with Grand, and it looks as if I am doomed to appear in front of my friends looking like some deranged dressed-up baby doll. I may have to wear a dress, but I swear that I am going to mess my hair up and refuse to brush it. I have to save my reputation somehow."

Jane gave her tomboy sister a comforting pat on the shoulder and, feeling wise as the older sister, offered some sage words of advice. "Ann, you know how much Babcia Grand loves you, and you know that her dream of seeing you develop into a proper young lady is just about hopeless." Ann smiled devilishly. "So, the least that you can do is to make her happy, if only for a little while. There is some redemption. We do have the pig feed tonight." Jane felt quite pleased with her words as her sister's face twisted into a gleeful smile.

"You know, Janie," Ann conferred a bit smugly, "I sure am glad that you feel this way about making Grand happy, because Mom said that since I was wearing a dress for this special occasion, you should too." With these words, Ann jumped up and began a wild sprint up the stairs with Jane close behind. Doors slammed, drawers slid noisily, and then as the storm quieted, both Ann and Jane entered the hallway in their skirted finery complimented by their favorite tennis shoes; there may be a chance at redemption yet. They locked arms in an exaggerated manner and headed down the stairs as if they were princesses headed to the ball. Wilma was waiting for them at the bottom of the stairs, and to the girls' shock and surprise she was also wearing a dress. This was a monumental moment as it was storied in the Krysochowski family that Wilma had always refused to wear dresses, even on her own wedding day, though she did finally acquiesce for the occasion. The girls' shock promptly faded as they noticed that their mom too was wearing her favorite tennis shoes. They all joined arms and headed for the kitchen for Babcia Grand's approval.

Babcia Grand smiled broadly as they entered the kitchen and eyed with approval their neatly brushed hair, their crisp pastel dresses, and as her eyes froze in their downward view, she spotted the tied canvas monstrosities on their feet; at least they were clean. She sighed, and her shoulders lowered slightly, but only for a moment, as she realized that even in her perfect and orderly world not everything was orderly and perfect. She gave all three of her girls—she did include Wilma as one of her wayward children—a big hug and told them that they looked lovely. The sound of approaching guests reached the kitchen, so the Krysochowski ladies headed outside.

Friends and family gathered around the colorful picnic tables that were crowded with all sorts of delicious edibles. The Krysochowski family was rather small; Wilma's parents were deceased, and Filip's mom, Alena Kaleen, was his only living relative in the States, so the rest of the partygoers consisted of friends. There was Ann's best friend, Alexandria Christina Iverson, or Al as she liked to be called. Al was a tomboy, like Ann, and she liked to refer to her abbreviated name as her "exandrafication," though never within hearing range of her mother. Bob Iverson, Al's dad, was also a guest and was the local banker. Mrs. Natasha Iverson, Alexandria's mom, never attended outdoor parties as she felt that they were rather common and far too uncivilized for citizens of standing, and boy did she consider herself a citizen of standing. A displaced relative from Czar Nicholas's doomed family—at least as she told the story—she had no memory of the events, as she was not even born at the time. Her mother, a very close cousin of the czar, told Natasha of her regal history as she lay dying from consumption when Natasha was only twelve years old, no one else having heard her confession except for Natasha. So, to honor the memory of the family that she had never known, she was committed to carrying herself and behaving with the utmost of propriety. This commitment extended to her unfortunate family, as both Al and her dad had arrived in their Holy Communion finery. A quick change of clothes remedied the problem, and a picnic mood prevailed.

There were also David and Lisa Everly, both friends of Jane's. Lisa was Jane's same age and David was two years older. Their parents, Ellie and Sam, were also friends with Jane's parents. Sam Everly owned the gas station in town, which, on hot days, was crowded with children buying cold soda from the new soda machine. Babcia Grand's friends from her quilting circle were also in attendance. They stood admiring Wilma's new-quilted tablecloth, although it wasn't quite clear whether or not they were admiring the needlework as much as the food that was resting on top of it; they were big eaters. It was a happy group that gathered that day to celebrate Ann's ninth birthday, to enjoy the company of good friends, and to surely enjoy a good meal.

Enjoy the meal they did. Babcia Grand received one compliment after the other, and even though Wilma piped in at times to say that she had helped, everyone there knew better, and laughter always followed. Filip rose to make a short speech, as was the custom. Jane respected her father immensely. Wilma was a wonderful and a fun mom who always made her feel that anything were possible, no matter how zany, but Jane's dad, Filip, was as warm and as reliable as the sun. She knew that she could depend on him no matter what. No problem was insurmountable when Dad took out his pipe, sat in his big comfortable chair, and gave it his full attention. She clung to his words as a leaf to a tree, and she waited for his words now. He cleared his deep voice with slightly self-mocking importance then began.

"We are all gathered here today to celebrate the ninth birthday of Ann Kaleen Krysochowski." There was clapping and snickering as Ann did not like her middle name and her friends knew it. "The first thing that I want to do is to thank my mom, Alena, for preparing such a delicious meal." There was loud applause. "I want to also thank my wife, Wilma, for her moral support in its preparation," he added with a wink at Wilma. There was a mixture of applause and laughter, especially from Wilma. She always enjoyed a good joke, even if it was at her own expense. "Ann"—he looked directly at his youngest daughter—"one of my greatest joys in being a parent is seeing my children grow into unique individuals. You are full of life and the wonder of it, just like your mother. You are creative, inventive, fast on your feet, and have the ability to get as covered in dirt as any child that I have ever seen."

There was more laughter, and Ann beamed. "Your mother and I love you now for what you are and anticipate with pride whatever it is that you have yet to become. Although, we are sure that, whatever your future holds, it will probably involve dirt. Happy birthday!"

There was great applause as Filip went over to kiss his youngest daughter. Wilma and Alena also rose and went over to give Ann a kiss and a hug. It was a short-lived gesture as newly anointed nine-year-olds are not receptive to kissing parents and grandparents, especially when the nine-year-old has a tomboy reputation to maintain.

"Now for my usual and might I add unusual special gift!" Wilma added excitedly. Wilma, Filip, Bob, and Sam disappeared into the large barn that was far removed from the rest of the farm. Soon a loud humming sound was heard, and the children, with the exception of Jane, began to scream with delight. The doors of the barn were spread open wide, and slowly a small propeller driven plane began to emerge from the barn. *Wilma's Wings* was the name flamboyantly written across the side of the plane, and the pilot, of course, was Wilma. The children ran toward Filip and then stopped, because they knew the rules. Each child, one turn at a time, was guided by Filip and helped into the plane; then, as the rest watched, Wilma took to the sky and gave them a brief flight that encircled the farm. Ann was first, as she was the birthday girl, and with the calm of a well-seasoned traveler, she climbed into the plane and waved to her cheering revelers as she took to the sky. There was no party game in existence that could match this one.

Jane stood back from the other kids, as she did not fly in her mother's plane. She had flown with her mother only once, and once had been enough. No matter how steady her mother had tried to fly the plane, Jane had become so ill that, even after landing, she had been unable to keep any food down for two days. Her mom had encouraged her to fly again, as she felt that she would have grown accustomed to it and would have overcome the sickness caused by it, but Dad, in his kind yet firm way, had said no more flying for Jane. Wilma never argued or tried to persuade him. She understood that he did not want to see his children ill, and neither did she.

Everyone having received their rides, including a few of the adults, the plane was carefully put back into the barn. It was time to sing happy birthday and to enjoy the cake baked by Babcia Grand. Alena could make a wonderful meal, but her cakes were legendary. They defied any verbal description, and the only responses by the more than willing guests who consumed her cakes were ones of rolled back eyes and tasteful moans.

They were decadently sweet and visually stunning. The singing began, and Alena carried her granddaughter's cake, illuminated with candles, and presented it before Ann. The singing completed, Ann made her wish, and then Grand sliced and served the cake, with ice cream of course. The slices were not too large, as Grand felt that the consumption of too much sugar was unhealthy, but they were ample in size and, when eaten, met with the usual moans and the rolling of eyes. The plates were scraped clean of every crumb, a few seconds were requested and honored with an even smaller piece, and then every guest just sat back, quietly for a few moments, in complete contentment.

The party was winding down just as the sun was getting a little sleepy as it began slowly sinking into the hills. There was just one party tradition yet to be carried out for the event to be complete: the pig feed. The pig feed was a tradition that had always caused fierce debate among both family and guests, but it was a debate that Babcia Grand always won; after all, she had baked the cake. Alena had very definite ideas about eating; one should not eat too much or too little, and one should definitely not indulge in too many sugary foods as it was bad for the health. It was perfectly all right to indulge in a sweet confection on special occasions, but once the sweet was consumed and the occasion was complete, the sweets had to go. This was as it had been and as it would be. So there were no arguments presented at the end of the lovely gathering as they knew that the tradition would be fulfilled no matter what was said; the rest of the cake was going to the pigs.

The Krysochowski family was a family of strong traditions; Babcia Grand made sure of it. Traditions were like the roots of a tree; they were a reminder to the tree that they were there first and that it was from them that the tree grew and thrived, not the other way around. It was okay to branch out and to even thrash and to bend wildly in the wind, but the only thing that kept the tree from toppling in the strongest of storms was its roots. The roots, at this particular moment, were saying that the remainder of the cake should go to the pigs, and the tree bowed to the wishes of the roots, well sort of.

The children were given the job of feeding the cake to the pigs, which was not such a bad job. They whined and complained convincingly for Grand's sake, then grabbed the remains of the cake and headed for the pigpen. The pen was obscured from the adult's view by the big storage barn and silo. The setting was perfect as they gathered in a circle to discuss their plans. Ann was the first to speak.

"First, does everybody have their change of clothes in the barn?" Everyone gave a nod. "Okay, David, you are the only boy here, so you're first in the barn to change, and don't waste a lot of time fixing your hair like you did the last time. We know that you want to look good for Janie, but we don't have time for that." Both Ann and Al snickered as David's face went red; they both knew that David had a crush on Jane. Jane was not amused.

"Gee, Ann, if boys are changing first, you and Al should join David. It may be a little hard to tell though since you both shaved this morning. Just think, if you and Al stopped shaving, you could both get jobs as the bearded best friends when the circus comes to town." Ann sneered sarcastically.

"Look, you idiots," Lisa chimed in, "fight about this later. David, go get changed." David ran into the barn and was back out quickly, then stood purposefully in from of both Ann and Al and messed up his hair. His actions brought a laugh as the rest of the party ran into the barn to change. In moments everyone was changed and stood outside of the barn ready.

"Okay," Ann began, "I am the birthday girl, so I get to go first. Everybody else line up in front of the pigs' pen." Some may say that animals are stupid, but those pigs knew something was up as they were all bunched at the fence where the children stood. "Now, we all know the rules, but just in case"— she gave David a sinister glance—"I'll repeat them. I throw the first piece of cake, and whomever I hit changes places with me. Whomever the next person hits trades places and so on and so forth. It is quick, yet orderly. The rules must be followed!" The kids all smiled and nodded their heads in agreement because Ann made this same speech every year, and they knew that as soon as Ann threw the first piece, it was every boy or girl for themselves.

Ann aimed the first piece at David, a direct hit in the head. Then everyone scrambled for the cake. Cake flew everywhere with the frustrated pigs getting a few vagrant crumbs here and there. Their screams could be heard by the assembled adults, who were now enjoying their coffee. Babcia Grand commented that she could not understand the children's enjoyment in feeding pigs. Wilma patted her shoulder and just smiled. The cake was soon dispersed—on the fence, on the ground, on their clothes, in their hair, and even on the pigs. They laughed uproariously at the sight of each other, complimenting each other for having completed another successful pig feed. They hosed clean their hair, their faces, their hands, and even the pigs and their cake-speckled pen. Then they changed back into their original clothes, as if nothing had happened, and returned to the party grounds.

Wilma spotted them first and with a wink asked whether or not the pigs had enjoyed the cake. "Mother," Ann responded solemnly, "I have never seen pigs enjoy any cake more." Grand rolled her eyes and continued with her conversation. The children ran off to try out Ann's favorite birthday gift, a flying model airplane. As their voices faded, the small plane took flight and hung silhouetted in the twilight of day's end.

CHAPTER 4

The hot days of July gave way to the blistering days of August. Even Babcia Grand seemed a flustered and impatient version of her usually calm and collected self. Everyone seemed just miserable except for Jane and her dad. Filip just accepted everything in his easy manner. He had felt hotter days, and he had felt cooler days, so why was any given day any worse or better than any other? Farming was in his blood, and he rolled with the rhythm of the earth and its seasons, be they hot or cold, rainy or dry. The good earth provided sooner or later, so why begrudge it a day or two of hot temperament? Jane, on the other hand, was just happy no matter what. She could not explain it, she just understood that she felt such joy and appreciation for where she was, who she was with, and what she was experiencing, that even the heat seemed to make the world shimmer brightly. Lisa did not quite see things as her friend did as she sat fanning herself in misery while they watched David fishing in the farm pond.

"You probably have temporary brain damage from heat stroke," Lisa commented. She had a tendency to be a hypochondriac and found mental illness most dramatic. "You know, I read in a newspaper once about a teenage boy that spent a whole day fishing in hot weather and then went totally crazy and tried to poison his whole family." Jane looked at Lisa with guarded interest.

"Well, what happened to the family?" Jane asked of her friend. "Did they all die?"

"Just about, you know, food poisoning has been known to kill people."

"Food poisoning!" Jane yelled. "I thought that you said that he tried to poison his family, like with arsenic or something?"

"He did try to poison his family," she continued quite indignantly. "A person would have to be crazy and bent on murder when trying to serve his family dead fish that have been sitting all day steaming in an old wicker fishing basket. The only reason that he was not convicted was that it was blamed on heat stroke, you know, crazy in the head. Let that be a lesson to you."

Jane burst into laughter even though Lisa felt that she had shared some valuable advice. David turned around to see what all of the laughter was about and then, checking his watch, realized that it was time to go home. He packed up his fishing tackle, his rod, and his basket, walked over to where Jane and Lisa were sitting and took a seat himself. David was a watcher, an observer who was not often taken with the art of conversation. Everything had its time and place whether it was an action or a deed, and there was no need for excess in either. Jane was still laughing, and Lisa had begun to join in.

"You know, Jane," David observed, "your face is getting awful red."

Jane was abruptly serious. "Do you think that it could be heat stroke?" That was it. Jane and Lisa roared with laughter and rolled in hysterical agony over the grass. David shook his head, picked himself up, and started walking home; girls' humor, he just did not get it. Lisa yelled for him to wait for her as she headed off after him. Jane could not resist one last quip.

"Hey!" she yelled after her friend. "You better not eat any of that fish." Jane could hear more laughter, which slowly faded into the quiet of the afternoon. A breeze began to move the blades of grass and the green leaves of the trees. There was no better place to enjoy a breeze than up in a tree, so Jane began to climb and perched herself onto a high branch with a nice view. The wind gently swayed the branch that Jane rested upon and as her eyes began to relax their gaze they unexpectedly began to fix onto a figure that was moving across the fields. The figure, moving closer, was that of a young boy, about Jane's age. He approached the tree where Jane rested and, to her surprise, sat down at its base. Jane watched him as he buried his face in his hands. He appeared so despondent that she felt compelled to call out to him.

"Hi there," she called out amiably as she began to climb down from the tree. His tearstained face peered up at her as she came down from the tree, and he seemed so exhausted that even her sudden appearance could not motivate him to move. Jane sat down next to him, a bit uncomfortable herself as she was not usually so familiar with strangers, especially strangers that were boys! And yet, reaching out to this strange boy, who was obviously in pain, seemed the right thing to do, something that she must do. He had turned his face from her in embarrassment, and in a movement of familiar comfort Jane reached for his hand and, cupping it in her own, gently patted it. He quickly pulled his hand from hers and faced her with an angry look. How dare this strange girl hold his hand, but looking at the kind concern in her face, his own harsh look softened. Jane spoke first.

"My name is Jane. What is yours?" There was no response, only a stark stare, so Jane continued. "I live at the farm behind us, so if you are hurt or anything, I can take you there for help. My Babcia Grand can fix anything that hurts, and my mom can make you laugh, so it will not hurt as much while it's getting fixed." The young boy smiled slightly but shook his head.

"I'm not hurt," he started to say as he slowly rubbed the swollen red marks on his legs. "I just did something wrong."

Jane looked at his legs and grimaced. "What did you do wrong?" she asked.

"I don't know," the boy added with a bitter laugh. "Since I never seem to do anything right, it's hard to tell exactly what I do wrong."

"Who did that to your legs?" Jane asked gently.

"My dad did." the young boy responded sadly but then continued defiantly. "But that is what dads are supposed to do, aren't they? They have to correct us when we do something wrong, or how else will we learn? How will we grow to be strong men if we do not learn how to be tough and learn how not to cry like babies when we are corrected? Isn't that so?"

No, Jane did not think that it was so. The worst punishment that she had ever received was one of Grand's lectures; the guilt was almost unbearable, so it was lucky that she usually forgot them quickly. It was beyond her imagination that anyone that she loved, and who loved her, could ever do anything to her like what had been done to those poor boy's legs. No, it definitely was not so, but she did not want him to feel worse than he already felt, so she did something that she had learned that sometimes made people feel better; she changed the subject.

"Are you hungry?" Jane asked as she reached for her lunch pail that was lying next to the tree. "Because I just remembered that I still have a piece of apple pie left from my lunch, and I am just too full to eat it, and my Babcia Grand makes the best pie, and she gets very offended if I don't eat her pie because then she thinks that I don't like it, so would you please eat this pie so that my Babcia Grand's feelings won't be hurt? You would really be doing me a big favor." And before he could answer, Jane placed the pie in his hands. He ate it willingly, and his spirits lightened as Jane got him talking about his hobbies, and before long it seemed as if they were old friends.

"Do you like airplanes?" Jane asked. "Because my mom has her own plane, and I can show it to you. It is in that big barn right over there." Now, Jane knew that she was headed for a lecture because it was a strict rule that no one was ever allowed to enter the plane barn without adult supervision. This could be really bad as her mother would give her a lecture, and then Grand would give her mom a lecture about the dangers of airplanes and then Mom would complain to Dad and then Dad would give her a follow-up lecture and then Ann would tease her about it for days. Well, the guilt would fade, and she would forget about it eventually, and this certainly seemed like a worthy sacrifice. The young boy seemed excited to see the plane, but then his face darkened.

"I have been gone too long already. I would really like to see your mom's plane but," he added gloomily, "I don't want to do something wrong again. I have to get back."

"You can come tomorrow if you want to." Jane added, "You can see the plane and eat some more pie. Grand loves to feed people."

"We are leaving tomorrow," he said flatly, and then he turned to Jane and looked at her. "I wish that I had a friend like you."

"You do," she told him, smiling while shaking his hand. "I hope that you can come back for another visit. Don't worry. No matter what your dad says, someday you are going to do something great. I can just feel it." He smiled brightly then turned toward the fields and ran, giving one last wave to Jane before disappearing from sight.

Jane lay awake in bed that night, long after darkness had fallen and long after everyone else had fallen asleep. She was troubled by the young boy she had met that day. Her eyes grew teary as she thought about the pain that he must have felt, not just from the welts on his legs, but from the welts on his heart. It was difficult for her to see any person or any creature suffer. Her young mind held the principles and the feelings that would guide her throughout her entire life. The attributes of a healer were within her, and a hurt, any hurt, mandated a cure or, at the very least, a reason for its existence. Thoughts continued to swirl through her sleepless mind when she felt someone sit at the bottom of her bed. As she sat up with renewed clarity, she swung her legs over the side of the bed and found herself sitting next to Golden Boy. This was not a bad thing, as she felt that she needed to talk.

"Why are people capable of such cruelty, even to the individuals that they are supposed to love and protect?"

"You are thinking about the young boy that you met today." Jane was startled, as she had not been aware of how closely he had been watching her. "Oh, I keep track of you," he added with a smile. "It's my job to make sure that you are all right. I have no intention of failing at my first job as a guider." He patted her shoulder reassuringly. "Now getting back to your question, this was the first time that you saw this type of behavior, but it was not the last."

"Yes," she responded grimly. "And it is not 'behavior'; it is abuse, and I do not understand it anymore at fifty-six years of age than I did at ten years of age."

"There is something more that is bothering you." She nodded. "You spoke to your father about what had happened, and you were disappointed and confused by his response." Again, she nodded.

Jane had wandered down to the barn after her meeting with the young boy, and she had found her father there, as she had hoped. She had poured her heart out to him about the boy, his injuries, and the cruelty of his father. She had been angry, and she had expected her father to have been as angry as she was; he was not. He had spoken calmly to Jane as he told her that although he did not believe in that kind of punishment, it was a parent's right to discipline their child as they saw fit, within reason. He had received a few whippings of his own as a young boy, and he was sure that he had probably deserved them. What did Jane really know of this boy or what he had done to warrant his punishment? Jane continued to argue, but her father held firm to his conviction; a parent had the ultimate say over the discipline and the guidance of their own child.

"I remember how disappointed I was in his response. My father, one of the kindest and the most compassionate people that I knew, was telling me that it was okay to treat a child in a way that he would not treat his own horse."

"You should know that, being a parent yourself, parents are people, and they are not always right," Golden Boy responded. "We can learn as much from when they are wrong as from when they are right."

Jane smiled. "That is true, but when you are used to looking up, it is hard the first time that you have to adjust your view down a little." She paused. "You know"—she pointed her finger at him—"you have a habit of diluting the topic. Now, can you please answer my original question? How can people be so cruel and hurtful, even to those that they claim to love?"

"Well," the young man began, "maybe they do not view what they are doing as hurtful; maybe they view it as responding to a situation in the only way they know."

"Maybe"—Jane's voice grew heated—"that is a load of horse manure, and maybe—"

He interrupted before she could continue. "Maybe," he said

calmly, "what they view is not your view. Your sky is blue and filled with light; their sky may be gray and laden with shadows. Where you see joy and happiness, they may see anger and rage. We are each a painter and our life a painting in process, and we can only paint with the colors that we carry on our pallet. Some of these colors are already selected for us, and some of the colors we create ourselves. This does not excuse the outcome of the painting; it only explains the process. The stroke of the brush is far reaching though, isn't it, Jane? It touches more than just one canvas, doesn't it? How it touches depends on the pallet, for it is all that the painter has to work with."

Jane shook her head. "You know, you speak so beautifully and with such complexity." Golden Boy was about to thank Jane for her kind compliment when she continued, "But do you think that for once you could just keep it simple and stick to some good old-fashioned good guy/bad guy stuff, where the bad guy just gets punished and goes to hell?" It was Jane's turn to give her golden-haired companion a pat on the shoulder, which was a bit of a reach for her. He smiled good-naturedly and told her that he would give her suggestion some thought. "I understand what you are saying," Jane continued, "but how can you change the colors so that they no longer hurt those that they touch?"

"You can't; only the painter can change the pallet. When he is unwilling or incapable of changing it, the only way of preventing the hurt is by removing the painter. You understand this all too well, Jane."

Jane did understand all too well as her memories bore witness to its truth. It was very late, and Jane's eyes finally began to grow weary as she allowed her head to rest gently back onto her pillow. The swirling thoughts that had whirled in her head were finally quieted. As the last of the tumultuous memories settled into yesterday, she slipped peacefully into sleep.

CHAPTER 5

The summer revelries came to a sudden halt when the last free day before school arrived. It was a somber day though the sun shone brightly. As was the custom, Jane, Ann, Al, Lisa, and David gathered in the early morning to collect the picnic basket prepared by Babcia Grand and to travel to their favorite spot to enjoy lunch and their last day of freedom. Jane enjoyed the challenge of school, while David and Lisa were impartial to the teachings of reading, writing, and arithmetic. Ann and Al, on the other hand, would have preferred toiling on a chain gang. No matter their likes or their dislikes, they gathered together to partake in their last day of unfettered fun.

It took some time to get to their favorite spot, as it was a secret, and they were cautious in making sure that no one was following them. They walked down the hill, behind the grove of trees, under the bridge, through the brackish water, carefully down beside the small waterfall, under the willow marked with the skull and cross bones, where the petrified log rested carved with the word *dogelwail*. It was a mystical place given its mystical designation by this loyal band of seekers that gathered there every year on that same day and only on that day.

"It's your turn this year, Lisa," Ann instructed as she pushed Lisa toward the petrified log. "Now reach your hand in there and get the eye."

Lisa looked at the bug-infested soggy log with the ominous hole at one end and shook her head no. "Do you realize that there is probably a venomous creature in that dark and soggy hole just waiting to sink its viperous fangs into some plump flesh like my hand. I remember reading about a girl that had to have her hand cut off after something bit her when she put her hand somewhere it did not belong."

"Let me guess," Al added sarcastically. "She went crazy after it happened."

"That's right. You see, Ann," Lisa continued, wide-eyed, "Al read about that girl too."

David politely brushed the girls aside and reached his hand fearlessly into the hole and withdrew the eye. It would have been considered gruesome had it not been made out of stone. It was a white, round-shaped stone with red veins running through it and a perfectly black circle marked right in the middle of it, just like an eyeball. The friends had found it a few years before and were convinced that it had been used by a pirate as a fake eye long ago. It was believed that the eye had the ability to see into the future, and thus the friends gathered each year on this day to tell the tale of the pirate eye and to ask the eye one question each.

"Who shall tell the tale?" asked Ann solemnly.

"I will tell the tale," answered David with equal reverence, and so he began.

"The evil pirate, Captain Dogel, was cast ashore by his mutinous crew. He was condemned by them to live the remainder of his life upon the land, a living death for a seafaring man. He wandered on the land, dying a slow death of thirst as the only thing that would quench his parched lips was the salty spray of the sea. Here, on this very place, he finally dropped and died, and the only part of him that remains is his eye. It searches still for the sea."

David rotated the eye slowly as if it were looking at each one of them. "Listen," he whispered. "Do you hear the wind wailing? It's not the wind that you hear; it's Captain Dogel crying out for his eye, his ship, and the sea."

Just as he finished, a rush of wind rustled the weeping branches of the old willow tree. The friends were mesmerized. Lisa, terrified as usual, asked a question, the same question that she always asked no matter how many times she heard the story.

"Can't we take the eye back to the sea and throw it in so that Captain Dogel can have his eye back?"

"No!" the rest responded loudly. It was time to continue and to ask the eye their one question about the future. Each person would ask the eye their question and then roll the eye on the ground. If the eye stopped with the black circle facing upward, the answer was yes. If the black circle was facing to the side, the answer was uncertain. If the black circle was facing the ground, the answer was no. One by one, they each asked a question and rolled the eye until there was only one person left; that one person was Jane. She pondered her question carefully until Ann began to roll her eyes and Al began to huff impatiently.

"Good gosh, Janie," Ann called out in exasperation. "This isn't a matter of life or death. Why don't you just ask your usual question, whether or not you will be the teacher's pet this year ... again?"

Jane stuck her tongue out at her sister and then proceeded to ponder her own question even further, to her sister's annoyance. The question came to her suddenly and from where she did not know. It was strange how some thoughts came from a place of unfamiliar origin. Where did thoughts and ideas come from? How did things just pop into the head, and where did they pop from? Jane was so taken with this question that she almost forgot the original question that she was going to ask Captain Dogel's eye.

"Will I meet someone new?" Jane asked in sudden recognition as she let the eye roll from her hand. The eye wobbled across the ground until it finally rested. The all-knowing black circle had stopped in a rather cockeyed stare halfway between up and to the side; looking at Jane in an ominously uncertain fashion. They all gathered around the eye to ascertain its answer.

"I say it doesn't know for sure," commented Lisa. "It is a wonder that it tells us anything at all considering the disrespectful way that we use it. All that it wants to do is to go back to the sea. I have an idea! Why don't we make a little boat with a little sail and take it down to the river and let Captain Dogel's eye sail back to the sea?"

"No!" the rest responded again loudly.

"I say it doesn't care," Al said, taking a closer look at the eye, "because it knows that the only thing that is ever new around here is the fresh cow poop on the fields every year." They all laughed as they knew that nothing much happened around their little town. It was a small farming community where generations were born and lived their entire lives. The few that left never came back lured, as Babcia Grand would sometimes lecture, by the flashing lights and the loud sounds of a world that had forgotten how to feed itself, physically and spiritually. The little band of friends that stood gazing at the stone cared little for what happened outside of their little circle of life, for as much as they asked about the future, what was important to them was here and now; the rest could wait.

The school year started, and Jane immersed herself in her studies. Ann and Al, as usual, complained and limped along, finding little use in the type of knowledge being taught. Lisa, though an above average student, was more interested in the sweeping novels that she continuously checked out of the local library, and David just did what was needed or expected.

Through the falling leaves and the howls of Halloween, Jane lived through two versions of the same life. Most of the time she lived in the blissful innocence of a ten-year-old, while on many evenings, in the quiet of her room, she sat with her golden-haired companion, fully aware of the reason for her journey into what had been. She had stopped trying to understand it and had begun to accept it as a gift. How fortunate she felt to have had such wonderful experiences to relive. It was odd though to sit and reminisce about the same events twice! There would be and had been sad times, she knew, but that was a part of living.

"It is sad to think that some people have no happy memories," Jane commented as she sat with her guide in her room on a cold, quiet evening. It was the first snowfall of the season, and the house was dark and silent except for the wind that wailed as it swirled the frantic snowflakes. He smiled at her as he sat comfortably in her reading chair, his usual spot. Their conversations were always enjoyable, though he never lost sight of their purpose as they helped to provide Jane with comfort, fortitude, and clarity on her journey. He had, however, taken her advice and tried to make his responses a little less complex.

"Yes, it is sad not to have happy memories. Do you really think that some people have no happy memories at all, or do you think that they only choose to focus on the unhappy ones while they push the happier memories aside?" he asked. Jane gave his question some thought. She thought about some of the individuals that she had met in her life or was yet to meet in her life. Even the meanest and the rottenest person she met must have had at least one or two happy memories. What were memories anyway but just the sweet or the bitter aftertaste of a moment lived? *How seldom it is realized,* Jane reflected, *that in the boiling pot of living day to day lies the flavor that will last as long as memory.* Jane paused; it was better to have more sweet than bitter.

"You are deep in thought," Golden Boy commented to his distracted companion. Jane pulled Babcia Grand's quilt tighter around her shoulders and inhaled the soft scents of home: cinnamon, Grand's light perfume of sweet lilac and the still lingering freshness of newly cut grass of a summer bid farewell. She could touch it, sense it, and remember it all at the same time. She turned her attentions back to her companion.

"You know," Jane began, "when I was a child growing up, time seemed to move so slowly. It took forever for school to end. It took forever for the holidays to arrive, like Halloween or Christmas. Christmas Eve must have been the longest night of the year! I can remember how Ann and I used to get up before the sun was even awake on Christmas morning, and we'd rush to get Mom and Dad, and then we would rush downstairs, and the Christmas tree would be ablaze with light, and there would be Grand waiting for us, dressed properly with the coffee already perking pleasantly in the pot." Jane laughed at the vision she held so securely in her mind. "We swore that Babcia Grand must have either slept in her clothes or hadn't slept at all just to be ready for us Christmas morning." She enjoyed another laugh at the memory, and then the smile slowly crept from her face. Jane seemed to not notice her companion as images seem to pass in front of her eyes. Watching them, she continued although it appeared as if she were talking to herself. "Then, when we became adults, time seemed to speed up: faster and faster. College, marriage, children, grown children, grandchildren, there were no brakes to slow it down, and instead of one night lasting for what seemed like forever, a lifetime seemed to be gone in one night." She stopped speaking as tears began to fill her eyes.

Golden Boy rose from Jane's reading chair and sat next to her on her bed, taking her hand in his, patting it gently. This was part of what he was there for, not just to guide her, but also to comfort her. To take this journey with her made him feel as if he were almost as much a part of her life as she was. His own life had been so brief, and he had so few memories of his own that, somehow, Jane's experiences and memories were becoming a part of him. Leaving his own thoughts, he turned his attentions once again to Jane.

"Do you remember when you said, just a few minutes ago, about how sad it would be not to have any happy memories?" She nodded a sniffling yes. "You have so many happy memories, Jane—yes, sad ones too—but so many more happy ones. They comfort you, and they comfort your family. Is a butterfly any less beautiful because it lives only a few months? You have lived a full and a happy life no matter the number of years. We seldom die wanting less of that life; we usually die wanting more of that life. Your melancholy retrospection is understandable, but realize that your feeling of melancholy reflects the journey's end, not the journey itself. You and your life were and continue to be a gift, whether that gift lies in your memories of a Christmas morning or in the memories left behind to the ones that you love, comforting you and comforting them, a tribute to a life well lived and to a woman well loved."

Jane smiled, and the sadness that had tarnished her face disappeared. She knew that his words had been heartfelt, but she just could not help herself.

"I wish you had written my eulogy. You say things in the

most beautiful way. I never fully appreciated how wonderful my life was," she added with a regal outward sweep of her arms.

"How do you know that I didn't? Anything is possible you know," he said with a wink of his eye. He patted her hand, and then Jane snuggled down deep into quilts. The wind continued to howl and hurl its frozen ammunition, but it did not matter. Jane felt safe and warm and secure in the knowledge that tomorrow would surely be another wonderful day.

Many wonderful days passed for Jane. Though they were rather cold and frozen, Jane did not care. Thanksgiving Day dawned cold with only a light dusting of snow to dress its ground. It was a favorite family day, almost as good as Christmas Day, noting of course the word *almost*. The afternoon belonged to the family; the Krysochowskis would sit adorned in their finest awaiting Babcia Grand's perfectly basted and dressed turkey accompanied by the sides of plenty. Yes, Jane could almost see and smell the whole feast before her as she sat in her bed. It was true. The afternoon was devoted to family, but the morning, well she, Ann, and their friends had some holiday traditions of their own to attend to.

Jane dressed quickly and then knocked on Ann's door. There was no answer. She knocked again and when there was still no response entered the still darkened room quietly only to promptly trip over some undistinguishable objects on the floor landing with a pronounced thud accompanied by a loud curse. She lay as still as a possum waiting for the presumed inevitable calculated steps of Babcia Grand. *Darn,* she said to herself, *a lecture on Thanksgiving Day.* The silence of the morning continued, and, to Jane's surprise, no sound of footsteps could be heard. Her eyes having adjusted to the darkness, Jane spotted her sister still sound asleep in her bed. A quick and forceful shove was administered to the motionless lump under the covers.

"Hey!" Ann erupted with a sleepy froth still lingering on her voice. "What are you doing waking me up this early? There is no school today, and I want to sleep in celebration."

"Have you forgotten what day it is?" Jane said as she ushered in the blinking sunlight from the now pulled-back curtains. She could see Ann's face clearly now, and from its sleepy repose she saw a twisted grin begin to spread.

"Thanksgiving," Ann said with a chuckle. "Time for the parade. Time ... what time is it?"

"It's nearly eight!" Jane almost shouted. "Unless you want to parade around in your pajamas, you'd better burn rubber; they should be here any minute." Ann sprung into action and dressed quickly. As they went down the stairs together, the first scents of what was to come enveloped them. Babcia Grand was already at work in the kitchen and had been even before the rooster had crowed his good morning. They stopped in the kitchen first to wish a quick Happy Thanksgiving salutation, wrestled on their hats, gloves, scarves, and coats, grabbed the lidded tins in the mud room, and headed out into the frosty morning. Familiar figures had already gathered as the steam from their frozen breath hung above them like an Indian smoke signal.

Jane and Ann joined them. It seemed the usual crowd with the exception that the head count seemed to have increased by one. The addition was heavily shrouded in winter garb, his face having almost disappeared into his hat and his scarf, but to Jane he seemed vaguely familiar. David spoke first.

"This is my cousin. He is having dinner with us today, so I thought it would be okay for him to come along." Everyone shrugged in acceptance except for Ann.

"I don't mind as long as he joins the group and takes the oath." Ann's request came as a surprise as no one had been allowed to join the group since the group began. This was not unusual, as no one new had moved into town since the group had formed. Ann eyed the newcomer warily and waited for him to respond, but David spoke first.

"You are such a goof, Ann. He is only going to be here for today. His dad works for the government, and they travel all the time. They are leaving tomorrow to go out of the country."

"Oh, I don't mind," the heavily hampered boy spoke up. "It would be kinda cool to belong to a club. Maybe I wouldn't feel so homesick then ... " He drifted but then added, puffing himself up a little more, "Not that a young man of my age gets homesick, but it would be cool anyway."

Ann seemed to soften a little: just a little. As acting president of the group, Ann administered the oath, which was of great interest to everyone else as they had never taken an oath and they had no idea what she was going to say. Neither did Ann, but she was not about to let them know that.

"Raise your right hand, close your right eye, and stand on your right leg." The boy complied then waited. "Do you promise to ... " Ann continued a little hesitantly. "To ... to ... to do as you are told and to not tell anyone what we do and if you do tell anyone about what we do ... "—continuing with the most menacing expression on her face that she could muster— "know that you will be struck by lightning and your burnt remains eaten by a roaming dog." The boy nodded in agreement. "Now," she added, "everybody spit on the ground and spit in the air. Okay?" Everybody nodded and then spit. "It's done; you're in."

It was time to get back to the important events of the day. They traveled to the barn and, once inside, made their way to a dark and obscure corner in the back. Once their eyes had become accustomed, they spotted what they were looking for. With several "ooos" and a "yuck" from Lisa, they each picked up their respective items and then traveled back out into the chilled sunlight. It was then that they could fully appreciate what they were holding; their now one-month-old Halloween pumpkins. The only smiling carved pumpkin had been Lisa's, but it wasn't smiling anymore as its once upturned mouth was now buckled in and lined with some kind of greenish red fungus. They lined them up reverently, one behind the other, and then admired them.

"Whose do you think looks the best this year?" asked Jane.

"I like Al's best," Ann said. "That scar that she cut on the side of the face has caused it to split wide open, just as if it had been done with a hatchet. It's just lovely."

"I think that you are all sick," Lisa blurted. "Let's get on with decorating them so at least they won't look so awful!"

The tins that Ann and Jane had brought from the house were hastened forward, and as the lids were removed and the contents grabbed and placed on the putrid yet still noble pumpkins. Plumes pierced and adorned with popcorn and cranberries were placed atop the pumpkins like hats and twine strung with pinecones that had been rolled in peanut butter then in birdseed were draped around the pumpkins like necklaces. Bundles of suet were lined along the sides of the procession like spectators and handfuls of dried corn and seed were thrown up into the air like confetti, providing a festive clatter as it landed. Finished, they stood back and looked, well pleased with their efforts. It was the Macy's Day parade in miniature; well, a rather warped version of it.

The newest member looked at the scene with a mixed sensation of appreciation and shock. "Do you do this every Thanksgiving?"

"Yes," Lisa responded with a sigh of resignation. "It is a rather *disconcerting* sight." She accentuated her use of a big word. "I feel that is a possible sign of a sick mind."

Ann's mouth was poised for retort but was cut off by Jane's suggestion that they should all head inside so that the birds and whatever other visiting critters could have their feast. Ann and Al grumbled but agreed as it was cold and they could always watch from the kitchen windows. Entering the house, they were greeted with piping hot cups of cocoa and freshly baked gingerbread cookies. They grabbed their cocoa and their cookies and headed for the windows that faced their parade. Some birds had already gathered and had begun sampling the fare set before them. A few wintering geese joined the party, and even a sleepy-eyed squirrel decided to stop for a snack before retreating for a long nap. The children were joined by Wilma and Filip, who also chuckled and laughed at the panorama unfolding before their eyes. Babcia Grand continued with her preparation not fully in agreement with the morning's strange activities, but she had come to accept them and even smiled, ever so slightly, at the sound of their gleeful exclamations.

The sun was stretching a little higher into the sky, and it was time for the friends to head home to their families. Jane slipped away from the chattering group and grabbed a piece of paper and a pencil and quickly jotted something down. Returning to the group, who were now at the door ready to leave, not empty handed as Babcia Grand had made them each a small sack of cookies to take, Jane gently and discreetly placed the piece of paper that she had written on into the hand of the group's newest member. "If you ever need a friend," she whispered to him. He looked into her eyes with recognition and appreciation. He had remembered, and so had she. They all filed out of the door then, once outside, spread out into different directions heading for home. Ann and Jane continued to wave from the window and, as their friends disappeared from sight, turned their attentions from the outside to the inside.

Preparations continued, and soon it was time to dress appropriately, a Babcia Grand version of appropriate. This was one of the few days of the year when there were no arguments about dresses and, yes, even dress shoes. Wilma embraced the spirit of the day, and she alighted from the stairs wearing a simple, straight lined but vibrantly red dress. There was a simple single strand of pearls gracing her neck accompanied by pearl post earrings. Filip smiled broadly when he saw her; the same smile that he always gave her, so filled with love and appreciation, even when she was dressed in jeans and covered in grease. Alena nodded an approval, eyeing the pearl set that she had given Wilma when Wilma had married Filip, the same set that she had worn when she had married Filip's father. The girls soon followed in their holiday finery, and all was ready.

They walked together into the dining room and stood, as they always did, to appreciate the scene set before them. The table was adorned with an heirloom lace tablecloth of white, and fine china from the old country, with its delicate border of roses, resting upon it regally. Small bundles of fresh flowers wrapped with ribbon graced the table in no apparent pattern, as if they had been swirled and softly laid to rest by an autumn wind. Candlelight danced across the crystal goblets and landed with playful importance on their intended focal points—the food. The turkey, with its russet sheen, glistened amidst many dainty platters and bowls filled with sugared sweet potatoes, beet and shredded cabbage salads, sausages, stuffing, still steaming freshly baked rolls, and many other delectables waiting to be tasted. To the side of the table was the server overflowing with pies, cookies, nut candies, and, of course, *Makowiec* or poppy seed roll. It was an inspirational sight that would cause the most finicky of stomachs to grumble with delight

They took their usual places at the table, chattering quietly yet excitedly. Filip was at the head of the table facing Wilma at the opposite end. Babcia Grand sat to Filip's left with Ann sitting beside her. Jane sat to her mother's left, and an empty place setting remained next to Jane. It was set with the same finery as the rest, still expecting its patron. Once settled, they each placed their clasped hands in their laps, waiting for the prayer. Filip began.

"We gather in thanks and in memory. We are thankful for the bounty that we enjoy, the good health that continues to bless us, and the love that we share. We thank you, God." He paused briefly to enjoy an appreciating glance at his family. "We also gather together in remembering those that we have loved and who have passed from our lives. We are thankful for the time that they were with us, no matter how brief." He paused once again as his voice always stumbled with emotion at this point. Nodding to the empty place to his right, he spoke. "This seat at our table is not empty, as it reminds us that they are with us still in our memories and in our hearts. We trust them, God, to your care." They paused again at this moment to remember, to utter the names softly and to sweep their hands to their hearts. "Thank you for every day that we are together and thank you for Babcia Grand's good cooking. Nobody takes the Lord's bounty and makes it taste as good as she does." The prayer and its final tribute were greeted by smiles and appreciative amens.

That night, Jane sat upright in her bed, smiling and reliving the day's events. It had been a wonderful day from start to finish. Even the tumble in Ann's room brought forth a laugh. The memories, so seemingly fresh, seemed to deepen and age as Jane became aware of her golden-haired guide sitting comfortably, once again, in her reading chair. She was resentful at his intrusion into her reflection as it changed her blissful reality into the memory that it was. He sensed her dissatisfaction at his arrival and thought cautiously before he spoke.

"You know," he started in a self-conscious tone, "I have to admit something to you." Jane's somewhat defensive stance changed to a more curious one.

"I do not have too many memories of my own," he continued, "and I have really enjoyed sharing yours. Jane, you are so lucky." Jane smiled broadly. Her thoughts shifted briefly; only a moment ago she had been brooding over his arrival, yet now he had her smiling. What was it about this young man that prevented her from remaining mad at him! She should be furious and resentful of this messenger of bad news, but— she gave an audible sigh at her inner thought—there was just something about him.

A crooked smile inched across her face as she stared at him. Then feigning a suspicious tone, she inquired, "Was there something that you wanted to ask me?"

An airy wisp of relief escaped from his lips as he nodded. "How was the food?"

They spent what seemed like hours together as Jane described in scintillating detail the day's feast. He sat mesmerized and asked many questions. How wonderful it must have been, he thought as Jane's face seemed to glow with increasing intensity with each word that she spoke; he could almost taste it! He had another question for her that did not really involve food. "Jane, tell me about the empty place setting? Why is it there?"

"It is there for a happy sad reason." Jane began. "Every family has sad times, even the happiest of families. Before I was born was one of those sad times. Did you know that I had an older brother?" Jane asked. The young man nodded. "I never knew him because he died before I was born. We don't talk about that too much, I mean, about his death. Both my brother and my grandfather, Dad's father, got sick from diphtheria. Dad got sick too, but he made it through; Dziadek Grand and Charles didn't."

"Charles was your brother's name?" Golden Boy prodded.

"Yes." Jane continued in a lighter tone. "Mom named us all after aviators; Charles for Charles Lindberg and Ann for Ann Lindberg, Charles's wife. Mom always thought that Ann was underappreciated. She named me after her mentor Phoebe Fairgrave Omlie.

Golden Boy was puzzled. "But your name is Jane?"

"Jane was Phoebe's middle name. Grand thought that Phoebe was a bit too theatrical, so Mom and Grand compromised, and I was named Jane. Dad didn't mind though, you know, how our names were chosen." Jane stopped for a moment to get her thoughts back on track.

"So that's what I mean by a happy sad reason. We don't talk about the way that they died; that's sad, instead we want to remember how they lived and that we love them and that they are special to us; that's happy. The place setting is not really empty, because they are still with us in our memories and in our hearts." Jane finished with an expression on her face that radiated an innocence and an optimism that was ageless, an expression undaunted by worry's wrinkles or life's cloudy skies. Golden Boy looked at her and felt, as he often felt, more the student than the teacher.

A yawn interrupted the silence, and Golden Boy took his leave of her, as he always did, exiting into her deepest memories. She blinked sleepily, not quite remembering her last thought. Oh, yes, she recalled, she had just scraped the last bit of Babcia Grand's poppy seed roll off of her plate. It had been delicious! Her eye lids closed on a satisfying vision of a family happily full, her family and a budding anticipation of the next day's leftovers.

CHAPTER 6

The last of the fall leaves escaped on the cold breath of the December wind. December brought with it not only the heightened anticipation of a certain gentleman's visit but also the added celebration of Jane's birthday. Although she was born on the second of the month, there was no shortchanging on her birthday just because Christmas was only a few weeks away! No, everyone's birthday was special in the Krysochowski family, especially Jane's as there had been so much loss and sadness before she was born. There was a grand meal, a grand cake, lots of friends, and lots of presents. Like all special days, Jane's birthday created its own unique reason to smile and then, like a precious jewel, was tucked into memory.

Trees decorated in their holiday finery and illuminated with rainbow-colored lights twinkled through windows trimmed with mosaics of ice. Christmas Eve had finally arrived, and the excitement in the Krysochowski house was as unbearable as in any other home that harbored children wrought up with the anticipation of Santa's arrival. It was nearly four o'clock and time for the family to leave for church. Ann was in her shepherd's costume for her part in the annual Christmas play. The Baron was at her side, barking at all of the excitement and ready for his role as sheep herder. Jane was not participating this year. She felt that as a grown-up eleven-year-old, she would rather watch. Babcia Grand hurried everyone into their coats and out of the door, as she made it a point never to be late.

"I look like a real goof," Al said despairingly as she gazed at her own reflection in the mirror on the wall of the church's makeshift dressing area. She was dressed in a gown made of white satin that flowed from her neck down to her feet. Wings were attached to her back and a glittering halo rested snuggly on the top of her head. Ann stood next to her friend, patting her shoulder to console her.

"Why do I always have to be the Christmas angel every year?" Al continued. "Why can't I be a shepherd with a flock of filthy animals? Maybe I still have time to change; no one would miss the Christmas angel, would they?" Al's last chance at emancipation from her plight as the Christmas angel was swept aside by a rustling of skirts ushering the entrance of Natasha Iverson, Al's mother. A vision of grandeur, she was adorned in a regal purple taffeta dress that puffed perfectly just above her slender ankles. Holding a silver-colored handbag that matched the color of her shoes, of course, she gently swept her perfectly manicured hand to her perfectly bouffant hair in a mock and insincere gesture, suggesting that some wisp of hair may be out of place, which it never was. Her glacier blue eyes fixed their gaze immediately upon Al, and with another swish of her skirts, Mrs. Iverson was quickly at Alexandria's side, adjusting this and that as if Al was part of a window display.

"My angel." Mrs. Iverson cooed and then, eyeing Ann, quickly commented, "Why, Ann, how nice that you are the shepherd again this year." Turning her attentions back to poor Al, she continued to tuck and tinker, which only increased Al's irritation.

"Why do I always have to be the Christmas angel? Why can't I be a shepherd like Ann? Or how about the little drummer boy?" Her eyes narrowed in a devilish slant. "I would love to bang the drum."

"Pish posh, Alexandria!" Mrs. Iverson continued, unabated by Al's pleas. "Shepherds are common and rather masculine. You are certainly not a boy. You are the angel because it is in your blood to rise above the ordinary and to glitter like a precious jewel. We must always be prepared to step into the role in life to which we are ordained." Her oration complete, she stood straight, her eyes fixated upon something that only she could see, as she seemingly waited for a crown to be placed upon her head. It was a coronation scene that Al had experienced too many times. An abrupt pat on the back brought Mrs. Iverson crudely back into reality as she shuffled a step forward from its force.

"How are you, Natasha?" inquired Wilma robustly. Without waiting for a reply, she turned to Al and said, "Are you the Christmas angel again this year, Al?" then adding with a wink, "I bet that you would rather be a shepherd." Mrs. Iverson inhaled deeply and straightened her carriage similar in pose to a cobra about to strike. The situation was saved by the intuitiveness of Mr. Iverson, who suggested firmly that they take their seats. Natasha gathered herself, blew Al a kiss, and regaining her composure, turned to leave the room first but not without incident as the Baron gave her a most inappropriate sniff on her way out.

The church, resplendent in the golden glow of candlelight and the red flora of poinsettia, was filling quickly. A gentle chatter echoed throughout, and Jane, catching sight of the back of the perfectly coiffed head of Mrs. Iverson, turned to

Babcia Grand. "Babcia Grand," Jane whispered, "what makes Mrs. Iverson carry on the way that she does?" Now, Babcia Grand made it a point not to gossip, especially in the house of the Lord. She had her own opinions, certainly, but she usually kept her opinions to herself. However, she also felt responsible for guiding her two young granddaughters in matters of propriety and felt this type of question should not be left for Wilma to answer. She turned and leaned toward her granddaughter.

"Jane," she began softly and discreetly, "when the Lord made each of us, He thought that He had created a perfect pie, but somehow, after we leave the baker's case, we all seem to have a slice missing."

She added in an even lower voice, "Some have larger slices than others missing." Jane let a little giggle escape. Babcia Grand gently cupped Jane's face in her hand and added, "I may have sounded a bit silly, but God knows that we, not one of us, is perfect. We all have our little oddities, Jane. To accept them in others gains acceptance of our own. It is our differences that make each of us uniquely who we are. Can you imagine Mrs. Iverson as anyone other than who she is?" Jane pondered a moment. She would not be Mrs. Iverson then. Jane took her grandmother's hand and gave it a squeeze. She felt lucky to have Babcia Grand just as she was although she did have a new appreciation for Mrs. Iverson, oddities and all.

The lights dimmed slightly. Mary, Joseph, and the baby Jesus were already in place in the stable at the front of the church. The earthy fragrances of hay and pine scented the air as the procession of the night visitors began its journey from the back of the church. All of the roles were played by the children of the church, and their proud parents whispered and pointed discreetly at their costumed progeny. Ann, the shepherd, passed the pew in which her family sat, although Jane thought she could barely recognize her as her face was almost obscured by her costume. The Baron trotted proudly beside her and sat majestically as they all took their places in the front of and at the side of the stable. It was the big moment as the light directed its focus on the holy family and on the much-anticipated arrival of the angel over Bethlehem. She appeared, as the prophets had foretold, but not in the form of the person that was expected. Standing in all of her angelic glory above the biblical scene was Ann. There was one audible gasp from the audience, and as Jane turned toward her mother with a stunned expression on her face, her mom gave her a quick wink and a smile. Jane returned her smile as she now knew full well who was in the shepherd's costume giving the Baron an appreciative pat and who was responsible for the unexpected transformation of the less-than-angelic Ann. Just one of Mom's oddities, Jane thought to herself, but there would sure be hell to pay for it this time.

The play was lovely, regardless of the surprise, and even Mrs. Iverson, having recovered from her initial shock, left the church with a gratifying smile on her face but not without extending a tight-lipped glance at Wilma. The Krysochowski family piled into the car and enjoyed a rousing ride home singing Christmas carols and reliving with laughter Ann's ascension to the heavenly hosts. It was Christmas Eve 1956, and as usual, life was not at all usual for the Krysochowski family.

CHAPTER 7

Lisa and Jane sat quietly at the kitchen table sipping sweetened coffee and poking absentmindedly at the small plate of leftover Christmas cookies. They were each lost in their own thoughts, and only the laboring grunts of the old furnace broke the silence as it tried to fend off the insurgence of the bitter cold. It was a quiet New Year's Eve. Babcia Grand had retired early, Wilma and Filip were celebrating at a friend's house, and Ann and Al were doing what they usually did to bring in the New Year.

"Do you think that 1966 is on fire yet?" Lisa pondered out loud and then continued. "It's a miracle that no one has drowned as a result of pushing that huge outgoing-year wooden pyre out onto the pond and then setting it on fire. You would think that Al and Ann would have outgrown their urge to set the old year on fire as its final farewell. After all, they will be entering their second year of college this coming fall!" Jane, rising from her chair, walked half-interested to the window to search for wisps of smoke pasted like cotton candy against the winter sky. Still searching, she responded.

"Oh, you know those two. They have to pass on the tradition of the outgoing year's Viking funeral to the younger generation; at least that's what Ann claims. I personally think that the real reason is that they are the same mischievous brats that they have always been; only now they have boobs." The friends shared a nod and a laugh as Jane's eyes caught the first sign of smoke in the darkened sky. "Well, there is the smoke. We better check our watches; 1967 must be fast approaching." The mood of the room grew pensive as Jane looked at her watch and was the first to speak. "It's 1967; happy New Year, Lisa." They could hear horns blowing and happy shouts.

"Happy New Year, Jane." The two friends embraced, and Lisa stared searchingly into Jane's eyes. "Why did you say no, Jane?" Jane turned away. "It broke his heart. I think that he has loved you since you were both kids. He worships the ground that you walk on, and he has been waiting for you to say yes to marriage for so long. He is a wonderful person."

Jane smiled slightly and turned back to face Lisa. "David is wonderful, Lisa, but he is not my Mr. Wonderful. I hate myself for hurting him now by saying no, but it is better than my saying yes and hurting him and having him hate me later."

Lisa placed her hand on Jane's shoulder. "David could never hate you. I don't think that David has ever hated anything in his life." Jane's eyes began to fill with tears. "He would do anything for you, you know that, don't you?" Jane nodded. "He loves you."

"I know that he loves me, Lisa, and I love him too, but not in the same way. Not in the way that a wife does, not in the way that a lover does." Jane's gaze was firm but kind. "I know that I am what David wants, but I am not what David needs. And as far as what I want or need? I'm not sure. The only thing that I am sure of is that I will be graduating next year and my life is too uncertain beyond that. David needs certainty. He needs someone to have his dinner waiting for him when he gets home, to sit at his side by the fire, and to have and to raise his children, a simple, yet wonderful life. Could I ever be that person? I don't know. I don't know what lies ahead for me. I do know that I will not have him waiting for someone and for something that may never be. It is better this way, Lisa."

Lisa put her arm around her friend's shoulder. "I understand, but don't expect me to be happy about it. Come on, let us pop the champagne and make well-intentioned but seldom-fulfilled promises and toast what lies ahead. Who knows, you may yet wind up fixing dinner, sitting by the fire, and raising a bunch of brats like your sister; Lord, help us, as Babcia Grand would say. Just promise your old friend one thing. Don't take life too seriously; leave a little time for fun, especially the guy kind of fun." Jane huffed slightly. "No, I mean it! You are far too intense. I read about a case like yours in my psych class." Jane started to laugh because she knew what was coming.

"You laugh, but people like you who are driven and don't have any fun can often go ... " Finishing the sentence together, they said in unison, "nuts." The bittersweet mood was broken as the kitchen door flew open accompanied by a blast of cold air and the loud entrance of Ann and Al. Resigned to the intrusion Jane and Lisa turned and asked the accustomed question. "How was the funeral of 1966?"

The house was quiet as Lisa and Al had gone home, and Ann, still smelling satisfactorily of smoke, had gone to bed. Jane sat comfortably in the rocker, her eyes locked on the flickering flames of the fireplace though her mind was fixed on other thoughts, waiting for her parents to return. She needed to talk to Mom about something. A voice brought her mind forward and backwards at the same time. Her golden-haired guider was now also sitting warm and comfortable in the other rocking chair. It was the first time that they had met anywhere else besides her bedroom, and the sudden cognizant vision that surrounded her made her catch her breath. This room, this place, the old rocker that she now found herself sitting in; how many years had passed since she had enjoyed its secure comfort? She rubbed her fingers lovingly over the tufted arms of the rocker before rising slowly. Looking around, it was just as she remembered and just as it was now, even more so. She stopped at the fireplace, enjoying the warmth of its flame and of its memories. Her hand rested on the mantel, and as she let it glide soothingly to the right, her eyes closed, and it touched her dad's pipe holder, rattling it a bit. Startled by the sound, Jane's eyes quickly opened, and, spotting what she had disturbed, she reached for one of the pipes and brought it to her nose, inhaling deeply. Once again, she let her eyes close.

He watched her quietly. It was not his time to speak as he wanted her to experience this moment as she wished. "You know," Jane said softly to herself as much as to anyone in particular, "we all have a scent, a fragrance that lingers as a memory. I would recognize my dad by the smell of his tobacco as easily as I would by the sight of his face or the sound of his voice." She stood for a moment longer, then keeping the pipe firmly in her grasp, began to explore further. There was the dining room with its large well-worn furniture. Pausing at the hutch, she spotted the china, Babcia Grand's china. She placed her hands against the glass, her face shifting in all directions, gazing in wonder at the contents as if she were Alice staring through the looking glass. Still she continued to inhale; the smell of old wood and the slight fragrance of cedar used to protect the linens greeted her. Entering the kitchen, she stopped; it was all there. A plate of unfinished cookies sat on the metal, but properly linen topped kitchen table. Dare she? She reached for a cookie and took a bite. It was real and it was sweet and it was delicious and it was Grand's. She could never forget the taste of

Babcia Grand's cookies, and at this moment, she didn't have to remember. She only had to taste. Remember, she remembered everything. Quite suddenly she did remember everything, and the day was no longer a yesterday. It was a today, a very hard day. Jane wandered back into the living room and took her seat once more in the rocking chair in front of the fire, still holding the pipe tightly in her hand. It was at this moment that her companion chose to speak.

"Happy New Year of 1967. How has your year been so far?" he asked cheerfully.

She could not disguise the condescending manner in her voice. "Now, Golden Boy, you know exactly how my 1966 ended, so how do you think 1967 has been so far?" Suddenly remembering where she was and when it was, Jane lowered her voice to a whisper; Babcia Grand was upstairs, and she could hear everything, even in her sleep!

The young man looked at his sullen-faced companion. Perhaps he had used the wrong tactic to lighten the mood. "You said no to his proposal. That was the right decision, don't you think?" Judging by the increasingly disagreeable appearance of Jane's face, his new approach was incorrect as well. Jane, it was true, was becoming even more disgruntled with her guider. *What business is this of his anyway?* she thought. This was all part of the past even if it did feel like the present, a very unpleasant present.

"Of course it was the right decision ultimately, but I didn't know that at the time," she responded, exasperated. "I only knew that I was hurting someone that I cared about, my friend. How do we ever know that what we are doing is right and that the decision we are making is the right one? That's what regrets are all about." Jane began to feel bitter as she continued. "We are creatures of regret. We regret that we didn't do this or that. We regret not being able to love someone in the way that they wanted to be loved. We regret that we did too little or maybe even a little too much. We regret that we didn't have enough time to do or to say all that we wanted to ... " Her voice drifted off.

They sat in silence for a while longer—both deep in thought, both thinking of the right words to say. The sound of her parents' car crunching slowly down the snow-covered driveway broke the silence as Jane shot a startled glance at her companion, who appeared to be in no hurry at all to leave. She was about to speak, but he interjected before she could.

"You don't."

"I don't what, and do you realize that my parents are going to be coming through the door in a few minutes?" she added with panic rising in her voice.

He stood slowly and sauntered toward the door as if he were like any other guest about to leave. "You don't know whether any decision is the right decision because that would require an ability to see into the future, which we do not possess." He turned and looked intently at her. "We take all that we know and make the best decision that we can at any given moment, and whether that decision is right or wrong, we do possess the hindsight to learn from it. And as far as regrets are concerned," he added with a wink, "regrets are only unpleasant reminders of what we knew that we should have done but chose not to do anyway."

Jane was still sitting in the rocker when her parents walked through the kitchen door. "Are you sitting here all by yourself in the early morning of the new year?" her father asked as he spotted her upon entering the living room. Jane rose from her chair and accepted a warm hug from her dad. Wilma joined them with a cookie protruding from her mouth, smiling to give it an even more comical affect.

"Actually," Jane responded, "I was waiting to talk to Mom about something." Wilma, with a rather surprised expression on her face, pointed at herself to extract a confirmation from Jane. Jane shook her head yes and explained to her dad that it was girl talk. Filip shrugged with a good-natured expression on his face and, after grabbing the rest of Wilma's cookie and popping it into his own mouth, headed up the stairs to bed. Wilma motioned for her daughter to take a seat in the rocker and, turning the other rocker to face Jane, sat down and waited.

"David asked me to marry him today," Jane began bluntly, "and I said no."

Wilma responded reflexively with a firm "Good." Jane, shocked by her response, stared at her mother with a questioning expression.

"I like David," her mother continued in a softer and a more controlled tone. "His life and his future is right here, and that will probably never change, which is not a bad thing, but your future is just beginning."

Becoming defensive, Jane responded, "How can you say that, Mom? You gave up your flight and your freedom to settle here with Dad, and you have been happy, haven't you? How is what you did for Dad any different than what David is asking of me?"

Wilma gently patted her eldest daughter's knee. "I have been very happy. Your father and your grandmother have given me the home and the love that I was searching for." She looked at Jane with intensity. "I had already had my days of soaring through the sky. Your feet haven't even left the ground yet. Give yourself that chance, Jane. Give yourself the chance to fly into the unknown instead of staying grounded and always wondering what it would have been like to break through the clouds."

They sat quietly together for a while, watching the flames in the fireplace slowly wane. It was not an uncomfortable silence. Each was lost in her own memories and thoughts and not disquieted by the other's presence. Jane's gaze pulled itself from the fire as she looked searchingly into her mom's face. "How do you know, Mom? How do you know when he's the right one, the right man for you?"

Wilma squeezed her daughter's hand and then smiled. "I guess you want to know how I knew that your dad was the right one?" Jane nodded her head in an adamant yes. She knew the story of how her mother and father had met. Her mother had been a flyer. Wilma had made money any way that she could as long as it had involved her plane. She had given flying lessons, delivered messages and small packages, had done some stunt flying, and was a locater for aerial signs. Wilma had landed in the field right behind their house on a warm fall day in October of 1939. She continued flying for a while after she met Filip, but as she liked to say from the moment of their first encounter her heart had been permanently grounded. Jane stared at her mom, and she watched the sweetness of those memories passing across her face. Wilma drew in her breath and brought her focus back to her daughter's question. Her voice began so softly that its unaccustomed subtleness grabbed Jane's attention as intensely as if her mom's words were being shouted.

"I knew that he was the one the first time that I looked into his eyes," Wilma began as she again reached for her daughter's hand and stared intently at her. "It wasn't love at first sight, no; it was a connection, a spark, a feeling of finding what I had been searching for without even realizing that I had been searching for anything at all. And love"—Wilma stroked her daughter's face gently—"that's the flame that the spark ignited, and it has only grown brighter and stronger with time. You'll know when it's time to land, Jane. When the time comes and the right one asks you, you will not find a single reason to say no."

Jane stared at her mother through eyes that still harbored a few tears. She felt so blessed at that moment. This woman, her mother, with all of her seemingly carefree and unfettered ways had with a few words brought an unexpected clarity and peace to her daughter's confused and anguished mind. Jane had always thought that her mom had been the lucky one in her parent's marriage; she now realized that her dad had been just as lucky.

CHAPTER 8

The summer of 1967 was to be a catch-a-breath summer for Jane. It was the last summer of her college career. Her BS degree in nursing was almost complete, with only one year left to finish. The past year's rigors in academia had been brutal, and she expected no less intensity in the year to come. She longed for the quiet and predictability of the farm to soothe her nerves and her soul. Some quality time with family and friends was desperately needed. She wanted to savor this time and catch up on some good gossip and some good food; college had not been a culinary delight.

The trip back home from college was a talkative one as she and her dad rambled along in the family woodie wagon. When the pace of conversation slowed a little, Filip became serious in his tone. "I wanted to make you aware of something, Jane," he began with his eyes remaining focused on the road ahead. "Babcia Grand has had some health problems these past few months." Jane remained quiet and listened intently as her father continued. "She had a mild heart attack in April. Not to worry too much, the doctors said, and she seemed to recover quickly, but the past two weeks have not been good, so they are doing more testing." He glanced at his daughter. "I wanted to warn you before you see her, she has changed." Jane was furious that she had not been told about Grand, and no amount of parental concern over her stress and grades could excuse their lack of disclosure. She was still fuming when they came down the driveway as the sight of home filled her with joy and trepidation.

Wilma was alone on the porch waving as she had heard the car crunching down the driveway. Hugs were quickly exchanged, and they promptly entered the house. The figure that she saw tucked into the rocking chair by a quilt was barely recognizable to Jane if not for the ever present cameo at the collar. Kneeling beside the rocking chair, Jane gently stroked Babcia Grand's arm waking her from her nap. Alena, seeing that it was Jane, raised her arms and wrapped them around Jane. How weak her embrace felt, and as she looked into her grandmother's face, she saw that Grand's once porcelain skin had become pale and the unwavering expression in her eyes had given way to uncertainty. As the sound of sniffles began to creep into the room, Babcia Grand having none of it, gathered her strength and her pride, placed the quilt aside and slowly rose from the rocker. "Sniffles are for colds, and we are all healthy as horses," Babcia Grand stated as reached for Jane's arm. "Now by my watch"—she mentioned glancing at her wrist—"it's time for supper. Heaven knows what it will taste like as my current kitchen assistant has questionable methods." She finished with a slight wink at Jane and a nod toward Wilma.

Wilma quickly slipped her arm into Grand's other arm and, giving her a peck on the cheek, commented, "Well, at least I baked the cake this time."

Ann soon joined the family as they sat down at the table. The meal was lovely and thoroughly enjoyable as Wilma made great, exaggerated exclamations over her culinary contributions. As Wilma's cake made its way to the table and the coffee began to perk persistently in the pot, Jane felt that it was the perfect time to hear about the *whos* and the *hows* of the town. Ann, always ready to dish the dirt as well as cover herself in it, began her monologue immediately.

"Well," she started with a deep inhale of breath, "Mrs. Iverson is still driving Mr. Iverson crazy as she insisted that he buy her one of those brand-new really expensive television sets with the mahogany cabinet, and the people who own the bank became suspicious of all of the money that he was spending. Mrs. Iverson shouldn't have invited them all to one of her swank dinners, so they had him investigated but didn't find anything wrong except for the fact that he owes Mike's Appliances a lot of money for that television set, timed payments you know." First breath. "David, you know that nice guy that you dumped? His parents took a mortgage out on the gas station so that they could finance a small farm for him, got the inside track from Al, just happened to see some of her dad's banking papers. You can't blame her if he leaves them sitting out. Wonder if he could get in trouble for that, better keep it quiet. Anyway, David, four years of college to learn how to farm, what a waste, well whatever. He's dating Melissa Graves, you know that mousy-looking girl that ate nothing but cheese, but she doesn't look half bad now that she's older, and I think that she gave up the cheese." Second breath. "Lisa, well, you probably know about Lisa, but just in case, she's going to school to finish becoming a shrink and nobody needs one more than she does. She told Kelly at the deli counter that when she becomes a shrink she is not coming back here because the people are too normal and she wants to live where there are people that need her services like in a big city. No shortage of nuts there.

No, I was not there eavesdropping. Cheryl was waiting at the counter at the same time, and Cheryl has a mouth like a megaphone. Lisa should have known better." Third breath. "Finally, Al and I have made an important decision. We are not going back to college next year, we are bored to death, and we haven't learned a thing that we can do anything with, so we've decided to enlist in the navy, well, actually we've already enlisted. We leave in two weeks. Thought maybe I could slip this in under the radar, but judging by your faces …" Ann's voice faded.

The room was as quiet as a vacuum. Jane opened her mouth to begin a tirade expounding on her sister's stupidity, but she was interrupted by Babcia Grand. "You never did like college, Ann, not that I have anything against a college education, but it is not for everyone. There are a lot of young people out there learning but not doing anything with what they learn. There is a lot to be said for doing and learning from what you do." She rose gingerly from her seat, walked tenderly to Ann and gave her a kiss on the cheek. "Besides," she added, "it is an honor to serve your country. I'm proud of you." Wilma jumped out of her seat with a wild yahoo and going quickly to Babcia Grand's side gave her a gentle hug and gushed that she could not have said it any better herself. Filip also rose to hug his youngest daughter, and Jane, having thrown her arms into the air in exasperation, mustered a small smile.

"This has been an eventful supper, and I feel rather tired out by it," Grand commented in an exhausted tone. "I think that I will have a bit of a rest. You two girls don't mind …" Before she could finish her question, Ann jumped up into a rigid salute. "KP is our duty today, ma'am." Babcia Grand nodded her head in appreciation, but she had a few last words to put forth before she retired. "One last thing, Ann, gossiping is unsavory behavior. You have an image to protect now you know." Ann lowered her glance, trying to control the mischievous grin that was forcing its way across her face. Jane, despite all of the family rallying around the flag, thought that her sister and her friend were both nuts. Lisa had plenty of potential clients in this small town after all.

The sun was meandering low in the sky with the anticipation of setting as the last of the dishes were put in their places. Jane was tired by the drive and by the unexpected concerns that had greeted her, but it was far too early for sleep. Walking out onto the back porch, she inhaled deeply, filling her lungs with air scented sweetly of summer. A walk would do her good, she thought, as she ascended the back porch steps. The early days of June eclipsed the last of spring's uncertainty as the earth around her looked renewed. The birds chirped their final songs of beckoning night while Jane walked at a leisurely pace. Continuing past the barn, she caught sight of her favorite tree, the grand old oak. What a perfect canopy to sit beneath and enjoy the twilight dance of the fireflies. As she walked closer, Jane noticed, rather unsettlingly, that she was not alone. A figure stood leaning against the tree. Hearing a muffled greeting, Jane continued her approach tentatively. It wasn't until she was about twenty feet away that she realized that the figure standing in the thickening light of dusk was a young man. Not recognizing him at first, Jane closed within a few feet of him before she drew in her breath abruptly and came to a complete stop.

It was not by his physique that he was so familiar or by the color of his hair or the tone in his voice. It was his eyes that connected to hers in remembrance, at one time tragically sad though nearly obscured by a tightly wrapped scarf and an oversized hat. Now his eyes did not just connect to memories but also to a new sensation that swept through her body like a shock. His voice was level and smooth and without acknowledgement as he spoke to her. "I hope that I did not startle you. I am visiting my aunt and uncle just over the—"

Jane interrupted him, "Oh, you mean Ellie and Sam Everly."

"That's right but how did you ... " His sentence once again rested incomplete as Jane interrupted. She could not resist toying with him though she had never been so forward with a man before and she didn't know why she was doing so now, but she found the taste of this cat-and-mouse game tantalizing.

"Oh I don't mind you standing beneath my tree as long as you can recite the oath," she added coyly. He seemed lost for words at this point so she continued on. "You know, Thanksgiving, when we were just this high and ... " Jane motioned with her hand to about shoulder height.

It was his turn to play the game, "And I had to stand on one leg and raise one hand and close one eye and ... " It was now Jane's turn to look surprised. He lowered his head and let his laughter rumble in deep tones in his chest as it escaped through his lips in warm chuckles. "Jane, do you think that I could ever forget?"

Jane became unwilling defensive as she blurted out "Well, Mr. David Bell, you never wrote to me." His eyes broke from hers, and he stared out into the darkening horizon. Slowly he reached into his pocket and pulled out his wallet. Opening it, he extracted a well-folded and brown-tinged piece of paper and handed it to her.

"I never wrote," he admitted, "but I never forgot." Jane unfolded the paper and read the note that she had written to a friend so many years before. It was her turn to turn away and the flush that enveloped her cheeks burned brighter and hotter than the setting sun. Gently he took the paper from her hand, folded it, and placed it back into his wallet.

"I am here for the next few weeks. Do you have any room on your dance card for me?" he asked, staring intently at her.

Jane chided him warmly, "That's so old fashioned. Why don't you just ask me for a date?"

That night as she sat brushing her hair and staring into the mirror, it was not her face that she saw. It was his. Wavy, warm chestnut brown hair framed a strong-jawed face embellished with equally warm chestnut brown eyes. His lips were sincere in their intent, yet seemed gentle and willing to extend a kind word. Her eyes closed as she continued brushing her hair and the vision and memory of him intensified beyond just a first meeting, and she knew why.

"You know," she began fondly as she addressed the person that she knew was seated behind her. "He told me later, after we had dated for a while and when we knew, that he had stood beneath the old oak tree every night for a full week hoping that I would wander over." Jane turned around in her seat and faced her familiar visitor. "Can you imagine anything so romantic and so sweet?"

Golden Boy stared at the slight blush in Jane's cheeks and felt almost voyeuristic in his presence there. Sensing his discomfort, Jane rose from her seat, crossed the room, and patted his shoulder gently. "I'm glad to see you actually. It's almost like having a girlfriend to chat things over with." It was now his turn to blush slightly. Jane retracted her words a bit. "Well not really a girlfriend, just a good friend." He seemed much more comfortable with that designation as Jane sat on the edge of the bed opposite of her seated companion. He knew that she had had a full day that day. He knew everything about her and everything that had happened to her from the day that she took her first breath of life. Yet, it was still odd at times traveling with her on this journey. Knowing of something was a lot different than actually experiencing it.

"I guess that you know everything that happened today." He nodded. "It still amazes me, even though I have the strange benefit of knowing the outcome, that the decisions and the choices that we make at any given moment have the potential to change our entire future." She continued to ponder her thoughts out loud. "How would my life have been different if he had not stood under that oak tree all of those days?" She could not even envision how her life would have been without David in it. Instead she remembered what her life had become after that meeting under the old oak. Her thoughts changed direction abruptly to some of the other events of the day. "What if," she continued in a more somber tone, "Ann and Al had not joined the navy?" Her mind's eye, like a soothsayer, continued to see the road that had already been traveled. Options and alternatives for choices already made began to crowd her thoughts resulting in outcomes sometimes better and sometimes worse.

"You are journeying into the land of what-ifs and second guesses. Do you remember when we talked about regrets and hindsight and the differences between the two?" Jane motioned her head in acknowledgement. "We have to rely on our ability to make the best choice or decision that we can at any given time based on what we know. Beyond that, we pray that the choice we made was right and if not, pray that we have the grace to understand and to learn from mistakes in judgment."

Jane became very serious as she posed her next question. "If we die because of a decision or a choice that was made, was it the wrong decision or choice to make?" It took him no longer than a second to respond.

"Men and women have died throughout history for causes that they felt were worthy of their ultimate sacrifice. Were their causes any less worthy because they died as a result of them?" Jane knew that he was right, but it was hard to look at lofty ideas and acts of self-sacrifice and not have them tainted, even a little, by the painful vision of mournful shadows that stood beside freshly churned earth grappling with the realization that their loved one was lying cold, silent, and dead below their feet. Was anything really worth that? He could almost read her thoughts as his next question jolted her attention. "Would you have risked your own life to save one of your children if they were in danger?"

"You shouldn't even have to ask that question. Of course I would have."

"How about if it were the neighbor's child that was in danger or maybe even someone that you didn't know or maybe an older person, or how about a dog that ran out in front of your car, or have you forgotten about all of the times that you swerved to avoid hitting a squirrel? You could have crashed your car and died on any of those occasions." Jane smiled ruefully because yes, she did remember all of the times that she had swerved to avoid hitting a squirrel. "It's not about what actions or ideas are acceptable and correct as perceived by others." Could he read her mind? she wondered. "It's about doing what we think is the right thing for us to do, and what we think is right for us to do is not necessarily what everybody else thinks is the right thing for us to do. It's really up to the individual, don't you think?" She nodded her head in resigned agreement.

"You see, Jane..." He began to get excited. "So many of the living are unwilling to risk, to try, to take a step because they become paralyzed by negative what-ifs, like what if they fail or, worse still, what if they die? Every great invention, feat, or moment in man's history was preceded by the proverbial leap of faith or the figurative step off of a cliff. And the great black abyss of uncertainty becomes through application and perseverance a plane in which to fly, a vaccine with which to cure, or a great novel to entertain and to inspire. What would the world be like without those that were willing to reach and to attain that which was thought to be unreachable and unattainable? That life can leave us at any given moment without warning and through no act of our own; this is a fact not a risk. The only true risk is in not living at all, not living to the full potential of our dreams and our aspirations whatever they may be and regardless of the journey demanded to achieve them."

Jane thought briefly and then brightened. "Kind of like

why worry about the risk when it involves something that you are passionate about!"

"Exactly! We are all going to die anyway, so live, live, live with the time that you have. There is no risk at all in living because dying is inevitable! Now, this is not to say that one should drop from an airplane without a parachute. The frailty of our physical existence mandates our respect, but our potential for accomplishment is unlimited. There are no risks in life, Jane, only choices and the outcomes of those choices."

"So," Jane asked tentatively, "should I be content with the fact that I am dead?"

"No," he responded. "You should be exulted with the fact that you lived." He looked directly into her eyes and took her hands and held them firmly in his. "I hate to use a quote from an old movie, Jane, but you have lived a *'wonderful life.'* Could it have been longer? Most certainly yes. Could it have been shorter? Tragically yes. As I said before, we are all going to pass from this life as we know it, but when that time comes, if we can greet it with the conviction and the confidence that we have lived with a full heart and have lived a life equally full in actions and in deeds, regardless of the number of days or decades, then it is in those things that we will find comfort and contentment."

Jane could not help but smile. Somehow he always did it; she didn't know how, but somehow he always parted the clouds to let the sunshine pass through. "I have known you now for almost eleven years; should I add or subtract that to my first fifty-six years?" He smiled without answering. "And you know what? You are pretty smart!" He smiled again, and Jane took the opportunity to reach for his hands. "Thanks for being here for me." The smile broadened as their hands gently released. He stood and stretched.

"A comfortable cloud is calling my name." Golden Boy said with an all-knowing wink.

Her companion and the world in which he lived seemed such a mystery at that moment. Were there really clouds to rest upon? *What was his real name,* Jane wondered, *and even more importantly, who was he really?* She so wanted to ask, but before she could, he took his leave and with him the questions from her mind.

CHAPTER 9

August 28, 1967

Dear David,

It was so difficult saying good-bye to you on Saturday. This past summer spent with you was the most wonderful summer of my life. My life seemed so clear before I met you, I mean really met you. The last year of nursing school was before me. I had picked the hospital where I wanted to work. It was all neat, tidy, and organized. As I sit here alone without you and reflect on all of those neat, tidy, and organized plans, they seem perfect for a career but a little too sterile for a life. Oh, I am not knocking career women and I am committed to a future in nursing, but it would be missing passion without you as a part of it.

I feel breathless at times. Our feelings for each other just seemed to grow wild like the honeysuckle by the barn. Do you remember that fragrance? We stopped so often during our long walks together around the farm to take in its sweet aroma. Did our feelings blossom too quickly? Oh, that sounds so cliché and too much like a romance novel. It feels right though, doesn't it? It does to me. It seemed the most natural thing in the world when you placed the promise ring on my finger our last night together. I said yes without thought, without question, without doubt. I thought maybe that the distance between us would make a difference. It has. My question did not become if; it became when. I never thought that I would feel this way about anyone, but I thank God every day that I do. I thank God every day for you.

I hope that I have not frightened you with the intensity of my feelings for you, but it comes from my heart—no pretense. I have learned so many things over my past three years in school: how to help, how to heal, and how to comfort. One of the most important things that I have learned is that life can be fragile and fleeting. Life is too precious to waste it's moments on preconceived notions about time and what is too short, too long, or just about right. Here and now, that's what matters.

Excuse me for not even mentioning your new position; I think rather that my emotions have ruled too much of this letter. How are the children? Do they realize yet how fortunate they are to have a teacher like you? They will, if not today, someday understand how much you have touched their lives. You give so much of yourself and with such ease that it seems as if what you have to offer is boundless. I believe that it is, and it is one of the many things that I love about you. I am so proud of you and proud of what you are doing in your life.

It is wonderful that you can stay with your aunt Cathy while you search for an apartment. I cannot wait to meet her as you speak so highly of her. From what you have told me she seems so different from your mother; it's hard to believe that they are sisters.

I must leave now and try to get my mind back onto topics like clinical nursing and patient care. I will call you soon and until then will continue to write.

With love,
Your Jane

August 31, 1967

Dear Jane,

I hope that you didn't mind my impromptu call last night, but I had to call you and hear your voice after receiving your letter. I have been anxious since you left and wondering if maybe the distance would give you time to reconsider your feelings for me. It all happened so quickly, but as you said in your letter and I will answer with a resounding yes, it feels right, so incredibly right. I have read your letter over a dozen times, and I am somewhat embarrassed to say that I feel like a lovesick puppy, but I will take this kind of sickness every day for the rest of my life. How can I lose? I'll have the best nurse in the world to treat me. And as far as pretense is concerned, I promise only to use it as a vocabulary word for my students, never as a means of communicating my feelings for you.

My feelings for you—I don't know that I can put them into words. They can't be put into words because they cannot rest idly on paper. My feelings thrive when I touch you, hold you, kiss you, and look into your eyes. When we talk about our hopes and dreams, children, and growing old together, my feelings for you live in those moments. To write that I love you just wouldn't seem enough. To live the rest of my life loving you will barely be enough. We fit like two puzzle pieces: you healing, me teaching, and both joined by a love of children. I have had so little love in my life. It does not sadden me, I am over that, but to have so much love in my life with you now overwhelms me. Tell me that you love me as often as you like; I cannot get enough of your caring, your warmth, you.

The kids are great! They test me of course; I would expect nothing less. Fourth grade: can you remember any of those years? We were always on the move of course, or I was sequestered in boarding school. I remember sixth grade, though, because I had a teacher, Mr. Mourlin. I was boarded in a little school in England that year while my dad worked and my mom toured Europe. He was a wonderful teacher. Firm but always fair and he sort of took me under his wing. He lived at the school, and sometimes in the evening, he would sit with me and tell me about the local history—great battles, gallant knights, with a few dragons tossed in. Looking back on it, I am sure that a lot of what he told me was local lure or legend, but what I really gained was a love of knowledge and the joy it can bring when it's shared. He made me laugh, he made me listen, he made me imagine, and by giving me his time on those evenings, he made me feel as if I were really worth the time. Every one of my kids is worth my time, my care, and my attention.

Aunt Cathy is great as well, and she cannot wait to meet you. I am thinking that maybe you should meet Aunt Cathy before you meet my parents to somewhat temper the experience. This brings me to a rather uncomfortable question. I know how much spending the holidays with your family means to you and, believe me, I would prefer to spend the Thanksgiving holiday with your family as well, but Aunt Cathy mentioned that Mom and Dad will be stopping over at her house for Thanksgiving before they leave on their next trip, so she wanted to know if we would both join her and my parents. She is forever the optimist and always hopes that somehow she can reach my parents and join us together as a family. As I said before, she is forever the optimist. I know that it is a lot to ask, but I am hoping that I can convince you. I would like you to meet them once before I sweep you off of your feet, and Aunt Cathy's would at least be neutral ground. Say yes!

My love always,
Your David

Yes was the answer that Jane gave to David, and on a dreary Thanksgiving eve in 1967, she found herself away from home for the holidays for the first time. The train pulled into the suburban Pittsburgh station as an uninspired drizzle began to infuse the air. She spotted him through her misted window and in her excitement almost left her things behind. Running to him like a schoolgirl, she leapt into his arms as the packages that she brought fell in a mess at their feet. He pulled her gently from him and, looking into her eyes, tenderly cupped her face in his hands and kissed her. She was unaware if anyone else had arrived to greet her, and at that moment she didn't care. Jane did become aware rather quickly that there were another set of arms that began embracing the two of them together. She drew back in a rather embarrassed blush, though even that dissipated quickly as she knew at once the individual who had shared in their embrace, Aunt Cathy.

"I am so excited that you are here, although as much as David talks about you, I feel as if you have been with us all along." She smiled broadly, and her warm enthusiasm did not disappoint David's avid and frequent description of her. Catherine Olivia Bryer was a tall woman who shared David's deep brown hues in the color of her eyes and her hair. Her figure was softly rounded, very motherly in fact, though she never married or had any children of her own. Jane liked her immediately.

"So this is David's fairy godmother?" Aunt Cathy laughed and chided David for letting out her secret.

"Well," Aunt Cathy added a little somberly, "he needed a fairy godmother. I only wish that I could have done more." David put his arm around his aunt's shoulder and gave her a gentle shake to relieve her pensiveness.

"More? Who traveled all over the world to see me arriving as if by magic and wrote to me constantly no matter where I was?" Aunt Cathy's smile returned. Jane watched as their playful conversation continued abundant in sweet memories that were only slightly diminished by their briefness. She could now see, in just these few moments, the source of David's warmth, caring, and sense of humor. He had inherited some wonderful traits from his aunt Cathy, though she wondered with trepidation about the other two influences in David's life that she was about to meet. Voices broke through thoughts and moved her into action.

"Enough jabbering," Aunt Cathy insisted. "It's time to head home for some holiday festivities: turkey, stuffing, cranberries, all manner of gastronomical delights, and bromo-seltzer. Actually you may need the bromo-seltzer after meeting *the parents* rather than after eating the food." David gave his aunt a wary look. "I know that I shouldn't say such things, but I believe in speaking the truth. I am sure that you have talked to Jane about your parents, and I just want her to be a little prepared when she meets them."

The drive from the station was brief, and it was not long before they pulled up to the front of a lovely colonial home. It was all brick with black shutters and glowing electric candles that warmed every window. The slumbering grass on the hill that sloped gently toward the door seemed to lead the way in welcome. Jane forgot her concerns at the sight of it and squeezed David's hand in pleasant anticipation. Entering the foyer, Jane was struck by the sights and scents of a Nutcracker fantasy. She felt rather like Clara ensconced in a dream world as the whole house was dressed and draped in Christmas finery that would defy even the imagination of the very young. Jane's audible gasp brought Aunt Cathy to her side.

"I just love Christmas, don't you?" she asked. Jane nodded in opened-mouth, juvenile fashion. Wrapping her arm around Jane's shoulders, Aunt Cathy chatted gleefully as she guided her through the lower rooms. Each room had its own holiday theme, but by far Jane liked the library the best. A train drawbridge stood guard to the entrance to the library and rose regally to allow entrance. The train's track continued in a circle around the book-laden walls, and each depot was a festive literary stop. *A Christmas Carol, The Night Before Christmas, The Holy Night,* and many others each had their own station and scenes recreated from their story; it was extraordinary. Jane gazed at the woman beside her and was struck by the light-heartedness yet deep love and passion that must reside in one to create such a seasonal symphony of sight and sound. She looked forward to getting to know Aunt Cathy better.

The tour continued until they entered the last room—the family gathering room. It was decorated to glittering perfection, yet it had a coldness that struck Jane immediately. It took but seconds for her to realize the source of the drop in temperature as she saw two figures sitting stiffly refusing to succumb to the plump and cozy sofa in which they found themselves encamped.

"Jane," David began in obvious discomfort, "I would like to introduce you to my parents, Richard and Mavis Bell." They stood for a polite but detached greeting. Jane could see David's physical similarities in both of them. Richard and Mavis shared brown hair and eyes, strong yet alluring facial structure, and stately carriage in their physique. By all standards, they were quite attractive and more than acceptable if only they had not been as inanimate as dolls in their lack of emotion. Their appearance was chilling more conducive to plastic than to flesh and blood, causing Jane to recoil in a reflexive step backward. Despite the initial reaction, the two groups moved closer although there were no hugs or kisses exchanged in welcome; only curt nods of acknowledgement and a forced handshake between father and son. Aunt Cathy, suddenly quiet, faded to the back of the room, a temporary stranger in her own home, but the motion was only temporary.

"Well, everyone take a seat," she said, regaining her cheerfulness. "How about some eggnog to begin the festivities?"

"I would think that it is a little early for eggnog," Mavis responded in cool fashion.

"Oh, I don't know, Mavis," Aunt Cathy countered with a wink to Jane and David. "I think that some whiskey with a side of nog sounds perfect right about now." As the eggnog was being poured and served, Jane sat in shock at the sight of David's parents, who were seemingly carved from ice; she wondered that their breath wasn't frosted when they spoke. She had prepared herself she thought as David had spoken frequently of his parents' strange behavior and even Aunt Cathy had chimed in, but this initial experience was well beyond her expectations and worst imagination. Jane was at a loss as to what to do so she did what a proper upbringing dictated; she tried to make conversation.

"Mrs. Bell," she began shakily, "David has told me that you and Mr. Bell travel quite a bit."

Mavis turned mechanically. "Yes, we do" was the entirety of her response as silence again prevailed.

Jane looked at David, and though his posture was erect, some color had begun to drain from his face. Grabbing his hand discreetly, Jane squeezed it, and catching her glance, he smiled slightly. "What have been your most recent travels?" Jane continued as she was becoming combative in mind though still calm in tone. She was not about to let the arctic king and queen off of the conversational hook. Mr. Bell perked up at this question as he enjoyed, that is if he could enjoy anything, conversations concerning himself and his conquests. Thus began a brief dissertation on their most recent trip, which was to Egypt. Promptly, with very little effort and even less enthusiasm, he turned a region of historic and cultural significance into the most mundane place on earth. His business success, Jane pondered, must have been achieved through pure will and pained submission of the opposing party, certainly not by means of charm. Through the entire conversation, Mrs. Bell sat in her perfectly coifed, dressed, and manicured state, without movement or emotion. Jane's thoughts reflected back to Mrs. Iverson, who at this point, in comparison, had the warmth of Mrs. Claus.

Conversation started and stalled repeatedly until after days had seemingly passed, dinner was called. The food was delicious and the dining room magnificent, but the balloons had been popped and the magic wand sadly removed in Jane's mind. She just could not recapture the wonder and welcome, even with the upside-down Christmas tree merrily dangling from the crystal chandelier. She stared quietly at them as she ate. How could it be? How could David have emerged from the union of these two people? It was like a horrible experiment somehow gone right.

"Jane." The monotone source of her name shocked her to attention. "What are your plans?" Mrs. Bell asked with feigned interest. Jane responded reflexively without thought as to the source of the question.

"I will be graduating in the spring of course," she began excitedly. "Then David and I will be getting married, pursuing our careers, settling into our life together and with God's favor"—she couldn't help but smile—"having children." Her smile broadened as she caught sight of David's smiling face.

The response should have been expected.

"It sounds rather a hindrance—the children, I mean. How can one expect ... "

Jane interrupted Mrs. Bell's cold rebuttal with a rebuttal of her own. "It's all really a matter of perspective. I find living out of a suitcase rather a hindrance, and as far as children are concerned even you had to be born, Mrs. Bell." Jane finished in a sweet and innocent tone. There was a brief silence as the spell had been broken. Why should she care what these two people thought even if they were David's parents? David mattered, she mattered, and the people in their life that loved them mattered. She grabbed David's hand under the table, as he sat to her left, and, squeezing it, leaned over and tenderly kissed his cheek.

"I love your plans," Aunt Cathy boomed, defusing the tension. "In fact, I think that the wedding should take place right here. What do you both think?" Jane glanced hesitantly at David, who was beaming and actually laughed for the first time since their arrival. "Oh, we can discuss the details later. For now, how about some coffee and dessert?"

The finale to the meal was complimented by a merry three-way conversation with little added to or tainted by the glum duo that also shared the table. Jane smiled as the more that she looked at it, she really did like the upside-down Christmas tree; she would have to remember it.

The house was quiet as everyone had retired for the evening. The soft chiming of Christmas carols pealing gently resonated from some unknown source. Jane sang along softly as she listened. She nestled into an overstuffed chair and began to read through a collection of vintage children's Christmas stories that she had found in her room. A soft knock at the door roused her promptly from her seat. Upon finding David at the door, she grabbed his hand, pulling him into the room quickly. Before he could utter a word, she kissed him passionately, allowing the first question to melt worry free from his mind. She guided him over to the chair and after he was seated, without invitation, sat on his lap and wrapped her arms around his neck. He was no innocent babe, but her actions, regardless, left him temporarily speechless. Jane spoke first as she read his expression and responded.

"David," she began as her eyes locked with his. "We are not children you know. We are adults. Soon to be married adults, and though I do empathize with your current slightly awkward but overall highly pleasant position, there is little to worry about." She took her hand and caressed imaginary worry lines from his forehead. "Your parents seem as if they could sleep through the 1812 overture complete with cannon fire, and Aunt Cathy," she added in a whisper, "wouldn't see or hear a thing even if she did." David smiled and relaxed, pulling her closer to him. She was so warm and so soft and the scent that enveloped him he could describe only as the fragrance of her, and it intoxicated him. His fingers wandered through her supple brown curls as she closed her eyes and rested her head on his shoulder. He was there for a reason. What was it again?

"Jane…" His voice began to struggle a bit. "Nothing has changed, has it? You do still want to marry me, don't you?"

"When?" Jane responded in a preoccupied tone, not fully grasping the intensity of his question.

He pushed her tenderly away from him so that he could look at her. "No, I'm not asking when," he countered in pathetic frustration. "I mean when is important, and of course I want to know when, but before I can ask when, I need to know if the answer is still yes, yes that you still want to marry me." Jane looked at the desperate expression of seriousness on his face. Cupping his face in her hands, she responded in kind.

"Do you honestly think that my feelings for you and about us would change over a first meeting with your parents? This is what your question and concern is about, isn't it?" David nodded.

"What do you think of them?" David asked tentatively.

Jane's gaze softened as her once-cupped hands began to caress his troubled face. "I think that they don't know how fortunate they are to have a son like you, but I know how fortunate I am to have a man like you." She kissed his lips tenderly as his tension audibly escaped. "David, look, I'm not going to lie and tell you that this introduction to your parents was expected; even with preparation it was a shock, but I am marrying you, not them. Their lives and ours are complete opposites. They will be busy traveling to the ends of the earth, and we will be busy right here with our own goals and dreams." Her voice trailed as she insistently nestled again into the nape of his neck.

He tightened his hold, feeling the closeness of her heart next to his. They sat for some time without words, needing only the warmth of their emotions and its physical expression. The thought of leaving, even from the chair, was proving difficult. David's body was telling him to stay, though his conscience was telling him it was time to go. "I should go," he said, lifting her gently as he rose from the chair. They stood in embrace, staring at each other, neither wanting to be the first to break away.

"Do you want to have a sleepover?" Jane asked with innocence in inflection only.

"How soundly do really think they sleep?"

CHAPTER 10

Time began to pass quickly after Thanksgiving. Jane went through the rigors of her final days in nursing school while David, having settled into an apartment, continued with teaching. They saw each other as often as they could and wrote or spoke daily. Graduation day for Jane in May was celebrated with everyone in attendance, except for David's parents. The joy of the event was crowned as David removed the promise ring from Jane's finger and replaced it with a diamond engagement ring. The flurry of activity and excitement of the impending wedding then began.

Thanksgiving Day 1968 dawned bright and briskly cold. Jane snuggled deeper into the soft, warm covers of her bed a movement that was promptly greeted with a swift nudge.

"Hey," a grumbling Ann said, "stop stealing all of the covers."

Jane's eyes lost their slumbering repose and flew wide open. This was the day! Her wedding day! And here she was lying in bed in Aunt Cathy's house as if it were just any day, and, oh no, what time was it? She rolled over without regard of her sister's proximity and began frantically grabbing for the clock that rested on the table next to her sister's side of the bed. Ann groaned in exaggerated agony as some of the other occupants in the room began to join into the early morning ruckus.

"Oh, Jane, don't worry. It's only six o'clock, and the sun is barely up," Lisa added promptly and then fell into a lamentable tone. "I just can't believe that you are the first in our little childhood group to be married. Oh that love should enter my life, but I will probably be old and senile before I am ever married."

Ann countered with a playful huff, "Senile yes, old no."

"Ann, you have just never matured enough to understand the complexity of the human mind," Lisa countered with sincerity. "If I did have the symptoms of senility before my geriatric years, it would not be caused by senility; oh no, it would be some other illness entirely like—"

"All right, all right, Doc, I surrender!" Ann interrupted, throwing her arms skyward.

"They are exactly as you described them, Jane," added a fourth matter-of-fact voice entering the fray. It was Melissa Talbot, Jane's closest college mate and hospital rounds companion. She spoke with a New England brogue. Tall and lanky, she and Jane had shared many late nights studying and many long days walking the halls of the hospital. A wry sense of humor found her amused by the bantering, but her common-sense upbringing required quick attention to the situation. "Now," Melissa directed, "everyone up and moving. It is time to get this young woman ready for her wedding, and tardiness is out of the question." She finished, sounding the matron but ending with a playful wink of her eye.

Jane stood alone in the room, trying to be calm as she felt the walls that surrounded her and the floors beneath her feet vibrating with excitement. She stared again at the reflection in the mirror. It was the reflection of a woman, yes, a woman, dressed in white from the lace veil on her head to the pearl luster shoes on her feet. Was this woman really her, herself, Jane? A knock at the door interrupted her thoughts but not her jitters. There was a slight pause as Ann entered the room.

"Oh, Jane," Ann gushed without a hint of sarcasm, "you look like a princess. You look beautiful."

Jane returned a nervous smile accompanied by an equally sincere compliment. "You look quite beautiful yourself, Ann." And she did in her dress of layered velvet and chiffon in the color of frosted cranberry with small burgundy rosettes scattered across the bodice. Ann smiled and patted her dress gently and then quickly returned to the reason for her arrival.

"Dad will be up in a few minutes to get you, so try not to be too nervous." Looking at her sister's face, Ann knew that the consolation of Dad's arrival was not much help. "And Grand wanted me to give you this," she added, handing Jane a small box. "She wanted to come herself, but as she put it, 'There are too many steps for God's use in this house.'"

Jane opened the box and lifted the delicate pendant from its soft resting place. She recognized it immediately; at least she thought that she did. It looked just like one of the beautiful pearl and crystal drop earrings that Grand had always worn on special occasions. They were so regal and delicate. Jane and Ann, as children, used to hold them up to the sunlight and marvel as rainbows refracted and scattered playfully on the walls. Holding up the pendant now as it hung suspended from a single strand of pearls, Jane stared at it in the same childlike fashion as it twirled.

"Do you remember them, Janie?" Ann asked as she took the pendant from Jane's hand and helped to place it around her sister's neck. "Grand had her earrings made into two pendants; one for each of us when we marry. Isn't it just to die for?" She gazed in admiration and then continued in a curious tone. "Do you think that it would be worth it?"

Jane, holding the pendant in her hand and touching it gently to her heart, felt warmth infuse within her that caused her jitters to melt away. "Is what worth it, Ann?" she responded with a welcome deep breath.

"Grabbing a husband to get the pendant. You know that I have never been patient and ... " Jane's laughter interrupted Ann's rant. She gave her younger sister a hug, which proved somewhat crushing to both of their dresses.

"You are just the funniest, Ann, and I love you for it." Jane chuckled as she attempted to straighten her slightly disheveled appearance. "I don't know if you will ever grow up," she continued softly, "but I hope that you never do, not completely."

"What do you mean?" Ann countered with inflated indignation. "I am the maid of honor."

"Honored yes ... " Jane smiled. "Maidenly never."

Ann high-fived her sister, and both of their heads turned toward the door as a familiar voice said, "It is time."

Her feet never touched the steps as she ascended on the arm of her father. They entered the grand foyer that was dressed in such grandeur that it had exceeded even Aunt Cathy's expectations. Bowers of fragrant pine entwined with fresh poinsettias in colors of red and white glistened under resplendent illumination. Wilma took Jane's other arm as the jubilant threesome, guided by ribbons garnished with lilies, proceeded down the aisle. David was waiting calmly without a misstep or a stutter. The vows were exchanged, and it was during this point that David seemed anxious as he could not seem to say "I do" fast enough. He then kissed his bride and lifted her in his arms, setting aside the tradition of walking back down the aisle as husband and wife. Family and friends surrounded them, and though Jane felt a bit silly, it was wonderful.

A small string quartet playing as a pied piper led the guests into the reception. Embraces were shared and words exchanged as everyone took their seats. Quiet suddenly prevailed as Filip raised his glass and tapped the crystal gently.

"I want to first thank all of you for joining us on this Thanksgiving Day to celebrate the marriage of David and Jane. This is traditionally a day that celebrates family and togetherness, and although we all know each other in many different ways, as friend, as new acquaintance, or as relative, today, and I hope in the days to come, we will know each other as family."

Welcome verbal acknowledgement greeted Filip's words as he continued. "There is an empty place setting next to me, and I thank Cathy for honoring our tradition. It represents those that have passed and touched our lives." Babcia Grand nodded her head gently forward. "And though we must always honor and remember the past, today"—a broad smile began to fill Filip's face—"today is about the future—Jane and David's future."

There was applause as broad smiles washed across the faces of everyone in the room. "When I held Jane when she was first born, I had so many wishes for her, oh my, health, happiness, no pain, no hurts. I did not wish for her love because I knew that she already had our love and always would."

His eyes teetered softly with tears as he paused briefly to compose his thoughts. "But today and for all of the rest of the years of her life, she takes into her heart the love of her husband, David, and he takes into his heart the love of his wife, Jane, and with that love they will face today and tomorrow together as one. There may be an equal love, when children come, but there will never be"—nodding his head to Wilma—"a greater love." Jane and David both stood and went to Filip and dissolved into one big hug.

Jane composed herself quickly and, taking control, continued with lightened spirit as she added her own memories. "Dad always gave the toasts and prayers while we were growing up, and he still does. He always says the right things in the most wonderful way, and I thank you and I love you, Dad, but," she added with a squeeze to her father's hand, "he was frequently expansive and the food was on occasion cold." Filip released a sheepish grin as the rest of those in attendance joined in Wilma's laughter.

Aunt Cathy rose from her seat as on cue and with pride and excitement began ushering the attendants into the dining room bearing trays filled with culinary delights. Circling continuously to assure that everyone was delighted with their delicacies, Aunt Cathy paused to touch her cheek softly to David's and Jane's, needing no words to convey her love, joy, and affection.

As the cake was cut and the bouquet thrown, as tradition would dictate, the evening begrudgingly found itself waning. It was time for David and Jane to depart as an overnight honeymoon train ride awaited them. Leaving behind enthusiastically waving arms, they stepped into the cold night as crystal rice fluttered and fell in blessing at their feet. Everything was happening as it should have and had before.

CHAPTER 11

It was a quiet spring evening. The birds had silenced their song early as the persistent chill of winter still clung to the night air. Jane sat in contented solitude, her hands cupping a warm mug of coffee and her ears listening to the rhythmic breathing of David sleeping soundly in the bedroom. He had gone to bed reluctantly at Jane's insistence contrary to his ritualistic recent late nights. She would be leaving soon to face her own late night, paying the early dues of her profession.

Sipping her coffee, she sensed him. It had seemed ages since they had spoken. She smiled, not minding the intrusion and warmly amused by the realization and memory of her surroundings. Looking at her own attire, she was the first to speak.

"Well," she began lightheartedly, "my feet aren't hurting, so I would imagine that I am on my way to work rather than coming from work." Golden Boy smiled in acknowledgement as he knew that it always took Jane a few moments for past and present to meet in her mind.

"I have not looked in on you for quite some time," he said. It was Jane's turn to smile in acknowledgement as she rested her mug on the side table and began to walk casually around the room.

"Oh my goodness." She chuckled. "Our little apartment. I had forgotten how small it was." She continued her brief tour. "I remember those stacks of books though. Between David's books used for studying for his masters, he wanted to become a principal you know, or did, well you know..." Her voice trailed slightly but then regained its strength. "And my reference manuals and textbooks, and all of those students' papers for David to grade, and oh, this apartment was more library than anything else. I always loved the library."

He watched her as she continued. She paused but a moment at the bedroom door and then went in. She crept to David's side of the bed. Leaning over his sleeping body, she tenderly swept his face with her fingers and touched her lips to his cheek in an angel's kiss. How warm and wonderful he felt. He stirred only slightly at her knowing caress while a contented smile spread across his face. She wished that she could slip into the bed beside him and just sleep, without thoughts, without memories, without dreams. But there was no forgetting what was and what had been, so, kissing him again, she straightened and withdrew from the room.

Golden Boy was seated now in her chair waiting. Jane looked at him in mild consternation. "How is it that you always wind up sitting in my chair?" she reproached him.

"It was still warm," he countered with a grin. Exasperated, Jane flopped down into the only other chair in the room.

"You have been married almost two years now. How has married life been so far?"

Jane stared at him rather incredulously. "Well, I do have

the benefit of knowing the outcome, don't I? It has been great!" she finished loudly but then softened a little as she continued. "I don't mean to be snippy. This all seems so new and wonderful, yet it's not new; it muddles my mind sometimes." She looked at him and shifted uncomfortably in her chair. "It's not you, I mean, not personally, but when you are not here, it's just like any day, any day in my life, but when you are here, I remember that this isn't real or maybe this is real and I'm not real. I don't know; it is hard at times, so hard."

"You know, Jane," her guider responded kindly. "You can stop this at anytime. You need not continue if it is too hard or too painful or if you feel that you have accomplished what you needed to."

"Just leave, just like that? Just end it right here and leave the rest of my life incomplete? Should I end it today or wait a day or two? What part of my life should I drop out on— the tenth anniversary, the kids, the graduation, or the birthday? No!" she shouted with no danger of waking anyone. "I don't want to drop out, and I don't want to miss a thing. This started as a simple good-bye, but it's more than good-bye now. It is my life!" The tone of her voice began to mellow. "My life, with all of the happiness and the sadness, the laughter and the late nights, the kids and the tearstained faces, the surprises welcome and unwelcome, and I do not want to miss a single moment of it. Not until there is nothing left to miss."

Words were beyond vocalization as she closed her eyes and cupped her head into her hands. Thoughts ravaged her mind. This room and this day and all of the places and the days that were to follow were all that she had known and all that she would ever know until that moment when memory stopped. Leave? Drop out? Vanish? To where? Beyond memory was the unknown and the unseen. It is said that when the time comes, when breath leaves the lips, one leaves the darkness and goes into the light. For Jane, it appeared the reverse. She would stay as long as she could, feel as much as she could, and love those that she loved as long as she could.

Golden Boy rose from his chair and, kneeling beside her, wrapped his arms around her slumped shoulders. "I did not mean to upset you," he whispered. Raising her head, Jane's tortured eyes met with his and found reprieve in his calm. "I just wanted you to know, maybe not in the best words or phrasing that on this path, I will support you in any choices that you make. Okay?" Jane nodded as a child to a father.

Giving her one last hug, he rose and looked at the watch on his wrist. Jane could only wonder what the face of it must look like and, catching her eye on her own watch, jumped to her feet. Rushing to the bathroom, she looked at the mirror to straighten her disheveled appearance, not understanding how she could be in such a state from just sitting leisurely with a cup of coffee. Breezing back into the empty room, she smiled, blew a kiss toward the bedroom, and, slipping on her coat while clutching her purse and keys, disappeared through the door into the night.

This particular evening found Jane attending to the needs of the patients in the maternity ward. It was Jane's favorite duty. The sight of just-born babies snuggled in warm blankets nestled in loving arms was intoxicating to Jane. She loved babies and longed for one of her own.

"Screaming women, squeamish husbands, screeching babies, and me, did you think that your night could be any better, Jane?" The straight and stalwart New England-boiled delivery nurse was both recognized and welcomed. Jane greeted Melissa Talbott with a quick wink and a hurried hello as there did seem to be a variety of loud vocalizations and few sounding in the best of spirits. Fortunate enough to be working at the same hospital after graduation, it was not very often that they found themselves working together on the same floor on the same night. Melissa, having been at work two hours already, gave Jane a quick overview.

"It's going to be a busy night. We have ladies in rooms 15A, 14B, and 12A with another lady looming large downstairs in reception and on her way up; charts are all posted, updated, and ready for review." Jane nodded. "And," Melissa continued, lowering her voice measurably, "we have Mrs. Williams in 10B. This is her third, but she is having a rough time. The labor is slow considering it is her third, and her blood pressure is a little elevated. You might want to do a check in now as Dr. Blevins is with her, and you know—" Jane raised her hand signaling her complete understanding as she immediately headed to 10B. *Dr. Blevins,* she thought with distain, *good doctor, lousy bedside manner.*

She entered the room quietly but with intent. Dr. Blevins looked at Jane briefly as his only form of greeting and then returned his attentions to the monitors. Having already reviewed her patient's chart before entering the room, Jane went immediately to Mrs. William's side. Gently taking her hand, she stared into her worried and wearied eyes.

"How are you feeling, Mrs. Williams?" Jane asked warmly. Before she could answer, Dr. Blevins interrupted.

"Mrs. Williams has been given medication to move this labor along. Check the chart please and stay with her and keep me apprised as to her progress. I will be back shortly, and I expect to see some movement, or we will have to consider other options." Adding his last two cents of misery and forcing a terse smile, he left the room.

Jane put a quick smile on her face, belying the myriad of descriptive obscenities that she was mentally directing at Dr. Blevins. Circling the room, she checked the monitors and then, returning to Mrs. Williams' bedside, repeated her question.

"Oh, I am a little tired." Mrs. Williams began with unconvincing lightness. "This has been so different from my other two pregnancies."

Jane patted her patient's hand reassuringly and smiled. "All pregnancies are different just as all children are different. It is completely normal. You have two children, don't you?" Mrs. Williams nodded with a smile. "Do you have two boys, two girls, or a combination?" Jane asked as she began to move around the room again to check her patient's progress.

The question accomplished what was intended. "Two girls" was the cheered response. "And you know I never thought of it that way. Our Vicky is five and our little Leslie just turned three last month, and yes, they are very different just like my pregnancies, just as you said." One of the readouts caught Jane's attention as Mrs. Williams continued, buoyed by the conversation. "Jimmy and I—Jimmy is my husband—we are hoping for a boy this time. We have his name all picked out, and you know boys, well maybe that's why ... "

Jane, cued by the sudden pause, turned to look at Mrs. Williams. Seeing her face, she knew exactly what to do—move and move fast.

The distant sound of the wake-up alarm greeted Jane as she walked into the begrudging lightening apartment. Her coat, purse, keys, and shoes fell one by one in rhythmic thuds as she headed straight for the bedroom. Clothing slipped to the floor as she entered the still darkened room. Giving the snooze button a slap, Jane slid into bed next to David and entangled herself within his warmth and security.

"How was your night?" he asked, wrapping his arms around her and kissing her forehead.

"Rough," she responded, sinking deeper into his cocoon like

embrace. "We almost lost a patient ... Mrs. Williams ... third baby ... needed a complete hysterectomy. Blevins did a good job ... still a jerk."

"How about the baby?" David asked, his eyes and mind becoming more alert.

"A screaming baby girl." Jane answered with a sleepy smile. "They were going to name him Matthew, but instead they are going to name her Mary."

David paused in confusion for a moment then quickly caught her meaning.

The alarm began to wail again as Jane tilted her face to meet David's. "Give me a screaming baby, David."

David eyed her coyly. "I thought that you said that we should wait for the right time?"

Jane forcefully raised herself on one elbow and responded directly. "Is there ever a right time, I mean completely right?" Lying on her back, she continued. "Right time: is that when we have a house or when you are a principal or when my biological clock is about to explode?"

David chuckled. Jane was beginning to become impatient and slammed her palm down onto the snooze button to silence the insistent and intruding alarm.

David asked casually, "What time is it?"

"That's your answer: what time is it?" Even more irritated, Jane rolled over and glared at the clock. "It is six thirty-five on Saturday morn ... wait a minute. You don't have school on Saturday. Why did you set the alarm?"

Smiling with self-satisfaction, he answered, "I wanted to be awake when you came home." Jane's irritation melted as she rolled over and kissed him.

"It is six thirty-five you said?" David asked, holding Jane tight in his arms. "I would say that that is the right time, wouldn't you?"

"Perfect," was Jane's only verbal response.

CHAPTER 12

The leaves on the trees were poised and still resplendent in their fall colors of gold, orange, and auburn. Jane's dampened eyes saw none of the visual splendor. The scenery and her soul were in two different places. David drove in uncommon quiet, pensive in his posture with frequent sideward looks of concern for Jane. They had received the call about Grand late in the last evening and had frantically secured their schedules for a quick departure early the next morning.

Babcia Grand, Jane knew, had been troubled by heart problems for some time. Individuals could live for years with heart problems, the lay person in her insisted. The nurse in Jane rebuked the simplistic lament. She was all too aware. She had spoken with the doctors, and she had seen the test results. All that was new and all that they knew could not always cure or fix. The last drawn breath was as intrinsic to life as the first drawn breath, and no pill or scalpels incision could indefinitely stay its ultimate inevitability.

The up-and-down bumpiness of the road to the farmhouse resonated through Jane's body, a physical expression of the year as it had passed so far. So much had happened that it seemed as if the year should have already been over. She replayed everything in her mind, like a record with far too many skips. David had received his hard-earned master's degree in education and was anticipating his first offer as vice principal. They had purchased and moved into their first home, small and humble but so warm and welcoming. In unexpected celebration of their new home, she had become pregnant after trying for over a year. A little boy. She lost him in the first trimester of her pregnancy. Devastated, she and David were comforted only slightly by the doctor's consolation that first pregnancies often have complications and his confidence that the next pregnancy would be successful. And then the somber call from Filip about Grand. Jane inhaled deeply; the year of 1971 could not end soon enough.

Wilma and Filip walked out onto the kitchen side porch as the car slowed to a stop. They all embraced in welcomed hugs and paused in brief conversation before entering the house. Jane had expected them to leave immediately for the hospital but discovered in the words exchanged that the trip would not be necessary.

"What do you mean that she is here?" Jane responded incredulously. "Babcia Grand should be in the hospital where she can be treated properly."

Filip placed his arm in consolation around his oldest daughter. "There is nothing more that can be done" was his simple response. He continued before any further protest could be made. "She wants to be in her home when the time comes, not in a hospital. It is what she wants, and it is what she will have," he finished in a shaking voice but a convicted tone. Jane shook her head in acknowledgement and then buried her head in her father's broad shoulder. He placed his other arm around her and wrapped her tightly in his embrace. She lingered in the security of his arms, feeling as a child again and knowing that with him a part of her always would be. Gathering herself and her emotions, Jane raised her head and met her father's gaze with a weak smile. Leaving her dad's side, Jane reached for David's hand as the small group proceeded into the house.

They entered the kitchen, and the scent that met Jane's nose made her stop in amazement. There were so many memories in this room and many of them extremely tasty ones, though even a memory could not be this intense. Never intense enough to smell just like Grand's spice cookies. It was as if Wilma was reading her daughter's thoughts.

"No, you are not imagining it," she commented with pride. "I baked some of Grand's spice cookies."

Jane looked at her mother in understandable shock. "Don't tell me you..."

"Oh God no," Wilma was quick to respond. "I only baked them. Grand made the dough. She has been mixing, cooking, preparing, and freezing all sorts of things. The extra freezer in the cellar is about ready to burst! Even up to the day... this last time in the hospital... she was in the kitchen..." Wilma's voice failed as her words were overcome with emotion. Jane went quickly to her mother, hugging her as tears began to fall from the eyes of both mother and daughter. Wilma began to smile through her tears. "You know, Jane, I think that she's afraid that we are going to starve, your father and I."

Jane returned her mother's teary smile. "She may be right." There were needed chuckles all around. They all picked up a cookie and tasted with pleasure its spicy sweetness.

"These are Grand's favorite, Mom." Jane smiled. "They are wonderful and not the least bit burnt."

Wilma quickly placed a few cookies on a plate that had

already been garnished with a cup of hot tea then whispered quickly in passing, "This was my second batch. Not a word."

Jane did not know what to expect when she entered Babcia Grand's room. She had learned from her years at the hospital that one never grew accustomed to death, one only became familiar with the sight of it. When she leaned over to hold Grand's hand and to kiss her cheek, she recognized it, but it was different. It was not someone else's loved one that she was staring at. It was her own, and the finality of it she was not prepared for.

Drawing back from the bed, Jane, still holding her grand-mother's hand, looked lovingly but helplessly into Grand's weary eyes. A determined twinkle peeked through the weary gaze as Grand swept her delicate thin hand in the direction of the plate of cookies that had been placed on the table next to her bed. "Did you taste them?"

"Yes, I did, Grand. They were just lovely. Not a bit burnt," was Jane's somewhat overexuberant response.

"It was her second batch you know." Babcia Grand squinted knowingly back. Jane laughed as did everyone else in the room, including Wilma. Babcia Grand turned her face toward Wilma and reached out her hand for her daughter-in-law. Wilma was at her side in an instant and holding Alena's hand, stroked it gently sharing a moment of mutual love, respect, and affection.

"Do you remember the day, that first day that you landed that plane of yours at the edge of the cornfield? You took out at least two rows of good feed corn." Wilma smiled and nodded in recognition. "Oh you were a wild sight with those goggles and your curls tousled about. How Aurek and I laughed about it that night. And then you came to stay. How many times you made me laugh and how many times I needed to even when you didn't mean to." Babcia Grand took Wilma's hand to her cheek and then kissed it. "You are the sun on the cloudiest day in this family, and if I have never told you before, know it now and always remember it." Wilma's eyes were fixed on Alena as the words just spoken seemed to illuminate her face as a new dawn. It was a gift given of love and admiration never to be forgotten.

"You remember everything, and you never miss anything either, do you, Grand?" Jane interjected softly.

"No," was the confident response, "and I never did. Especially those cake fights that you, your sister, and your friends used to have. Covered in cake you must have been. The icing behind the ears always gave you away. Feeding the pigs indeed!" was the feigned indignant response.

"You never said a thing! You couldn't have ... " Jane gasped in disbelief as her face flushed in recognition.

Babcia Grand smiled contently. "You two girls never got anything past me even when in your devilish delight you thought that you had. Speaking of getting away with things, where is Ann?" Grand asked with building strength in her voice.

"She is in transit, Mother," Filip said. "She will get here as quickly as the navy will send her."

"There is a 'delivered via naval air stamp' on my butt as I have arrived," came the boisterous addition to the chatter of the room. Indeed, in the door stood Ann in full uniform. Briskly she made her way to Grand's bedside. Planting a warm kiss on the face of her beloved grandmother, Ann looked at her in an exaggeratedly critical manner. "What do the doctors know! You look great!" Before a word could be spoken by anyone, Ann, eyeing the cookies next to the bed, picked one up and promptly popped it into her mouth. Her smiling expression changed into one of discontent. "These aren't yours, are they, Grand? They taste a little burnt." Babcia Grand smiled with satisfaction. She could never have heard a more fitting eulogy without its intent of being one. Her culinary legend would be preserved for many years to come. Reaching her hands upward for Ann to come to her, she brushed an appreciative kiss on her granddaughter's cheek.

The afternoon warmed itself with memories, smiles, and laughter. There was no verbal sadness shared, as Babcia Grand would have none. They were all gathered, she made it a point to say, not to participate in a wake, but to enjoy a time of togetherness and happiness. It was her wish and her word, and it was to be followed. There may have been an ache of heart but not of words.

The sun finally bowed to the evening's moon as the group chatted quietly, and Grand slipped into a quiet and a contented sleep. "Perhaps we should let her rest for a while and go to the kitchen for something to eat," Filip directed softly. "I am sure that everyone is hungry." There were nods of acknowledgement as one by one they touched Alena gently then left the room.

They gathered around the old and familiar kitchen table and enjoyed a light meal of cold meats and salads. It was a brief time to get caught up on what was new in each other's lives. Even though they all spoke to each other frequently, events in life seemed to move faster than their phone calls could catch. As they finished the meal, David and Filip remained at the table while Wilma sat with Grand. Jane, feeling a need for fresh air, stepped out onto the side porch. She was soon joined by Ann. They sat down next to each on the porch step, their knees tucked to their chest to buffer the chill of the autumn evening. "Do you remember all of the times that we used to sit here as kids, Ann?"

"We hatched some great plots from this old step, Janie. But it seems that we had more room on this step back then." Jane smiled. She had noticed the tight fit as well.

"Nothing will be the same without, Grand!" Ann burst out tearfully and then continued stormily. "I'll be able to cuss all that I want, and eat all of the sugar that I want, and gossip shamelessly all that I want."

Jane put her arm around her now sobbing sister. "But, Ann," she tried to reason, "you can do all of those things now anyway. You are all grown up. You can do whatever you want, even if it is what you shouldn't."

Ann turned to her sister with tears streaming down her face. "Yes, I can do all of those things and more, so much more. That's the grown-up part of me, the part of me that stands at attention. But I couldn't do those things here, Janie. Not here. Not with Grand. She is the only person that lets a little piece of me still be little. I'll miss that so much, Janie. I will miss her."

Most of the family had gone to bed, except for Wilma and Filip, who sat at the kitchen table, checking frequently on Alena. It was deep into the night, but Jane still could not sleep. No consoling hug from David could calm her restlessness as she lay wide awake while he slept soundly beside her. Frustrated, Jane slipped from the warmth of the bed and, wrapping herself in her robe, went quietly down the stairs. She saw the muted light of the kitchen and heard the muffled conversation of her parents. It was not their company that she sought. Unnoticed, she entered her grandmother's room and found her still asleep. Kneeling next to the bed, she placed her head tenderly next to Babcia Grand's hand. Jane had no wish to awaken her, only an unyielding need to touch her and to be near her.

"Have you done something wrong, Miss Jane, that causes you to be kneeling at your grandmother's side?" Babcia Grand spoke out quite unexpectedly. Jane raised her head but did not speak as her words would have only come as tears.

Cupping her granddaughter's chin lightly in her hand, Babcia Grand said, "I have not seen you since you lost the baby. You are hurt and troubled. I know how desperately you want a child, David's child." Jane tried to turn away, but Grand held her face firmly with unexpected strength.

"What we want may not always be what we get. But sometimes it can be so much more than we could have ever asked for or expected." Her memory was still so clear as Alena continued. "When we lost your brother and your grandfather, it felt as if our hearts were broken, that love was lost. Then you were born and then Ann. Those that we love leave us, Jane, sometimes sooner and sometimes later, but our love for them never does, and new life reminds us that our ability to love never ends; it is boundless. You and Ann were proof of that. Your heart is broken right now, but you must have faith and believe." Gently Alena stroked Jane's face. "Have faith and believe. You have the love of a good man, and you love him; trust that from so great a love will come more love in all forms. Don't narrow your view, Jane; expand your heart. Remember my words; you will come to understand." The words exhausted but contented her grandmother's fading spirit.

Taking Babcia Grand's hand in her own, Jane promised that she would remember, and suddenly she did—everything. This time, this place, her words, the past, and the future; it was all happening too quickly. She saw him, Golden Boy, out of the corner of her eye. He walked to the other side of the bed and reached for Alena's hand. Smiling, Alena clasped his hand as the pigment of her face began to fade and the breath became shallow, leaving her lips as a whisper. There was little time to say anything. Grand's eyes were fixed, staring. Jane needed to know. She yelled out in panic, "Wait, Grand! What do you see? Tell me? What do you see?"

"Exactly what I wanted to see" was Alena's simple response.

And in that moment as hurried footsteps approached, he was gone and so was Grand.

CHAPTER 13

"You are kidding, aren't you?" Jane asked. Looking at David's beaming face, she could not tell if his smile reflected a joke or a joy. Sweeping her into his arms, he whispered into her ear that he was not kidding and that, yes, he had been offered a position of vice principal at a school in Maine and that, yes, he wanted to accept it. He was smiling; she was not.

"David, for goodness' sake, of all of the schools in all of the states, you have to consider a school in Maine? It might as well be on the moon!" Jane dropped her head in an exhausted thud onto David's chest. David continued to hold her tight.

"There were not any positions open on the moon," he added playfully. Jane pulled away from him in anger.

"I am not in a joking mood, David. You are asking me to leave everything behind—my home, my job, my family. I don't know if I can do that." Jane was certainly not in a joking mood as it had been another tough year. She had miscarried yet again, and it had not been any easier, rather much harder. David had been so loving and supportive, but her optimism was failing her. How could David ask her to leave the love and the support that she needed now more than ever! She needed to be with her family, her whole family, not just David. Maine was just too far; it might as well be the moon. Jane lowered her face into her hands despondently. Reaching for her, David gently lifted her face to meet his gaze.

"I know that I am asking a lot. I know that you will be away from your family, but I just thought..." He reached for just the right words to say. "I thought that we could start fresh in a new place, like a new world. We can't change what has happened, but we can move forward and change what lies ahead. You remember that old phrase 'a change will do you good.' Let's do it, Jane; let's make a change." Jane looked at his hopeful face warily but with a little more interest.

"And look, I checked it all out. There is a hospital near where we would live, near the school. You can still work and do what you love to do. And the school, Jane, it's grades kindergarten through twelve! And the principal is going to retire in about eighteen months, so he would be training me to be the new principal. And I got this book all about Maine." He stopped just long enough to breathe and to hand her the book. "It looks beautiful. What do you think?"

Jane took the book into her hands and skimmed through the pages. It did look beautiful, but there was more than atmosphere to consider. She was so very unsure, but then again she was unsure about almost everything right now. Looking at David's encouraging face, she knew that she was sure about one thing, one person, David. Maybe, just maybe he was right. Maybe a change could make a difference. She had no more to risk and maybe, just maybe, something to gain. Jane continued to stare at him as her thoughts raced through her mind. Seizing the opportunity of her silence, David spoke.

"I am not saying this to be hurtful, but," he continued once again holding her close, "we don't have little feet to chase after right now, not yet. And I do mean not yet because I know in my heart that we will. So let's do this. Let's make this move to Maine and chase little feet there, as many pairs as we can." Jane held onto David tightly, trying to let his confidence and conviction quell her insecurities.

"Okay," she responded softly. "It is worth a chance, and just maybe the change will make the difference ..." Her voice weakened then faded. David held her in his arms as the tears came as they too often did.

They left on a brilliantly sunny but hot day in June. This was not to be the final move as that was not to occur until late July. David had accepted the position and had already made several trips to Maine in introduction and initial training, but this was Jane's first visit. There was much to be done before July as they needed to find a house and Jane needed to find a job. The good-byes had been building as their eventual departure approached. It was almost an emotional relief just to be getting away from the trauma of constant farewells, so Jane found some unexpected pleasant anticipation in their trip.

The car traveled with ease, unencumbered by emotion or memory. The landscape changed as they left behind the gently sloping farmland, the aging steel towns, and family. It was hard for Jane to imagine any other place as home; there had never been any other. Yet, the car's rhythmic motion soothed her unsettledness. The windows engaged her in a panorama of scenery unfamiliar but intriguing. *Oh brave new world,* Jane pondered. A new world to be sure, but the bravery would need to come from her.

Moving her gaze from the window, Jane looked at David

sitting comfortably behind the wheel. A smile had not left his face since she had said yes to this adventure, and it was still firmly planted as he drove. Catching her stare out of the corner of his eye, he was gratified by her grin, a crooked one but a grin nonetheless.

"Is that smile stuck, or are you really that happy?" Jane inquired a little cynically. Almost impossibly, his smile broadened even more as he responded.

"No surgery necessary. I really am that happy and plan on being even happier because I have a surprise." David's smile took on a Cheshire cat quality that made Jane nervous. Before Jane could ask about the surprise, she paused. They both saw it at the same time, the bridge that would take them over the waterway into Maine. The crossing took but a moment or two, but it was as if one life had been handed off to another as the car's tires changed tempo, transitioning from bridge surface to road surface. It was done. They were in Maine.

Jane and David were without words for some time as their eyes took in their surroundings. Seeing a sign for a scenic pull-over, David took the turn. Pines quickly enveloped them but then just as quickly gave way to the promised vision. Leaving the car parked, they strolled, stopped, then stared. Wrapping their arms around each other's waist, they gazed in awe at the vista before them. The Atlantic Ocean lapped almost passively on the rocky shore. There was no sand to fling by wind; only rounded stones in mass lined the shoreline, many speckled in shades of gray and black turned and beautifully polished by the Master Jeweler. Tall pines towered in a protective embrace beyond the rocks and bowed only to the prickly primrose adorned in pink blossoms that settled as sea sirens at their feet. Though Jane and David stood in sunlight, a light fog wistfully kept its distance offshore as if heeding the stern warning of the foghorn of a nearby lighthouse. Jane had never seen anything like it. It was nothing like home, but somehow she knew that in this place, she could make a home.

"It is just so beautiful, David!" she exclaimed. "The ocean, the rocks, the pines, it's just beautiful," she repeated.

"I knew that you would fall in love with it," David responded, his spirits heightened by her positive reaction. "And wait until you see our house. It is right on the water as well."

It only took a few seconds for David's statement to sink in. Jane turned, stunned, toward David. "What house?"

David continued smiling confidently. "I bought a house, our home. It was an incredible opportunity, and I knew that you would love it." Jane's arms slowly folded in front of her as her jaw began to set in consternation; still David continued. "Look, before you abandon me on some deserted shore and head back to Pennsylvania, just promise me one thing. Before you condemn me and the house, look at it first? I know that you will love it. You trust me, don't you?" David finished imploringly.

"David," Jane began with the voice of a teacher brandishing a ruler. "This situation has nothing to do with trust. Well, actually it does. I trust you not to make major decisions on your own that impact our lives. And, David, a house is a major decision that impacts our lives; personally and financially. These are together decisions, do you understand that?"

"I know." David's smile dissolved into sincerity. "Buying a house is a major decision. I want your input in everything that we do, but this was not a decision. It was a gift. You have had so much on you lately, too much. You made this move for me, and I wanted to do something for you. I wanted you to have a home to come to, not a home to search for."

Jane turned from him and focused her view back out onto the water. He watched her as her eyes seemed to be searching for answers. David waited, and as he observed her once taunt demeanor relax, he seized his opportunity. Moving softly behind her, he wrapped his arms around her waist and locked his hands protectively. Reflexively she leaned into him as he whispered into her ear.

"This is the conch shell speaking," he began playfully. "Look at it first. I know that you will love it."

Jane chuckled then countered by whispering into his ear. "You are echoing just like a conch shell. I have heard, 'I know that you will love it,' or some slight variation of it at least four times since we have stopped. Who knows, maybe the conch shell will be right, or maybe I am just being brainwashed."

David turned Jane to face him. His serious expression had faded as his smile triumphantly returned. She loved his smile. She loved him. Reaching for his face, she kissed him, letting her fingers tangle in his warm brown hair. "Okay then?" he asked hopefully.

"Let me look at it first."

Their first stop was to be their half-approved but nonetheless fully owned home before anything else was seen. David pointed out sights of interest as they came closer to their destination. The sights, like the gas station and the grocery store, though unimpressive, thinned as their surroundings became dotted by homes and the occasional farm. What could one do around here? What would she do?

"Lilac Lane," Jane commented as David made the final turn onto the road. "At least it has a nice smell to it." The road continued lazily curving from left to right. Houses appeared, comfortably resting on one side of the road or the other. In fact, they looked as if they had been resting for some time.

"These houses look a bit weathered." Jane observed with a hint of discomfort.

"Oh," David answered with ease. "They are showing character that comes with maturity. Many of these homes have stood for well over a hundred years. There is no flimsy modern construction in those good old bones."

"The key word here is *old*, I would say," Jane commented as her brave-new-world resolve began to erode. The road came to an end and with it Jane's teetering optimism. The only option that remained at the end of the line was an overgrown driveway anchored by scraggily pines and valiantly guarded by a dilapidated mailbox. The car stopped at the mouth of the driveway.

"Well," David exulted. "This is it! Shall we go in?"

Jane stared at him as if he had taken leave of his senses. "David, is there any way that we can get out of this?" she asked flatly. Smiling, he patted her hand and, reminding her of her promise to look at it first, confidently directed the car into the driveway. As they passed the dilapidated mailbox and squeezed through the pines, Jane felt as if she were entering a nightmare. The car proceeded on a slight upward climb of the rutted road while pine branches scraped and grabbed at the sides of the car as if desiring to consume it and its passengers. Suddenly the evergreens released their hold and parted, revealing a house sitting aged but regally on an overgrown lawn scattered with unattended shrubs. David pulled in front and parked the car. Leaping from the car, he ran to the passenger door, pulling his somewhat shocked spouse from the vehicle.

Jane stared. The old Victorian stared unashamedly back. It was not at all what she had expected given the introduction, thank God. It was a grand home actually from a grand time. Jane's gaze softened, but the house was not so forgiving. The towering turret on the northeastern side of the house glared down, daring any thought of transgression. An array of windows in rounds, rectangles, and octagons mirrored back mutual curiosity. *Years of neglect have been unkind but,* Jane thought, *not unfixable.* Half smiling, she was not even aware of David's intense gaze as he had been so quiet that he had dissolved into the background of her observations. *Yes,* she continued to evaluate in her mind, *there is something stalwart and inviting in the old bones of this house.* She liked it, not loved it, not yet. Words came as Jane's eyes finally left the house and met David's.

"It is a huge house." David nodded silently in agreement. "It needs a lot of work, new paint, and, oh my, who knows what else." David again nodded in agreement. "Structurally you had it checked out, right?" she added in a startled voice. "It's not going to fall down or anything, is it?" David nodded yes then no. Jane looked sternly at David. "Are you going to say anything at all, or are you just going to nod all day?"

"What do you think of it?"

"Well," Jane began reluctantly but warmly, "I have to see the inside, but so far it has possibilities. Can we go in?" David reached into his pocket and, pulling out an old skeleton key, offered it to Jane.

"It's yours" was his answer. Jane reached for the key with her left hand and with her right hand reached for David. He grasped her hand and kissed it sweetly. It was just what she needed as she instantaneously swung and wrapped her arms around his neck, kissing him passionately and whispering into his ear that everything was okay no matter what. There had been so much tension over the move and then the house. They fell to the grass in release, laughing as children then kissing as lovers. Rolling onto their backs side by side, they looked up at the beautiful blue sky laced with carefree clouds of white.

Jane inhaled deeply and then exhaled. "I feel as if I have taken my first deep breath in a very long time." David, nuzzling her neckline, teased her that he agreed with the benefits of deep breathing. Jane pulled away. It was private here certainly, but not that private. Jumping to her feet, she chided him. "Am I ever going to see the inside of our home?" Reluctantly he rose to his feet and then reached for her, kissing her and sweeping her into his arms.

Wide steps led them to the porch, which wrapped around

the sides of the house. Despite its wear and frequently buck-ling planks, it seemed to invite wood rockers, potted plants, and a good book. Double oak carved doors looked unyielding, but as Jane turned the key in the lock, the right side sepa-rated from its twin with only a slight groan. Upon entering the foyer, they were greeted by a sweeping staircase. Hand in hand they began in the first of the double parlors, a schematic so common in the architecture of the time period. David had already seen the house, but as this was Jane's first time, they progressed slowly. Her eyes widened in awe. It needed work yes, but the craftsmanship! Beautiful wood floors, crown mold-ing, wainscoting, large rooms for entertaining, small rooms for intimacy, and even a library: how she could picture her beloved books there with room for more! It just needed some care, a lot of work, love, and again a lot of work. It was as if a clock had stopped somewhere and she need only wind it to bring life back again. Life: renew, a new; it was what David had tried to tell her. Little feet would scamper across old floors made new again; she just knew it.

"Wait! Wait!" David practically shouted. "I saved the best for last!" They were standing in the kitchen. "Close your eyes," he commanded gently as he guided her from the kitchen out onto the back porch. "Now open your eyes," he instructed with a hint of magic in his voice. Jane's eyes fluttered opened, tak-ing a few moments to adjust to the bright sunlight. Focusing her gaze, she stared in amazement. A stubby stairway led from the back porch to an expansive patch of crabby grass. The intermittent pines that moped nearby seemed unimpressed, but Jane most certainly was. The fringe of languishing land-scape before her spread its tired arms toward the majesty of the sea. The slight salty breeze caught her breath as she stared in awe, and she felt, that no matter how long she lived and no matter how many times her eyes and her soul took in this view, it would always feel as it did right now: new and wondrous.

They went down the steps together and walked quickly to the spot where the rocks, nestling in tall grass, sloped gently to the equally rocky shore. The waves lapped so casually as if to appear ordinary. Jane held onto David tightly as words raced through her mind and passed her lips without sound, unable to find their voice. How could this all be? The question broke through her maze of thoughts and finally gave way to speech. "David, how ... this view ... all of this ... and the house. How could we ..." She finished in fragmented confusion and disbelief.

"Afford it?" David completed in quick summation. "These big old houses don't sell as well as they used to. What is new is what is wanted, and as you can see, this house is far from new and it does need a lot of work, *but* it is pretty amazing to the right eyes, isn't it?"

"Amazing?" Jane responded wistfully as she turned to look at the house and then turned back again to inhale the oceanic painting before her. "It's a definition of infinite description." They stood together arm and arm in peaceful quiet, joining as if by a painter's brush, the magnificent mural that encompassed them. *How nice it would be to stand here forever,* Jane pondered in silence.

Putting the next few pending minutes in order, Jane left her fanciful meanderings as one more little issue had to be addressed before moving forward. "There is just one item that I would like to clarify." Jane began. "The next time "see it first," no matter what it is, means before we buy, not after you buy. Okay?"

David looked at Jane sheepishly. "Understood, *but* you do like it, don't you?" He accepted the hug and a kiss as a yes.

"Now," Jane continued, "why don't you show me that new school of yours and ... oh no, what time is it?" David quickly looked at his watch.

"Now don't panic. It is two thirty, your interview is not

until three, and we are only twenty minutes from the hospital." David saw the lack of confidence in her expression. "We better run just in case I am a little off." And so the sprint began.

The hospital was not too hard to find as it was the only one in Portland, Maine. It was somewhat small, unlike most of the hospitals in which Jane had trained and worked. There was a coziness to it that unfortunately did not reflect in the décor of the room in which Jane now found herself. She sat in one of two straight-backed chairs that faced a large metal desk that was anchored by two potted erect and straight plants; nothing was allowed to slouch. There were no pictures, no clutter; not even an errant pen or pencil seemed to be allowed. Bright fluorescent lights seemed to unwontedly illuminate Jane's building nervousness. It had been a long time since she had felt this unsteady as she didn't know whether to expect an interview or an interrogation. The door opened behind her, and promptly rising, Jane turned to greet the nurse administrator of PM Northeastern Medical Center—Sylvia Laithe.

She was a woman in her early fifties of slight frame without an ounce of fat to spare, yet her lack of girth in no way reflected her stature; she was not a woman to be taken lightly or in jest. Greeting with a firm handshake, her steel blue eyes met Jane's gaze with sincerity and intensity. Motioning for Jane to take her seat again, she briskly moved behind the desk and then with military precision sat down addressing Jane without pause.

"I appreciate the extensive information that you forwarded with your application for employment. Your qualifications, experience, and educational background are exemplary. You would be an asset to the staff and the patients of this hospital, and I want you to join our team." There was no time for humble acknowledgement as she continued. "I am sure that this hospital is smaller than the hospitals that you are accustomed to, *but* PM Medical prides itself on service rather than size." Jane did not waiver at the last comment but wondered whether mind reading was also one of Sylvia's talents. There was no time to wonder further as Ms. Laithe continued again with barely an audible intake of oxygen. "I have a particular position in mind for you which will require some additional study on your part, which I feel sure will not be a problem. Your portfolio also included your personal medical information." Sylvia glanced upward from Jane's paperwork in brief and direct acknowledgement. Jane was unflinching. "I hope that you will not consider this insensitive as I need draw attention to the fact that you have lost two pregnancies through early miscarriage."

Jane maintained a steady gaze, unwilling to recoil from the matter-of-fact statement. She sat unbending and surprisingly unaffected as the straightforward manner of this woman thankfully eliminated the need for tender treading or tears. Jane matched her in response.

"Yes. That is correct, and how exactly does my medical history segue into a position here?" Rising from the desk, Sylvia Laithe walked to the front of the desk and, leaning lightly against it, crossed her arms with conviction.

"You are a bright young woman. Life teaches what the books cannot. I want you to pilot a new program at this hospital. As I said before, PM Medical is about service, not size. We seek to address both the physical and the emotional needs of our patients; the two are really inseparable. I want you to be our new high-risk pregnancy nurse specialist. You will be assigned cases and will be an in-hospital patient advocate through pre and post natal. High-risk pregnancies are becoming more common, unfortunately, even in the smaller hospitals like ours. It will require specific additional study on your part, as I mentioned earlier. Are you interested?"

Jane was both shocked and honored. To offer a specialized position of this nature to an individual with no prior experience and new to the hospital was most unusual. "Yes, I am very interested and very flattered that you would offer me this opportunity." Nurse Laithe turned to her desk and lifted the expansive file that Jane had forwarded.

"It has nothing to do with flattery, I can assure you," Sylvia responded sharply. "I know your qualifications. I know that what you have experienced in your miscarriages gives you unique insight into the emotional and physical issues of the woman for whom you will be entrusted. The knowing part of it will come in time, if you accept the position."

David had not been waiting long when Jane exited the hospital briskly. He smiled optimistically as she got into the car. "Yes," she responded to his unasked question. "I have a job. I can't even call it a job; it's an opportunity. It will be challenging but"—she caught a glimpse of paint cans and a menagerie of brushes and rollers in the back of the car—"I, we like a challenge or challenges, right?" Looking at David imploringly, Jane had but one request before the challenge of the paint brushes commenced. "Can we at least eat first?"

Quick to respond to his wife's needs, David lifted a bulging sack from the seat, which seemed to be slightly stained with grease. "It's in the bag." Jane smiled contently, considering the days ahead. It had been a good day, a very good day.

CHAPTER 14

Jane sat in the same straight-backed chair, more comfortably though than she had the first time almost two years earlier. It was spring 1975, and as Jane waited, she admired the yellow potted tulips that she had placed on Sylvia's gray desk, the only splash of color in the room. It had become a good-natured joke between them. There was always something blooming on Nurse Laithe's desk, and although she feigned indifference, the one week that Jane had forgotten the flowery foliage, she was promptly reminded by her superior that commitment required consistency.

The door opened spritely as Nurse Laithe briskly entered the office and motioned for Jane to remain seated. It was Friday, their customary meeting day to discuss the hospital's high-risk pregnancy cases. The routine never changed; it was always business first. As Sylvia began scanning the charts before her on the desk, she began an adjacent verbal overview.

"Mrs. Vincent lost her little boy last night," she began evenly while eyeing the second chart. "I was sorry to hear that."

"Yes," Jane responded on an equally even keel. "He was stillborn. An emergency C-section was immediately performed when the erratic heartbeat was detected on the fetal monitor. Resuscitation was administered upon delivery but was unsuccessful. He was a beautiful little boy; they named him Adam." Jane finished with softness in her voice.

Sylvia raised her eyes from the charts and observed Jane with intensity. It had taken the nurse only a week or two to determine that she had chosen appropriately. Now, almost two years later, Jane had continued to excel and even expand the program to home-care visits as well. It was still a hard job to be sure. She had watched Jane commiserate over the loss of each infant as if it were her own yet unselfishly give comfort and support. In the sweet reward of healthy cries Jane drew inspiration and hope for the next difficult case. Sylvia realized from her own experience, that nursing required strength and compassion, though marred many times by despair and regaining balance only through a degree of detachment yet always remaining fortified by indomitable commitment. It was a skill that once learned sometimes left one emotionally remote for as a maternal pride welled in Sylvia's heart for Jane, it remained unspoken; it was her way. The review continued, and once completed, only one order of business remained for Sylvia to address. "Am I invited to dinner this Sunday?" she inquired more matter-of-factly than as a question.

Jane smiled. "You know that there is an open invitation any evening for dinner, but, as this Sunday is the third Sunday in April and as it is a ritual for you to come to our house for dinner on the third Sunday of every month, the logical answer would be yes." A small upward motion threatened the corners of Sylvia's mouth. How Sylvia reminded Jane of her Babcia Grand! It was a pleasant remembrance as she had come to rely on Sylvia's strength and healthy endowment of common sense. They were firm friends, though they always maintained as Babcia Grand would have observed, the appropriate measure of propriety and respect. Another question interrupted Jane's thoughts.

"Am I to witness any new wonders of improvement on that behemoth Victorian of yours since my last visit?"

"Oh you know the house is coming along." Jane sighed then smiled. "I have come to the conclusion that this house will always be in a state of becoming rather than completing. But I have also come to the conclusion that it is the same plight for every homeowner." Another thought quickly came to Jane's mind. "It may be fortuitous that you are coming this particular Sunday." Sylvia responded with only a quizzical look. "David has informed me that he has a big surprise for me this Sunday."

"Was not his last big surprise for you the house?" Sylvia countered dryly.

"Yes. That was a big one, wasn't it?"

Sunday came, and the house was immersed in flavorful smells. Babcia Grand had trained Jane well as she was an excellent cook. Jane had pummeled David relentlessly as to the nature of his surprise, but his only hint was that Jane should prepare ample for dinner; nothing further could be pried from his sealed lips. It was not difficult to surmise that there would be additional guests for dinner, but she could not imagine what guests would require such secrecy. It was unsettling as David was equally reliable and unpredictable; it was the unpredictable part that worried her. Thirty minutes before dinner, David entered the kitchen where Jane was working and kissing her sweetly, exited the kitchen again without a word. Hearing the front door creak open and then shut, she shook her head and wondered what was in store.

Sylvia arrived and was uncharacteristically early as Jane was quick to note. The always steady respondent acknowledged the accuracy of the observation but maintained that it was better to be early rather than late, though they both knew that she was never either. Thinking momentarily that Sylvia knew something that she didn't, Jane shrugged the idea off as improbable. David was totally intimidated by "General Laithe" as he occasionally called her, so a behind-the-back alliance was out of the question.

They were upstairs in the turret room looking at the newest completed paint project that had followed the newest completed plaster project when they heard David call out in greeting. Promptly leaving the room, they walked down the hallway and began the descent down the stairway. Sylvia reached the foyer alone as Jane had slowed and then stopped completely several steps from the bottom. Three boys stood staring up as she stood staring down. They were standing with David just inside the door and were actually three surprises, not one, the tallest one not reaching the height of David's shoulder.

Jane recovered quickly from the sight of her unexpected guests as she traveled the last few steps and joined her company. She smiled at them warmly. They were probably just students at David's school, and in fact she was sure of it even though she had never met them before. It was completely normal even though David had never brought students to their house for dinner before. She continued smiling as she shook each one of the boys' hands and waited for an introduction. Noticing that David's face was beaming, Jane's internal smile began to fade; his look was too familiar.

"Well," David began, "let me introduce our honored guests for the evening." Like a modified version of duck, duck, goose, he gently tapped the youngest boy on the head. "This is Robert, and this young but growing gentleman is four and on his way to kindergarten this fall." Robert smiled and wiggled pleasantly as if ready for take-off. "And this," he continued by tapping the head of the next tallest in line. "This is Eric, a second-grade scholar and an excellent speller. He is seven." Eric broke rank and, coming to Jane, reached for her hand. "Thank you for having us for dinner, Mrs. Bell. Mr. Bell says that you are a very good cook." Jane smiled in appreciation but waited for the third introduction before speaking.

"And the senior member and leader of this pack," David finished with a hug of affection, "is Michael, and he is ten. And they are all members of the Stanford family." Michael seemed to be the most stand-offish of the three, saying nothing and barely mustering a smile.

Jane did not understand the need for David's secrecy, but she had no doubt that at some point she would find out. Until that time she was going to do what she always did with her guests: make them feel welcome and at home. "I am so glad that Mr. Bell invited you three gentlemen for dinner tonight," she said warmly with a wink. "There is a bit of a chill in this April evening air, so I made pot roast and mashed potatoes for dinner tonight. How does that sound?"

Robert spoke up immediately. "Are there any vegables?"

Jane lowered to her knees to address his question. "Why yes, Robert. We are having carrots and peas."

"Do I hafta eat 'em?" was his equally rapid response.

Sylvia, who had been quietly watching, too quietly, now spoke for the first time. "Of course you have to eat them," she answered firmly. "You are a guest. Good manners require that you eat what you are given, and vegetables are good for you."

Robert looked at Sylvia quizzically but offered his next question generally. "Is she staying for dinner?" he added, resting his gaze firmly on Sylvia leaving no doubt as to who "she" was. Jane could only nod yes as she feared if she had said the word she would have burst into laughter. Without a word or resistance, Robert walked to Nurse Laithe and took her hand.

"Will you sit next to me and watch me eat my vegables?" he asked, tugging gently and insistently on her hand.

"Why ever should I watch you eat your vegables, I mean vegetables?" she asked incredulously as this young sprite had totally unnerved her, a sight Jane had never before witnessed.

"'Case I forget, you can 'member me" was the simple answer.

Enclosing his hand firmly in hers, more in affection than direction, Sylvia began leading him into the dining room as the others followed. "That is a very wise request, Robert," she complimented the youngest of the brood. "And have no worries, for I will remind you."

Dinner was a flurry of food, questions, and conversation. Robert did not have to be "'membered" to eat his vegetables, as he made it a point to turn his head to Sylvia each time that he took a spoonful. She smiled—yes smiled—encouragingly, though the sight of peas and carrots being ground in his frequently open mouth must not have been a pleasant one. Eric offered to help with the clearing of the table and even assisted with the washing of the dishes; the automatic dishwasher had not yet made the project list. Michael remained quiet throughout the meal but did timidly enter the conversation during dessert when David brought up the topic of baseball. After dessert, Jane brought out one of her old childhood games. Called "Flip a Lid," it was a modified version of tiddlywinks. Everyone joined in, Sylvia assisting Robert. It got rather raucous with lids flying everywhere for, despite Sylvia's guidance, Robert found it much more entertaining to send his lid flying in every direction except into the box for points.

It was getting late, and David suggested that it was time for the boys to be getting home. Warm hugs were exchanged along with Jane's sincere promise that they could come back again soon. The boys scuttled out the door and into the car. As

Jane and Sylvia stood waving, Sylvia suggested that she stay to keep Jane company until David's return. Eyeing her curiously, Jane accepted verbally, knowing that this delay would cause Sylvia to exceed her usual prompt nine o'clock departure, most unusual and putting Jane back on alert.

David returned shortly to find Jane and Sylvia seated in the living room, chatting congenially. In an effort to blend in, David quietly and casually took a seat but quickly realized that the conversation had abruptly stopped. Observing his companions in the room, he noted that Jane was sitting stiffly with her arms crossed in front of her while Sylvia appeared to be sitting calmly. David decided to remain silent. The furnace decided to speak first as it grumbled to life at the insistence of the quickly chilling evening.

"Why did dinner tonight have to be such a big surprise?" Jane asked David.

"Well," David began with unconvincing nonchalance, "I have never brought any of my students home for dinner before, and I was not sure how you would feel about it."

An unpleasant huff escaped from Jane's lips. "David, you will have to do better than that. Who are these boys, where do they live, and most importantly what are you up to?"

"Well…" David began again with a quick glance to Sylvia in hopeful support; Sylvia remained silent. "You know who the boys are, of course. They are currently living close to the school with good friends of their parents."

"Currently?" Jane picked up on immediately. "What do you mean currently? Where are their parents?"

"Stephen and Angela Stanford died in an accident two months ago" was David's level response. "They have no other family in Maine, so they are staying with friends."

Jane caught her breath and was flooded with immediate compassion and sympathy. "Oh dear God, no. Those dear sweet boys. What happened?"

David began to explain. Stephen and Angela Stanford were originally from Massachusetts; Stephen was a fisherman. They had decided to move the family five years ago to Maine to start a lobster business. Angela was pregnant with Robert when they made the move. They purchased a small home near the water and with the remainder of their savings purchased a lobster boat. The business was hard but was beginning to show a profit. To help out, Angela would occasionally go out with Stephen on the boat as the sternman. A little over two months ago, they had gone out together on the boat early in the morning. The boys were in school except for Robert, who was with a neighbor. The boat did not return that evening. A search was started early the next morning. The boat was found partially swamped; Angela and Stephen were not on board. The search continued, but they were not found and were presumed lost. The school of course was notified, and David was supporting the boys and trying to help with the situation in any way that he could. A sad silence enveloped the room. Jane's heart ached, but her practical mind began to address the most immediate issues.

"What will happen to them? I assume that there are family members more than willing to take them. I hope that they can stay in the community. It would be so much easier on them during the transition."

"Well," David began in the most delicate of voice, "there is no family to take them, so whether they stay in the community depends ... "

"Oh no, no, no, no, no, David, what have you done?" Jane began to stutter in panic. "Tonight, the secrecy, the surprise ... are we it, are they it, the surprise?"

"Well ... " David tried to begin but was abruptly interrupted.

"I want to be an aunt," Sylvia burst forth from her self-induced silence. "Robert is a jewel; he just needs some polishing. Overall, they are wonderful boys."

"You told her before you told me?" Jane responded incredulously glaring at David, then at Sylvia, then back at David again. "How could you? You said that she intimidates the hell out of you!"

"Nonsense." Sylvia once again intercepted David's intended response. "He felt that he needed some sound advice before he approached you, and I was the obvious choice. No decisions were made certainly."

Jane was stunned into silence. She knew that David could be a shaky limb at times but now Sylvia; they must be crazy. David used the temporary lull to speak at last.

"Now, Jane." he began with an easy sincerity. "Sweetheart, just take a deep breath for me, really. Calm down just a bit. This will all get sorted out." His attempt at calm was ineffective as Jane stood up and began to pace the room.

"Take a deep breath. I'd rather take your breath right about now. I'd rather..." She stopped abruptly and turned to look at David. "David," she addressed him pleadingly, "tell me that you didn't say anything to the boys. To get their hopes and then...their hearts have already been broken once. Tell me..." She saw his rapidly shaking head and hopelessly pleading expression. She softened slightly. "Oh, go ahead and talk!"

"Okay," David began with some relief. "Angela and Stephen were only children, so there are no siblings to take the boys. There is a great aunt on Angela's side, but she is in her late seventies and has said that she cannot take them." The speed and urgency in his words increased. "The friends that currently have them have four children of their own and have no means of keeping them either. One of the last remaining options is foster care with the hope of adoption, but there are no guarantees that they can be kept together."

"So..." Jane proceeded noticeably calmer. "What other option have you and *Sylvia*"—with an unpleasant accentuation on Sylvia's name—"decided upon."

"Well," David began amiably, "when I filled out the preliminary forms with child services—"

"You filled out what?" Jane yelled. "David, you picked out the house without me. Now you are picking out our kids! This has got to stop! You—"

"Enough!" was Sylvia's deafening demand. Regaining her composure in the next breath, she first addressed Jane. "Jane, I am quite shocked at your lack of control in this situation, especially when it is so easily remedied." Jane raised her arms in feigned defeat and sat down. She was on the losing side of this issue. She couldn't understand how, but she was.

"This is all quite simple," Sylvia began in her usual static voice. "These boys need a loving home with a caring surrogate mother and father. Is this not correct?" David nodded his head in willing agreement, and Jane didn't know how but somehow she was shaking her head yes in agreement as well. "You both are ably and amply capably of providing them with a loving and a caring home. Is this also not correct?" Again, two heads shook in agreement. Were there strings attached to Jane's head, she wondered to herself, or was she really starting to believe it? "You have a big enough home, and you have enough income, and when you have your own biological children, well, the more the merrier." The way that Sylvia explained, it all made perfectly good sense.

Jane and David stared at each other quizzically, trying to absorb and understand Sylvia's words and their impact. Sylvia again broke through the silence. "Now, Jane, I do not disagree that David should have consulted with you before filling out any forms. However, he is a man of action with a big heart, and he saw an immediate need." David smiled warmly at the "general." "And Jane," she added, rising from her chair and going to Jane's side, gently touching her arm, "the papers are truly preliminary. Nothing has been finalized in any way. David has said from the beginning that the ultimate decision is yours." David, hoping to further ease Jane's trepidation, added one final option.

"Jane," he introduced gently. "We can take them on a trial basis. A final decision to adopt does not have to be made for six months after they begin living with us." Jane sat for only a moment longer before rising from her chair. She walked to David.

"There are still quite a few things that I feel that we need to talk about. There is one thing for certain. There is no way that I, that is we, are bringing those boys into our home unless they are our boys permanently. There will be nothing temporary and nothing trial about them entering our home and our hearts." Kneeling, she placed her hands on David's legs as her eyes locked with his. "We need to talk tonight, and then tomorrow we can look at the paperwork together, okay?" David stood, lifting his wife off her feet. There was no yelling or brewhawhawing in exultation. Unabashed by the guest still seated in the room, David simply took his wife into his arms and, kissing her, whispered into her ear.

"I am so lucky, and so are our boys."

"Our boys," she repeated with tenderness, "my goodness that does sound wonderful, *but* there is still so much to talk about and so much to figure out and we have to be approved first before they are 'our' boys."

"Oh, I can assure you that you will be approved. I will make sure of that," Sylvia commented with completion. "I have my connections, and with the reference that I will give, they would let you adopt the president of the United States."

"I didn't vote for him," David joked.

"Neither did I" was Sylvia's quick response. "And that was not the point."

"You see," Sylvia rationalized as she began putting on her coat to leave, "this quandary cleared quite quickly with some added insight.

And the most important point is" she finished with a slight wink of the eye, "I am going to be an aunt."

CHAPTER 15

It was eleven p.m., and Jane would soon be leaving for a rare night shift at the hospital. Unplanned, Jane had received the call after dinner informing her that one of her high-risk patients had unexpectedly gone into labor. Jane requested that she always be notified about the status of her special pregnant moms, though her presence was not always mandatory. Sally Wants, the patient in labor, was a sixteen-year-old unwed mother. She was so young, inexperienced, and terrified, under-standably so, and she had come to depend heavily on Jane. Of course, Jane wanted to be there for her if only it had been any other night! Unfortunately such circumstances were rarely a matter of choice.

The windows were open only slightly on this cool evening in early June, but it was enough for the sounds of the night to seep in. As Jane left the kitchen with her cup of coffee and headed up the stairs, she could hear the subdued wrestling of the waves and the still unsettled cooing of the doves that nested in the pine next to the house. Entering her bedroom, she saw that David was still awake reading.

"Have you looked in on them lately?" Jane asked anxiously as she snuggled, in full nursing garb, next to David in needed comfort. Easily sensing her insecurity, David promptly put his book aside and wrapped his wife in a firm hug.

"I just checked them about an hour ago," he assured her. "They were sleeping soundly and appeared to have no intentions of going anywhere." Jane was not comforted by his attempt at levity.

"How do you think that our first day went? I mean..." She stumbled slightly "The boys as our boys. Do you think that they are happy here? Do you think that they like us?" Jane implored. David held firm in his hug and tried to reassure her.

"This was only our first day together as a family. Try not to expect too much too soon. They have been through a lot and still have a lot of uncertainty, as should be expected." He held her even tighter. "But, yes, they will like it here, and yes, they will like us and even grow to love us. It is a process like all relationships; try not to worry." He felt her body relax in his arms so he knew that his words had helped. "What time do you have to leave?" It was the wrong question to ask as her body tensed again. Rising quickly from the bed, she made a light sprint toward the door.

"I have to leave in about ten minutes, and I want to look in on them one last time before I leave. I will be home by six, no matter what, so I will be here to fix breakfast, to see you, Michael, and Eric off to school, and to take care of Robert," she finished in one breath as she reached the door. She was just about to leave when she heard a firm command.

"Whoa there!" David called out, causing Jane to pause. "Slow down a minute. You do not have to do everything yourself; I am here too, remember?" Jane responded with a crooked smile of acknowledgement. "I can fix breakfast and see to the boys if need be and whenever the need be. This is not a hundred-yard dash. Slow down a bit and enjoy, okay?" Jane nodded sheepishly and took a deep breath.

"And one last thing," he added coyly. "No kiss good-bye?" Turning on her heels, Jane made an exaggerated dash for the bed. Leaning over David, she kissed him lushly and then, straightening herself before he could respond, turned on her heels again and dashed for the door.

"I am still looking in on them one more time," she countered, not waiting for a response.

The boys' bedroom was down the hall on the right from their bedroom. There were enough bedrooms for Michael, Eric, and Robert to each have a room of their own, but David and Jane had felt that sharing a room at first would aid in some feeling of security. It was strange, Jane thought as she walked down the dimly lit hallway, that Michael, Eric, and Robert were now their boys, their family. She had imagined and dreamed so many times of family: hers and David's. A child, their child, growing inside of her, being born, first steps, and all of the growing, knowing, and learning. This was so different. So many steps were missing, and she wasn't sure how to catch up. She paused at the door and prayed, *Dear God, let me not just love them, but let me also know them and help them fulfill their needs and their dreams.*

Entering the room, Jane's eyes were guided by the warm glow of the whimsical nightlight that Aunt Cathy had sent. She saw, with comfort, three beds and three little bodies nestled contently in them. The room became a little more crowded as another presence entered the room. Her hands flew to her mouth to quell the gasp that threatened to escape with the full realization of what she was seeing. A familiar arm wrapped around her shoulder in knowing comfort as her eyes remained glued to the three little beds.

"Oh my," she whispered as much to herself as to him, "our first night together as a family, our first night!"

"Is it as you remembered?" Golden Boy asked softly.

"Oh my," she said again, "memory serves but not in proportion I guess. They are so small, so small, so much smaller than I remember." Jane felt frozen, afraid to move for fear of waking the boys. Sensing her hesitancy, Golden Boy spoke calmly.

"We will not disturb them. Don't worry."

Taking him at his word, Jane moved toward the beds. Stopping at each one, she tucked the blankets gently around their slumbering bodies and kissed them each tenderly. They felt so warm, so wonderfully warm. Returning to her companion, she touched his arm with affection. "What do you think of our boys?" she whispered proudly.

"I know," he answered immediately, "that they will grow to be fine men."

"You do have that benefit of insight, don't you?" Jane responded. "And I guess," she added with clarity, "so do I. It is so strange."

"Can you remember this night, what you were feeling, without the benefit of insight?"

"I remember how nervous I was those first few days—months really. We had an instant family, but it didn't feel like a family. Unknown and unfamiliar individuals with different likes and dislikes and all sorts of hurts and insecurities all gathered under one heading: family. David took everything in stride, calm and patient as always. I, on the other hand, wanted to fix everything at once. Love, understanding, and time was the remedy I soon realized and to each one of them"—she nodded toward her sleeping angels—"his own love, his own understanding and in his own time." Finishing, Jane slipped into the silence of her thoughts. Stirred by her memories, she continued. "Every moment with them was such a joy, such a blessing. There were times though that I felt guilty that my bliss should have come as the result of a terrible loss." Golden Boy seemed to be pondering some thoughts of his own.

"Everything turned out as it should have," the young man reflected cryptically.

"What do you mean by that?" Jane shot back. "Was it all part of the Master's plan that Angela and Stephen Stanford should die so that David and I could have an instant family? Is life and death really that easy and convenient, and by that standard what convenience has evolved by my death?"

Golden Boy remained calm and unaffected by Jane's indignation, which only intensified the heat of Jane's feelings. How dare this young kid take life so lightly? For that matter how dare God. They were more than pawns, and she was going to tell him so she stormed.

"Are you where you want to be?" he asked.

"What, dead?"

"You know exactly what I mean," the young teacher reprimanded. "This place and this moment, is it where you want to be, or would you choose to change something or someone?"

"For example?" was Jane's quieter and more curious response.

"For example, what if you and David had chosen not to adopt the boys? Certainly the deaths of Angela and Stephen would not have changed, but the outcome of three lives would certainly have changed."

"Three lives changed? How about five and even more! I can't imagine it, and I wouldn't want to! They were gifts to their own parents the day that they were born, and in their own passing they passed their gifts on to us. Life, every life is a blessing that touches so many other lives and causes an impact that can never be replaced." The young man did not recoil at her reproach. He knew that her words were never personal, and he never took them as such.

"And so I ask again: are you where you want to be?"

"Yes" was all that Jane could say.

"You see, Jane. Living life is not about understanding why things happen; frequently we never understand. Living life is about responding in the most positive and productive way to what does happen, even in the most extreme of circumstances like death. That is exactly what you and David did when you adopted Michael, Eric, and Robert. Isn't that the same wish that you would have for your own family as a result of your own passing that beyond grief they should still embrace life and the living of it? We only have the ability to create and change that which is creatable and changeable; that is our responsibility and our stewardship in life."

Jane took in his words but was not settled by them. An uncomfortable feeling of helplessness seeped into her soul. Was anyone ever really in control, or was the Great Puppeteer just pulling strings at will. How could any direction in life be chosen with certainty if the outcome was never really in one's own hands? A frown clouded her face as she left her companion's side. Going to Michael's bedside, she knelt beside it and placed her arm gently across his slumbering body in a protective embrace. Golden Boy followed her course and knelt facing her.

"You were not given the ability of choice without the faith to make one," he whispered to her as he gently touched her arm. "All is not known, and all will not be known. If it were, there would be no need to choose. There are no strings attached to life, only a guiding hand from time to time."

"Mind reading again?" she jested. Shrugging, he feigned innocence.

"I'll take that guiding hand," she added, smiling. "And for them as well," she continued, sweeping her arm to encompass her sleeping sons. "For everyone," she finished contently. *Perhaps things do turn out as they should,* she thought, *as long as one takes the steps that one should and has the faith that one can.*

"This feels like a Tiny Tim 'God bless us, every one' moment," Golden Boy added with a lightness of spirit.

Jane laughed, enjoying his melding of sincerity and humor. "Smart guy" was her only remark, which brought a wide smile from her companion. Still kneeling beside Michael's bed, she allowed her gaze to sweep over her sleeping little ones, reveling in the renewed realization of how much they had filled and fulfilled, not only her own life, but so many others. Rising, he left her there, taking with him the memories yet to come and leaving with her the pure joy of what was.

Jane was true to her word, for as the six a.m. alarm sounded, David heard the car door slam and the front door creak in welcome. There was no time to change as Jane entered the boys' room still in her nurse attire. Eric and Michael began to stir sleepily at Jane's gently prodding, but at the sudden recognition of their new surroundings, they became quickly wide awake. An attempt at quiet failed as the no-longer sleeping Robert was not about to miss out on any of the morning's excitement. David now joined the group and was designated to assist Michael and Eric as needed in the preparation for school while Robert assisted Jane in the kitchen with breakfast. The boys laughed as David saluted in acknowledgement and was promptly lectured on the importance of organization. Robert, always seemingly in search of the last word, looked up in awe at Jane. "She sounds like Aunt Silva" was the innocent comment to which everyone burst forth in some much-needed laughter.

Breakfast preparation ensued with an unending symphony of chatter from Robert. As Jane busily scrambled eggs and fried sausage, Robert was quick to comment. "Mikey and Eric won't eat that stuff," he said, shaking his head.

Jane paused in her endeavor. "They won't eat eggs and sausage?" Robert continued to shake his head no. "But why not? It is such a nice warm breakfast."

"Not dorin' the week" was the straightforward response.

There was no wish to sound flustered though the minute hand of the clock seemed to be pounding in Jane's head. Keeping a level tone in her voice, she pushed further. "What difference does it make if it's during the week?"

"Cereal dorin' the week; Sunday we get eggs and stuff. That's what Mommy always said."

Jane turned to the stove as she felt her cheeks blush. Some missing steps she reminded herself, and she was sure that there would be many more. She didn't miss a beat though as she quickly got some boxes of cereal out of the cupboard along with some bowls and the milk. It was just in time as she heard a chorus of feet cascading down the stairway. David, Michael, and Eric entered the kitchen with anticipation.

"Wow, something sure smells good!" David exclaimed enthusiastically.

"Cool," Eric added with gusto, "scrambled eggs and sausage during the week!" Sitting down, he eyed the boxes of cereal. "Cereal is good too," he added politely. It had not taken Jane and David long to realize that Eric was very sensitive to the needs and feelings of others, even at his young age. He was quite like David really—kind, compassionate, helpful, and quick to laugh. Jane gently placed her hand on his shoulder.

"Eric, you can have the cereal, or the eggs and sausage, or both. What would you like?"

Eric turned his encouraged face up to meet Jane's gaze. "I would like the eggs and sausage please but no cereal. Is that okay?"

"Not sapossed to," Robert was quick to correct. "Sapossed to eat cereal."

"Well," Jane addressed the concerned Robert with care,

"this is a special day, so special days should be celebrated, so we will celebrate by eating scrambled eggs and sausage, okay?"

Robert liked special days and inquired if this special day involved presents as well. Though the answer was no, he still seemed satisfied and was indeed pleased by the steaming plate of scrambled eggs and sausage that David placed in front of him, which he ate with his usual openmouthed enthusiasm; it would be a hard habit to break.

Michael sat next to David, his usual seat of choice. He seemed most affected outwardly by the loss of his parents. Quiet and pensive, a smile never came easily to his face. When a smile did come, David was usually the reason. Taking each boy under wing was a top priority for David, and he saw in Michael a special need. He saw in Michael himself, a boy again suffering with the loss of his parents, not by fate, as was Michael's situation, but by cold and cruel choice, yet the pain was the same. There was still love and laughter in the world. Michael just needed help to see it, and David knew that he could guide him to it.

Breakfast was soon complete, and bellies were full. Jane gave Michael and Eric an unaccustomed kiss good-bye as David scurried them out of the house. Waving good-bye, Jane turned and went back into the house hand-in-hand with Robert. Shutting the doors behind them, Jane let out a sigh of accomplishment, at least one so far for the day. Robert's hand was still warmly in Jane's as he began tugging insistently. "Watta we gonna do now?" was the simple inquiry. Sleep was Jane's first thought as she looked down at his little face with ruddy cheeks. He was a jewel as Sylvia once said, but to Jane's eyes there was no polishing needed. Lifting him up into her arms, she hugged him and asked him what he would like to do.

"Let's go see Aunt Silva" was the energetic suggestion.

Sleep was definitely not an option. Jane smiled. "How

about if I call Aunt Sylvia and ask her if we can have lunch with her?"

Robert brightened instantly but then suddenly wrinkled his nose. "At the smelly hosbital?"

Jane looked at his comical expression and tried not to laugh. "It smells like that because it is so clean."

Robert continued to wrinkle his nose. "I'm glad that our house in't that clean."

Laughing, Jane gave Robert a loving squeeze and then gently let his feet slide to the floor. She would be sure to share Robert's comments with Sylvia. Undoubtedly after a chuckle, she would respond by attempting to convince Robert of the importance of cleanliness and would undoubtedly fail. The call was made and a lunch time willingly confirmed; it was now time to do some reading with Robert. Nestling into the comfortable sofa together, mother and son began the tales of Pooh bear and friends.

CHAPTER 16

The adoption process had been remarkably quick with Sylvia's help. Settlement of the estate, however, proved to be more of a challenge. As there had been no will, the matter had rested with the court, but with no one to contest, the estate passed ultimately to the three boys. Jane and David, as the adoptive parents, were given the responsibility of determining what should be done. The house they decided would be sold and all money from the proceeds would be placed in bonds for the boys' college educations. The contents would be a family decision with the decision residing heavily with the boys. It was now time to tell Michael and Eric. Robert would be with Sylvia and would have the issue explained when he was older.

Michael and Eric sat quietly side by side as Jane and David explained about the sale of the house. Michael asked, "How about our things?"

There had been a few visits to the house to pick up some

clothing and a few toys, but aside from that, everything remained untouched.

"Well," David began tenderly, "we were thinking that we should all of us, including Robert, go to the house together and decide what should be kept and brought here." David could see Michael's eyes beginning to well with tears, and instantly he went to his side. Jane was quick to follow, sitting next to Eric. Hugging him affectionately, Jane continued.

"There are no limits here, right, David?" David nodded his head firmly in agreement. "Whatever you want, no matter what it is, we will bring it here and find a place for it. This is your home, and we want to do whatever we can to make it feel like your home. Okay?" Both boys agreed.

The planned weekend arrived, and the family of five filled the car joined also by Aunt Sylvia. Feeling that her help and organizational skills would be of use, she was welcomed but also cautioned in private that all decisions were to be made by the boys alone; she understood and agreed completely. Robert began to point excitedly as they came in view of the Stafford home. A light fog had settled, giving the cottage an ethereal look. The house was nestled among many other houses, most identical in style. Spilling forth from the car, the group stood silently in front of the little house, uneager to approach the task before them. Sylvia, of course, instigated action, "Who has the key?" David moved toward the short steps, extracted the key from his pocket, and opened the storm door and then unlocked the wooden door.

Robert raced through the door first with Sylvia keeping pace at his heels. The remaining two boys entered the house tentatively with Jane and David. "Now," Jane began softy, "I am going to give each of you your own color of stickers. As we go through, anything that you want..." Jane paused and made it a point to make eye contact with Eric and Michael. "Anything at all, just put your sticker on it, and it will come home with you. We will be right here with you to help." The boys took the stickers, looking a little more encouraged but still disquieted; Sylvia was already in possession of Robert's stickers. It was a small house, but as the boys began to branch off separately, Jane joined Eric, and David joined Michael.

The three small bedrooms, living room, and eat-in kitchen that comprised the compact house still seemed to be bursting with items to look at. As the day progressed, each boy would frequently call out upon seeing a familiar item and then happily place a sticker of ownership upon it. As Eric and Jane traveled down the hallway to the bedrooms, Eric caught sight of his parents' bedroom. No one had entered the room yet; as Eric stopped and stood staring, he seemed unwilling to be the first. Still curiosity and emotion kept him standing outside of the door and peering inside. Jane was quick to react to his pensiveness. "Do you see something that you want, Eric?" Eric was still unmoved. "I will come in with you if you want." Eric nodded and still hesitantly entered the room with Jane at his side. Walking to the corner of the room, Eric stopped and rubbed his small hand softly on the arm of an old oak rocking chair.

"This was Mommy's rocker," Eric said as he gently pressed the arm, causing the chair to rock. "She rocked Robert when he couldn't sleep or when he didn't feel well, and she would hum." He grew quiet as if listening to the sound of his mother's voice in his memory. "She rocked me too when I was much younger." Jane nodded. "But I guess we really don't need a rocker, do we?" Jane took one of the stickers from Eric's sheet and placed it firmly on the back of the rocker.

"I think that your room could use a nice comfortable rocker like this one." Eric's face brightened. "After all, you're going to be getting your own room soon, and you will need a good chair to read in." Eric took Jane's hand in his and squeezed it with affection.

"Mommy would have liked you," he said warmly. Jane

hugged him, feeling for the first time a bond of motherhood with a woman that she never knew. The moment was broken abruptly as Robert raced into the room with Sylvia tailing him close behind.

"Look, look!" he squealed excitedly, raising a box for Jane to see. "Aunt Silva found my pirate treasure!" Looking into the box, Jane gazed with enthusiasm at the assortment of rocks in all manner of haphazard colors, shapes, and sizes. "See how they sparkle?" Robert continued as he lowered the box to look at them again in rapture. "We found 'em on the beach." He motioned to his brothers. "And I hid 'em so nobody'd steal 'em, and then I forget where I hid 'em, and then Aunt Silva found 'em. She's a good finder!" The now quite familiar upward tilt of the mouth embraced Sylvia's expression as she affectionately tousled the top of Robert's head. The group was joined by David and Michael. Together they shared in the success of Robert's discovery and reveled in a happy moment, joining the many that had happened on that very spot not too long ago.

As they continued to share some of the other finds of the day, they heard a knock at the front door. As they left the room, Michael was the first person to see the as yet unknown individual peering in from outside through the glass of the storm door. Michael, recognizing the person instantly, raced for the door and, swinging it open, ushered the individual in. Their guest was an older woman, as they could now plainly see and a most welcome guest as Michael threw himself into her familiar and opened arms. Robert and Eric quickly followed as her arms widened to include all three of the boys in her embrace. Michael turned excitedly to introduce his guest of honor.

"This is Miss Mary. She is our neighbor and my friend."

"She's my friend too," Robert countered stormily.

Michael corrected his brother quickly and firmly. "I know. Now be quiet. Miss Mary took care of us when Mom and Dad were away, you know, on the boat. Her husband was a lobsterman too, right, Miss Mary?" Michael's face was beaming with pride. Mary Mallory was in her early sixties, and she bore the characteristics of a woman weathered by the sea. Her face was leathered and creased with lines that had gathered from looking searchingly out to the waves, time and time again. Her small, blue eyes, still sparkled with warmth and faith. Time had diminished her carriage but not her stature. Her arms were strong, and her chubby hands were still accustomed to taking care of herself and others as well. David spoke out immediately in welcome.

"You are quite the tonic, Miss Mary," he said warmly as he reached for her hand and shook it. "I have never seen Michael so excited." Mary smiled but still did not utter a word. "I am David Bell, and this is my wife, Jane, and our good friend Sylvia Laithe."

"Pleased," Mary finally responded. "Hope I'm not intrudin', but I wanted to see my boys. I've missed 'em." Michael continued to hold on tight as she spoke. Jane moved forward to shake her hand as well; she liked the firmness of her grip.

"No intrusion at all." Jane responded sincerely. "I am so glad that we have finally met. Robert talks about you all of the time," she complimented.

"Robert just talks all the time" was the matter-of-fact but tender response. They all had a good laugh, for it was certainly true. "Well," Mary added, "I'll be leavin'. Don't want to hold anything up." Her intent may have been to leave, but Michael was not about to let her go. Jane could see the love and devotion that Michael felt for Mary. She hated to see them separated. What a breakthrough it could be for Michael if they could see each other more often, even every day. Suddenly the solution became obvious, but she had to set the stage.

"Do you live alone, Miss Mary?"

"Yes. Lost my husband and my only boy fifteen years ago: lobsterin'."

"Well," Jane continued as David gave her a curious look, "David and I both work, and we could certainly use some help with the boys. It's obvious how much they adore you." Mary smiled at the compliment. "We have a nice room with a bath that I think would suit you nicely. I know that the boys would love to have you—"

Jane could not finish her sentence as the boys began jumping up and down yelling, "Yes, yes, yes!" David was shocked into silence by his wife's unplanned proposition. It was certainly not like her.

"I don't know" was the uncertain response. Mary had come to love the Stafford boys as her own. They had bonded immediately, and she had jumped at every chance to watch them and to take care of them. When they left after their parents' deaths, she had missed them terribly, and though she had been well accustomed to being alone as fate had dictated; accustomed was far from acceptance. She had nothing to lose by saying yes and maybe she could be a real help and Mary liked the idea of helping her boys.

The boys would not relent as they continued jumping and chanting, "Yes, yes, yes."

"Maybe we could try it for a spell, just to see. How about that?" she countered, which finally quelled the yelling and the jumping.

"Wonderful," Jane accepted enthusiastically. "We can discuss and work out all of the details a little later. Do you think that you can visit with the boys a little longer? I know that they would love it." Mary accepted willingly.

"We will be in the back room if you need us," Jane added as she, David, and Sylvia left Mary and the boys to enjoy each other's company. As soon as they reached the back room and were out of hearing range, a quiet riot erupted.

"What was that all about?" David whispered loudly, fairly bursting.

Sylvia quickly chimed in. "Jane, you don't even know the woman and to ask her to move into your home; that was quite impulsive." Jane crossed her arms in front of her ready for verbal combat and she had no intention of losing.

"David," her unflinching tone brought him to attention, "do we not need someone to help us with the boys, and was it not discussed?"

"Well yes," David answered, "but ... "

"Did the boys' parents not trust her with them?"

"Well yes," David acknowledged, "but ... "

"It is obvious that the boys love and adore her, would you not agree?"

"That much is obvious," David confirmed.

"And Mary said that we will try it for a spell. Is that not correct, David?"

"That's what she said," David admitted, finding nothing yet that he could disagree with.

"Therefore, there is no harm that can be done, but there is everything to be gained for us and the boys. It was an obvious solution." Glancing at Sylvia, Jane directed her next question to her. "How did I do, Teacher?"

"Checkmate, Jane," Sylvia responded immediately. "I must say very well done." Jane smiled broadly.

"Wait a minute," David interjected. "Shouldn't we have talked about this first?" He realized his blunder as soon as the word *first* left his lips. Blistering under Jane's "What's good for the goose" gaze and wilting under Sylvia's slightly softer "cooked in your own pudding" unflinching stare, David raised his arms in good humor. "I surrender," he offered. "Checkmate is accepted."

It was decided unanimously. Mary was stickered as well that day!

CHAPTER 17

The Bell family expanded once again, as Mary Mallory came
to try a "spell" at the big old Victorian by the sea. There were
cheers of delight as the Bell car carrying Mary and a few of her
possessions, including a tail-wagger named Blackie, pulled in
front of the house. It was pandemonium as the car door opened
and Mary and the somewhat stunned Blackie exited the auto-
mobile. The boys circled her like a net and, pulling their catch
into the house, anxiously began showing her all that there was
to see. Blackie, recovering quickly and following obligingly,
sniffed his new surroundings and then promptly took a nap.
David placed Mary's items in her room and then went to the
kitchen where everyone had finally gathered.

"This is a fine home you have here," Mary said.

Jane picked up on her wording and immediately responded,
"I hope, I mean we all hope, that you will see this as your home
too. We want you to feel comfortable and at ease."

Mary smiled, nodding in understanding and appreciation. Words were only needed when necessary for Mary, and even when necessary the fewer and more to the point the better. Looking at the weathered watch on her wrist, she said, "It's four o'clock. Getting close to suppah time. Better get cookin'." The boys began to chatter excitedly in anticipation of one of Mary's home-cooked meals.

"Now, Mary," David began politely, "we don't expect you to cook and housekeep. *Really,* helping with the boys is a handful." Mary rested one hand in the palm of the other and gave David an unfaltering and direct look. It would be a look that he would become familiar with and would usually be offered before a straightening out.

"Yor hungry, aren't yah?"

"Well yes, but ... " David's retort was to be left incomplete as Mary good-naturedly shooed him from the room with her hands. Eyeing a still unmoved Jane, she shooed her as well, though not before asking if the boys could stay with her to help with dinner. Jane willingly agreed.

"She doesn't say much," David whispered as they left the kitchen and headed to the front parlor.

"She doesn't have to."

Sitting comfortably, Jane and David chatted lightly though they more frequently fell pleasantly silent, preferring to listen to the muffled chatter emanating from the kitchen. They didn't know how this new union was going to work out, but it sure seemed to be off to a good start. It wasn't long before wonderful smells from the kitchen began wandering into the room where they sat.

"Whatever it is it sure smells good," Jane commented.

"What did we have in the fridge?" David asked.

"Well," Jane began with hesitation, "there were some leftovers I'm sure and ... " She paused again, feeling a tad flushed at her lack of ingredient knowledge. "And of course there are eggs, bread, butter, and milk."

"Blizzard fare," David correctly categorized. They both laughed. Their years in Maine had taught them the importance of the basics.

"Wait a minute. I have a nice chicken roaster in there. That must be it."

"If that's a chicken," David sniffed contently, "that's one good-smelling chicken."

Though it might seem fair for Jane to be incensed by his comments, Jane felt no threat from Mary as her upbringing had made her familiar with the idea of more than one cook in the kitchen. In fact, it made her reflect pleasantly on her memories of childhood—home, her mom, and Babcia Grand.

David caught her smile. "What are you thinking?"

"Oh, I was just remembering what it was like when Mom and Grand were in the kitchen together, not that it happened that often you know." David nodded knowingly as he had heard and enjoyed many of Jane's family stories. "Grand was certainly a woman to be reckoned with as Mom frequently tested, but they loved each other. When you love each other, the kinks always seem to get worked out or even overlooked." Looking a little pensive, she added, "I wonder what kinks Mary and I will have to work out."

"That depends on how 'suppah' tastes," David jested. Jane countered with an exaggerated "ha ha" though she always appreciated his knack for bringing the necessary levity to a situation. She analyzed while he simplified. Falling silent again, she listened with comfort to the chatter in the kitchen and the familiar clanging of pots and pans. There would be a few kinks, she knew, but she just had a feeling that everything would work out. How she hoped that they would all soon be a family, not just on an paper, but in love and in spirit. Mary too could be a piece of the family quilt; the boys loved her so.

There was much to admire in Mary. She was strong, a shoulder to rely on, yet she was childlike too without pretense. She was easy to like.

"I wonder how Mary is making out cooking with the boys? Perhaps I should go check," Jane questioned then answered unsettled.

"No," David responded firmly and quickly. "They're fine. Mary has handled them and can handle them. It's not like they're going to burn the house down."

"That sure helped," Jane responded sarcastically, raising an eyebrow but staying put.

They had nothing to fear for the kitchen was indeed well under control. The chicken was roasting in the oven. Eric was peeling the potatoes. Michael was helping Mary with the shucking of the corn. Robert was talking.

"What we havin', Miss Mary?"

"Chicken."

"What kind?"

"Cooked." The second one-word response drew giggles from Michael and Eric. Robert did not see the humor in the answer.

"Do we have to eat it cooked?" Robert asked.

There was no need for Mary to answer as Michael exasperatedly interceded. "For gosh sakes, Robert, you can't eat chicken raw!"

"Why not?"

"'Cause it will make you sick if you eat it raw."

"Is that why vegables make me sick? I eat them raw you know."

"Vegetables are different than chicken, you goof. Oh never mind, you're hopeless!" Before Robert could open his mouth with another question or comment, Mary changed his direction.

"Robert, please go ask your mother if she would like to have suppah in the kitchen or in the dining room."

"She's not my mom," Robert retorted angrily. "My mom's dead; she's Jane."

Mary was quiet after Robert's sudden outburst. Putting the corn that she was handling aside, she took a seat in one of the kitchen chairs. Motioning for Robert to come to her, she placed him gently on her lap and wrapped him in her secure arms. She did not chastise him for his words but rocked him gently in comfort. Michael and Eric stopped what they were doing as well and joined Mary. After a few more moments of silence, Mary began.

"You boys know about my boy, Paul; you saw his picture." The boys nodded. They had seen his picture many times as Mary always had her family pictures proudly displayed. Paul had died years before, and thus the boys had never actually met him, but Mary had made him come alive time and time again as she had told them so many stories about her Paul. "He wasn't my real boy, not from me, you know. He was my husband's boy, and when we married, he became my boy too. Do you understand?" Michael and Eric nodded their heads in tentative understanding, but Robert was confused.

"If you weren't his real mom, where was his real mom?" Robert asked, trying to understand.

"His real mom was in heaven like your mom. I was his mom here on earth just like Jane is."

"So you 'dopted Paul like Jane and David 'dopted us?" Robert reasoned.

"That's right, Robbie," Mary acknowledged as she hugged him tighter.

"You're sapposed to call me Robert like a big boy," Robert corrected.

Snuggling deeper into her embrace, he added, "But I don't mind."

It was now Michael's turn to be unsettled. "Did he call you Mom?" Michael inquired tentatively. Mary's response was instantaneous with a firm "yes."

"Don't you think that it made his mom in heaven kinda sad that he was someone else's boy?" Michael continued with a catch in his voice.

"To be sure she missed him," Mary answered easily and with conviction. "But she loved him so much that she didn't mind sharin' him, not at all. Paul was a lucky boy 'cause he had two moms that loved him so much, just like you boys do." Michael was silent as his mind processed Mary's answer. Mary continued to rock Robert in her arms. It was difficult, she knew. Paul had been just a small boy of barely two when she had married his father. He had adjusted to Mary quickly and easily and she had immediately loved him as her own. This situation was different, especially for Michael. He had loved both of his parents deeply, not that his brothers had loved them any less, but Michael was the oldest, in his age and in his soul. He felt things so deeply Mary realized as she came to know him, and that is why the loss had been so much harder for him. Perhaps the good Lord had sent her here to help in some way, to somehow help in the healing. She wasn't sure how at the moment, but she knew that she would be shown the way. Michael wrapped his arm in affection around Mary's neck and leaned his head gently into hers.

"Miss Mary," he whispered, "can I go ask the question that Robert was going to ask?" Mary nodded.

David and Jane were still sitting in the parlor. Hearing one set of footsteps approaching, they both turned to face the doorway. They smiled as Michael entered the room. It was not David that he approached, which was his normal custom. Instead, quietly and with intent, he approached Jane. Standing next to her, he softly touched her arm as he spoke. "Mom," he began, "Miss Mary wants to know if we should eat in the kitchen or in the dining room?"

Jane lost every word after he said the word *Mom.* She had hoped and prayed for so long, forever it seemed, to hear her child call her Mom. That the word should first be uttered by Michael surprised her into a dumb euphoric silence. He was the most distant from her of all three boys, yet that one word had spanned the miles in an instant.

"Mom, did you hear me?" Michael asked with a look of confusion on his face. Jane noticed that both Michael and David were staring at her with a degree of concern on their faces. A tremendous smile erupted across Jane's face as she jumped from her chair and embraced Michael.

"I think," she began, hugging him in her arms, "that we should eat in the dining room with our best china. This is a day to celebrate! Can I help?"

"No, Mom," Michael countered, feeling more comfortable with the word. "You and Dad relax. We can handle this." Jane released her hold and watched with joy and pride as Michael left the room. Turning to David, she observed his equally wide smile.

"Well, Mom," he said, speaking as a proud papa, "what do you think?"

"I think," Jane responded, "that I shall write in my diary tonight that our child's first word was *Mom* with *Dad* coming in a close second. *And,* I think that I know how this all happened. There is an angel among us."

"An angel that can cook," David added as he rose from his chair and wrapped his arms around his wife. Content in body and soul, Jane stood, taking in the warm feeling of completeness.

Dinner that night would be one that they would always remember. It was delicious, but it was not the taste that would linger in their minds. It was the gathering of family for the first time that would always garner fond reminisces. There would be challenges ahead, life's guarantee, but they would face them as a family, not as strangers gathered around a table. As dinner finished, the boys asked if they could take Blackie out for a romp in the warm evening. Jane willingly agreed. David was shooed again by Mary into the other room as she and Jane prepared to clean up from the evening meal. As they worked, few words were exchanged. It was not an awkward silence rather it was a comfort; the synergistic movements of two women bound by one purpose.

"That's done." Mary observed as the last dish was dried and put into the cabinet. Jane nodded in welcome agreement. "Shall we sit on the porch a bit?"

They made themselves comfortable in the rockers on the kitchen porch, rocking quietly as the breeze from the sea caressed them in cooling comfort. Listening, they could hear the boys as they played in the pines nearby, accompanied by barks of pleasure from Blackie.

"Michael called me Mom for the first time tonight," Jane said. "It was the most important word that I have ever heard in my life. I think that you made it happen in some way. I want to thank you."

Mary continued to rock and stare straight ahead, only pausing a moment to reach out and to pat Jane's arm fondly. "Michael did that himself, not me."

"I know, but I know that you must have helped."

"Oh, I jest told him a story. He's a smart boy; he figured out the rest."

"Would you tell me the story someday?" Jane asked. Mary nodded, but the sounds of the night began to entice their ears rather than words. Jane was soon to realize that today was not to be someday and that she should never question the timing or the wisdom of angels, and she wouldn't.

Mary had gone inside to attend to some knitting, and David was taking advantage of a quiet house to grade a never-ending supply of student papers. Jane sat quietly by herself on the porch, pleasantly rocking and listening to the boys and Blackie as they continued to play.

It was more than the sea breeze that caused the rocker next to Jane to renew its movement. Golden Boy had joined her. His presence, even in reminder, could not disturb Jane's sense of peace and completeness.

"How are you feeling, Mom?" Golden Boy addressed Jane by her newly attained title.

"Like a mom," Jane answered. "Finally like a mom. May I never grow tired of hearing it; tired in many other ways"—she laughed—"but never tired of hearing *mom*."

They continued to rock in easy silence. Jane had no fear of her companion being discovered. She had come to understand that she alone could see him.

"Tell me about your mother, Golden Boy," Jane asked softly as she continued to rock.

Her companion paused, unaccustomed to questions about his own life. "She was wonderful. I loved her with all of my heart, and I still do. I would do anything for her."

Jane jumped at his response. "Yes, yes, that bond between mother and child … father and child too but … a mother and her child. I only thought that it was physical at first, that the bond begins as a mother carries her child in her body, but"— she turned and looked at her trusted guider—"it is a bond of heart and of love, not exclusive to blood, that binds mother and child. Feeling what I am feeling right now and knowing what I know, it is true, so true."

Golden Boy smiled. "That bond can never be broken, not by a harsh word, misunderstanding, or even by death."

Jane settled once more into rhythmic comfort. "Never, no never."

CHAPTER 18

"I don't know," Jane commented with uncertainty. "Mom was very insistent that we come next week rather than our planned week. She would not give me a reason, only that it was important and she was quite mysterious about it all."

David was frustrated as he knew that moving the date of departure forward would prevent him from traveling with his family. The trip had been all planned for months! It was their first full summer together as a family and the boys' first trip to Jane's parents' farm. They were all excited, but David's excitement began to wane as he knew that his duties at school had to be completed before his summer vacation could begin. As of yet, he had not heard one solid reason to change their plans. "It is often a mystery how your mother thinks," he responded with noted sarcasm while shaking his head. "Did you speak with Dad?"

Jane scolded him with her eyes. "Yes, I did speak with Dad,

and he was just as mysterious in that he had no explanation and only referred me back to Mom. It all seems a bit strange."

"You and the boys should go. You won't feel right if you don't," David added with resignation. "It may not be so bad; you can take the train." Brightening visibly the idea began to form and to take hold. "Actually this could turn out to be quite an adventure. The boys would love the train, and I will join you by car in two weeks." David finished with enthusiasm as his idea had gained momentum.

Jane was not feeling his optimism over his budding plan. She pictured another kind of momentum as the vision of her alone on a train with their three boys, specifically Robert, became focused. Mary would not be there to help her, as she had decided to stay home to mind the house and Blackie. Jane's face clouded with concern; she just was not sure about this proposition. Reading her face, David tried to address her concerns before they reached her lips.

"The boys will love it!" he exclaimed. "Not to worry; between you, Michael, and Eric, the three of you will be able to keep Robert under control." Jane was not completely convinced, though she did agree that Michael and Eric were excellent helpers. It would be an adventure to be sure she thought to herself smiling. Perhaps it could work; perhaps they could survive the trip.

"Okay," Jane agreed hesitantly. "The train it is, but ... " she added, sternly pointing a finger in David's direction, "I expect to see you in two weeks. No delays!" David assured her that he would not be delayed under any circumstances.

Amid a flurry of rapid preparation, the day of departure quickly arrived. The family stood next to the puffing and impatient train as they exchanged their good-byes. There were no tears as the boys knew that their dad would be joining them shortly and besides there was that big steaming hunk of iron to think about.

"Now, Robert," David addressed firmly as he lifted his youngest into his arms, "listen to your mother and your brothers."

"Which one first?" was the next question asked that now rested on the dozens of others that Robert had asked on the way to the station.

"Whoever speaks first," David answered as he kissed Robert's cheek.

"But what..." The train whistled, offering a welcome interruption as David took the opportunity to place Robert into Jane's outstretched arms. Kissing Jane, he looked into her still uncertain eyes and met her gaze with confidence; she could do this and do it well. Embracing Michael and Eric one last time, David guided his family up the small steps to the train. Waving good-bye as the train puttered into motion, David hoped that the two weeks would pass quickly.

Before too many days passed, the train pulled into the Pennsylvania station. The boys were knocking heads as they tried to catch a glimpse of their grandparents. Though it was their first visit to the farm, Filip and Wilma were already well acquainted with their new grandchildren as they had visited at Christmas. There was no adjustment of introduction needed for their relationship had blossomed almost immediately. The children fell in love with Grandpa Filip's kind and gentle ways, though without offense taken, as Robert would often say, they had the "bestest fun" with Grandma Wilma. Ann could not get leave for Christmas, so they only heard stories about their aunt Ann. Michael was the first to sight a familiar face as he spotted Filip, an easy standout in the crowd.

"Look, look!" Eric chimed in. "There's Grandma Wilma with Grandpa." He began waving ecstatically to attract their attention. "She sees us." He laughed. "Look at the funny face that she is making!" Wilma had seen them for indeed she was making a comical face with her eyes bulging out in animated surprise. Jane was having trouble seeing as Robert, whom she held in her arms, was weaving from side to side in his own attempt to see. Robert suddenly stopped moving as he had finally spotted someone that he knew.

"I see Grandpa!" A puzzled expression quickly raced across his face. "He has his arm around a fat lady. I don't know her."

Jane was equally puzzled. Placing Robert in the seat next to her and firmly instructing him to stay put, Jane finally had an opportunity to see her quickly approaching family. She could see her dad, and she could also see just the head of her sister, Ann, next to him as they were surrounded by other people. Looking down at Robert, she corrected him. "That is your aunt Ann, and she is certainly not fat." Directing her gaze to the window once more, Jane looked as the sea of people surrounding her dad and Ann parted, revealing not a fat lady but a pregnant lady. "Oh my, I am sorry, Robert!" Jane gasped. "Pregnant women can seem fat, but they are not, Robert, and your aunt Ann is pregnant, very pregnant!"

Gathering their belongings, they struggled down the narrow aisle and then spilled down the stairs onto the train platform. Wilma made an unsuccessful but comical attempt to hug all three boys at once. Filip was right behind Wilma, guiding the waddling Ann to the welcomed party. The boys chattered in unison though not coherently, which kept her parents and Ann occupied, which gave Jane a chance to quietly observe her sister. Ann was thoroughly enjoying an animated conversation with her newly introduced nephews. She seemed completely unconcerned and unfazed by her bulging stomach and did not notice or did not care to acknowledge her sister's shocked gaze.

"Jane," Wilma whispered sternly with a pointed nudge, "stop staring at Ann."

Turning to her mother with an incredulous expression on her face, Jane fired back in a hiss, "Did you just forget to tell me about this, or did Ann simply defy all laws of procreation and this just happened?" Putting a quick finger to her lips,

Wilma mouthed the words *later*. Later might very well be at the hospital Jane thought as she took another look at Ann. A quick estimate put her at nine months pregnant. No wonder her mother said the trip could not wait. Shaking her head softly, Jane fell slightly behind as the chatting group finally began to move in the direction of the car. Jane always knew that she could expect just about anything from Ann and she was sure that this was going to be some story. Dropping back to join her sister, Ann joined her arm in Jane's as they continued walking in step.

"Thanks for coming sooner, Janie," Ann whispered in her sister's ear. "I really need you." Jane smiled and patted her sister's arm in comfort. The story could wait. What mattered now was the need at hand, and boy was she needed!

Arriving at the family woody wagon at last, the family quickly piled in and drove to the farm. Lush green fields burgeoning with the anticipated fall crop guided the road as they went. A familiar driveway opened its arms as the wagon made its last turn and bumped its way to the front door of the house. The car barely came to a stop before the car door burst open and three excited boys spilled out.

"Whoa!" yelled an exhausted Jane as her brood ran in all directions. "Let's go into the house first, and then we can discuss some rules for outside play and wait ... " she added as they attempted to sprint for the door. "How about helping with the luggage please," she finished in firm request rather than question. Michael and Eric followed obediently with luggage in hand, while Robert needed some assistance, which he received in the arms of his grandpa Filip.

Once inside, timidity set in as the three boys huddled together. "Now, boys," Wilma admonished good-naturedly, "you have not just entered a museum. We raised your mother and your aunt Ann in this house, and the walls are still standing. This is the fun house not the big house, so let's have some fun!" Wilma enthused but then eyeing Jane's warning glance added, "As soon as your mom gives the rules." Though Wilma was sincere in her acknowledgement of Jane's maternal authority, the word *rule* still left a bad taste in her mouth.

Smiling in thanks, Jane shared the few guidelines and then as her mother and the boys wiggled equally with anticipation, she let them loose. The boys had no idea what the big house was, but they could sure relate to the fun house. It was a grand day not to be wasted inside, so the pent-up crew immediately headed outside. Filip excused himself to attend to some farm duties, which left the two sisters alone at last.

Jane poured two glasses of iced tea, placing one glass in front of her sister as she took the seat next to her at the kitchen table. Quietly sipping the cool brew, Jane waited for Ann to begin. "I am pregnant," Ann said abruptly. Realizing the absurd statement of the obvious brought both sisters to immediate and much-needed laughter. The laughter transitioned into tears as Ann began to cry. Jane immediately tried to comfort her sister.

"Everything will be fine, Ann. How did it happen?"

Through her tears Ann, looked incredulously at her sister. "You're a nurse. Don't you know?"

The laughter started all over again. As they both finally calmed down, Jane tried a simpler approach. "Okay, Ann, let's have it."

"It wasn't for love or anything," Ann started. "I guess that I should be ashamed, but I am not. This is a modern world, right? Men and women get together, and they have needs right? Well, that's what happened." Jane observed her thoroughly modern sister sitting in an age-old condition looking most uncomfortable physically and emotionally. She had heard the story so many times before. A man and a woman or a boy and a girl, and the time-transcending need resulting in the inevitable biological outcome. Always the same just different faces, and now the face that Jane saw was her own sister's.

"Does the father know?"

Ann smiled. "Don't get me wrong, Janie. He's a nice guy. He said all of the right things when I told him—let's get married, and all that stuff—but I want to marry a guy because I want to, not because I have to. Okay?"

Returning the smile, Jane nodded in understanding. "What are your plans? Are you going to keep the baby or consider adoption?"

"Babies, you mean. They are twins," Ann added as she gently rubbed her plump belly. "And I am going to keep them. They may not have been made with love, I mean the husband and wife kind, but I love them even when they are kickin' the hell out of me." Her hand flew to her mouth in instinctual habit as she mouthed "Sorry, Grand."

Jane rose from her chair and leaning embraced her sister. It would not be easy; she knew from her experiences with other young women in Ann's position. She also knew, however, that commitment and love could overcome life's challenges. A lot of support and help never hurt, and there would be no shortage of either from her family.

"How can I help you, Ann?"

"Well," Ann answered immediately with noted anxiousness in her voice. "Will you stay with me and help when I deliver, when I have them? I'm scared to death." Jane nodded yes enthusiastically. "Is it really as painful as they say, Janie?" Ann asked, wide eyed. Jane looked at her sister and responded with some needed evasiveness.

"Let's just say that you've never experienced anything quite like it."

The heavy door of the barn creaked open with an ominous moan, and sunlight pierced the darkness. The three boys stood at the entrance, and as they peered in, a blast of musty air caught their breath. They didn't know exactly what was in the barn, but they liked the feel of it already. Moving in farther, their eyes adjusted, allowing their vision to catch sight of the prize in the box, and they gasped in amazement.

"It's a plane!" Michael exclaimed.

"I thought it was goin' be a aminal," Robert grumped in disappointment.

"A plane is much better than an animal," Eric countered as he moved closer to the winged wonder.

"Better than a bear? Why?" Robert asked.

"Because it's your grandma Wilma's plane, and she can fly it," Wilma answered proudly. She had been standing quietly behind her grandchildren enjoying their observations.

"In the air?"

"Don't answer him, Grandma Wilma. He'll just ask another one." Michael intercepted matter-of-factly. He wasn't interested in wasting time on a million of Robert's stupid questions; he wanted to hear more about the plane. Walking confidently to the side of the machine, he placed his hand, palm flat and fingers wide, onto the sleek metal. Expecting it to feel cool, he was surprised by its warmth. Michael stood motionless, his hand seemingly glued in anticipation as if waiting for a heartbeat. Wilma ushered Eric and Robert forward to join Michael.

"You know," Wilma began, "I wasn't much older than you are now, Michael, when I learned to fly a plane."

"Really? How old were you?"

"I was sixteen years old," Wilma answered as she affectionately patted the plane. "My brother and a dear friend taught me how to fly."

"Can you teach me?" Michael asked, visions of himself flying through the air forming in his mind.

"Oh," Wilma responded with a mist of memory in her eyes "Things are different now. To learn to fly today, you have to take classes and get a license and do all sorts of things. It was much simpler when I learned and I think much more exciting."

Then adding as she could imagine what Jane would say about her last comment, "But it is much safer the way that flying is taught today."

Robert eyed the plane warily. "Can this really fly? It looks old."

"She may be old, Robert, but your grandma keeps her in tip-top shape," Wilma defended immediately. "The engine purrs like a kitten."

"Does it have a kitten in it?" Robert asked hopefully.

"No!" Eric and Michael yelled in unison. Wilma placed a comforting arm around the still puzzling Robert. She could tell by the look on his face that he remained unconvinced of the airworthy abilities of the machine in front of him. Smiling, she ruffled his hair.

"Would you boys like to sit in her?" Robert's questions dissolved as he quite liked the idea of sitting in it even if he didn't think that it could really fly. Placing her foot strategically on the wing, Wilma lifted her body up with an agility that belied her years. Robert was placed in the back seat, where he could do the least amount of meddling. Lending a hand first to Eric and then to Michael, Wilma helped them into the front seat. Leaning over, she explained the purpose of the various dials and pedals to the fascinated Eric and Michael while Robert busied himself with wiggling and touching anything that he could reach, which thankfully wasn't much.

"Can you tell us about one of your adventures?" Michael asked.

"An adventure!" Wilma thrilled. "Well, of course, but we have to set the scene then. Michael, hold onto Robert so that he stays put." Turning in his seat, Michael gave Robert a look that meant business, and in rare cooperation, Robert did not move. Lowering herself to the ground, Wilma went to the double barn doors and swung them wide open. Sunlight spread like spotlights to every corner of the barn as if the curtain had risen and the star of the show sparkled in metallic brilliance. The boys' eyes widened as the blue of the horizon that now lay before them seemed taunting as if tempting *Wilma's Wings* to take flight. Strutting quickly back to the plane, Wilma, with the lightness of anticipation, swung herself up onto the wing of her plane. Leaning over again, she addressed her enraptured subjects.

"Now we are ready for an adventure!" And so she began the story, one of many, the same story that she had told her little ones when they were little ones so many years before, and for one solid hour her crew did not move, not even Robert.

It was two days before David was to leave to begin his journey to join his family in Pennsylvania, and he was excited. He had spoken with Jane and the boys daily and by their detailed descriptions of their activities felt as if he were there with them—almost. Ann's situation had also been shared, and as the eternal optimist, he had spoken with Ann and told her how much he was looking forward to being an uncle. Beaming, Ann relayed David's words to Jane and as Jane finished her own conversation with her husband added that she owed him a kiss for his kindness. There was a lot to look forward to, and David was ready to be on his way.

The summer's sun was still perched in the sky though it was almost six p.m. Mary had left for the evening to visit some friends and was not expected back until the next morning. No guests or visitors were expected, so David was surprised by Blackie's warning bark as a car crunched down the driveway and then stopped in front of the house. Quickly putting his packing aside, he ambled down the stairway and opened the front door. To his shock, the two people standing in front of him were his parents. He was speechless and could only motion for them to come inside. The threesome stood in the front hall, and though awkward was an inadequate description the familiar automated ritual began. Mavis Bell leaned stiffly toward her son for the expected kiss on the cheek, and once performed, Richard Bell extended his hand for the perfunctory handshake. David stood stunned in silence, so it was Mavis who spoke first.

"We thought this a good time to come as Jane and the children are visiting her family and their absence would avoid some discomfort." David was amazed by their apparent knowledge of their affairs though it seemed obvious that they were innocently informed by Aunt Cathy. Neither David nor Jane had seen his parents since the disastrous Thanksgiving dinner at Aunt Cathy's house almost ten years earlier. Richard and Mavis had not even attended their only son's wedding. An appropriate excuse, in their eyes, had been forwarded with a check of course. Having made it a point of not being a part of their lives in any way, it completely befuddled David as to any reason that would have brought them to their doorstep now. Sensing that further explanation was necessary, Mavis continued, "Catherine told us of your family's travel plans."

"May we sit somewhere for a few moments?" Mavis asked starchly.

Shaking loose a bit from his initial shock, David motioned his parents into the parlor. Glancing around the cheerful room, Richard and Mavis took a seat. David sat in the chair opposite his parents and waited, still silent and still very, very uncomfortable. Never one for pleasant chitchat, Mavis started immediately.

"Your father and I have engaged the services of an attorney to begin the process of preparing our last wills and testaments. As you can imagine, it is *quite* complicated as our estate is quite expansive." The emphasis on *quite* was not missed by David, though he really could not imagine anything with regard to their estate; he had never asked, and he had never been told. Richard continued.

"We feel strongly that a provision should be made for you as you are our only child and biological heir. We do, however, have a problem with the orphan children. After all, they are not of our bloodline."

David stared at his parents, wondering how he could possibly be part of their bloodline. As a child he had yearned for the bonding and belonging that he had seen in other families, but it never came. They sent him to the finest schools and to the finest camps, but they had never sent him love in any form. As he grew, he learned compassion and care from strangers and came to understand that there was love in the world though not from the two people that were supposed to love him the most. It had taken time and maturity for as he gazed at his parents he felt no resentment or bitterness as to their treatment of him; he had too much to be thankful for. They were the same, but there was one difference. These were his children that they were talking about, not orphans. He had taken their cold dispatch all of his life, but it was not a trait that was going to be handed down to the next generation. His bloodline was beginning to boil.

"They are not orphans," David responded. "They are my children—mine and Jane's. What is the problem?"

"Your father and I have not worked and acquired such a

measure of wealth over the years only to have it passed down to orphans of unknown breeding who you claim to be the parents of on paper. It is completely unacceptable," Mavis said indignantly.

"Certainly," Richard continued with misdirected commonality in thought, "you must see that some provisions must be made." David rose from his seat and faced his parents.

"Certainly some provisions must be made, and here they are." David began, his eyes flaming with anger yet his voice remaining steady. "You, the both of you, in my life, have never given me anything that I truly needed—not love, not care, not kindness. You have given nothing to me in life, and I want nothing from you in death." Richard stood as if he were about to strike David. Standing firm and unflinching, David stood nearly a head taller than his father. Mavis stood quickly as if to intercede, though she had never once in the past.

"A beating?" David addressed seeing his father's familiar stance. "Those days are passed." Moving back slightly, Richard paused. David was ready at last to finish what was never started.

"I give you permission to leave this house and to leave my life permanently. Leave your 'estate' to whomever and in any way that you like, but, do not leave me so much as a penny because if you do, I will give it to the charity of my choice. And one more thing, you both count wealth in dollars and diamonds, but the wealth that I have—the love of my wife, the love of my children, and the love of my family and my friends—can never be calculated in hand only in heart." Looking at them with sympathy, he concluded "You are both so poor in what really matters; I pity your poverty."

His parents were quiet. They had nothing to add and nothing to offer. They gathered themselves and left without a kiss on the cheek or a handshake. Their meeting was ended politely as if by strangers, as they were.

"I am a member of the finest fighting force in the world! I am navy! I am tough! Oh no, not another one!" Jane was by Ann's side. She had been in labor for almost six hours. The pain was starting to increase as the contractions were growing more intense and coming closer together.

"Ann," Jane addressed her sister in her calmest voice as her fingers were turning blue from Ann squeezing them. "Try to breathe through the contractions. I know that it is hard, so let's do it together. Come on, breathe with me." Ann turned her sweating and contorted face and looked at the relaxed and angelic face of her sister as she breathed rhythmically in and out. This was not helping.

"Are you kidding me?" Ann yelled. "I am breathing. You breathe when you scream, don't you?" As the contraction reached its peak, Ann made another plea. "For God's sake, Janie, get these babies out of me, and make it stop *now!*" Jane dared not tell her sister that the worst was on its way long before the best; she would find out soon enough. The contraction finally subsided, allowing Ann to rest a moment while she madly sucked on an ice chip. Her repose was interrupted as her doctor entered the room.

"How's Mom doing?" Dr. Williams inquired cheerfully. He enjoyed the blessing of bringing new life into the world, despite the pain of the process. Ann, however, was not feeling blessed at the moment.

"You should just be glad that I am not armed," Ann answered grimly. Dr. Williams chuckled as he had heard all manner of threats and angst from his ladies in labor.

"Now let us see how you are doing," he said to Ann as he snapped the latex gloves onto his hands.

"Oh this should help," Ann responded sarcastically while

he checked the progress of her dilation. Finishing his quick examination, he advised his patient.

"You know, Miss Ann," he said in his chipper manner. It was beginning to make Ann sick; she wanted to slug him. "Your dilation is slow, and while normally I would recommend medication to speed the process, this is your first pregnancy, and there is some risk in that." Ann became tearful as she had no idea what he was talking about or what was coming next. "You are also having twins, which increases the risk, so we are going to proceed now with a cesarean section. That way both Mommy and babies will be healthy and safe, okey dokey?" Ann, unable to take any more, stuck her tongue out at him. "She's a feisty one," he said with laughter as Jane blushed with embarrassment.

"I don't care if you have to gut me right here, Doc, just make this all stop!" Her pitch once again began to rise as another contraction began. He left her screaming but consoled her that it would soon be over and that the anesthesiologist was on the way.

It was soon over, as promised, and two healthy boys were delivered: Edmond Filip Krysochowski, six pounds four ounces, and Danny Joseph Krysochowski, five pounds eight ounces.

The hospital room had slipped into dusk, and Ann had fallen into an exhausted sleep. Jane had remained with her sister, allowing the babies to stay in the room for a time. Standing by their wheeled cribs, Jane caressed the babies gently as they cooed softly and reached their tiny covered hands upward in instinctive need. She was in love with them from the moment she saw them. How she secretly wished that they were her own and then smiling, realized that a part of them was. Suddenly she caught her breath as realized the full impact of what she was seeing and when she was seeing it. Tears of remembrance and joy crept down her cheeks as her familiar friend took his place at her side.

"They are so tiny," Golden Boy observed in awe as he stared down at the tiny bundles.

"Yes, they are," Jane agreed. "Would you like to hold one?" He shook his head in a panicked no, but Jane picked up one of the babies and placed the baby boy in his arms. After she showed him the proper manner of holding a baby, he relaxed slightly.

"He is so light. Are you sure that I am holding him right?" Jane nodded. It was certainly a switch in roles. She was usually the one feeling uncomfortable. Though he was insecure in his task, he was unwilling to release his hold. Gently raising the baby to his face, he felt the warmth of the baby's skin against his. Inhaling in curiosity, he glanced at Jane. "He has a scent that I have never experienced before."

"There is nothing else in the world like it," Jane answered contently. "A baby's fragrance is unique, the infusion of new life. There is nothing sweeter."

Still cradling his tiny charge in his arms, he continued to stare in amazement. Placing her arm in motherly affection around her companion's waist, she joined him in the admiration and the appreciation of where life begins not where it ends.

Jane's head dipped to the side as she drifted into sleep. Righting her head again, she tried to focus on the clock in the room; it was nearly six a.m. There had been no need for Ann to ask for Jane to stay. Having suddenly been presented with two babies and major surgery, Jane had insisted that she stay with her sister overnight even though the babies were now tucked back into the nursery. Still, Jane was so tired that her head, dipping once again, sought the resting place of her upstretched hand. The door silently opened, and Jane was momentarily startled by familiar lips brushing against hers. Her eyes flew open in immediate consciousness, and she jumped from her chair and embraced her husband. "Oh, I have missed you so much!" she whispered as she placed her lips once again on his. He smiled and kissed her neck, causing a giggle to escape.

"I guess that my timing was pretty bad," he observed with some accuracy. "I came into the door of your parents' house just as you and your screaming sister were coming out. Did you have to explain any of those words to the boys?" Jane laughed softly.

"Her labor had just started to intensify. You should have heard her later."

David looked over at the still slumbering Ann. "Everybody okay? Mom and babies healthy?"

Jane smiled broadly. "Mom and babies are just fine. One mom has delivered, and one is on the way." David looked at Jane quizzically. "I didn't want to tell you until you got here. I just had a feeling, and I had the test." David's eyes grew wide as he held onto his wife firmly as if needing support. "It was positive! We are pregnant. We are finally pregnant!"

CHAPTER 19

The only other person told other than immediate family was Sylvia. Jane, though hopeful and excited about her pregnancy, wanted to wait until she completed her first trimester before a full announcement was made. It was not up to argument as Sylvia insisted that Jane take an immediate leave of absence. The obstetrician and the best specialists in the area were consulted. All medical procedures and precautions were administered and advised to ensure a successful pregnancy. So Jane, with reservations but also with assurances that the hospital would manage without her, took her leave to put her feet up, to relax, and to wait.

A fall morning crisp and clear peeked through the curtains of Jane's and David's bedroom. Opening her eyes for the second time, the first having been a sleepy farewell to David as he left for work, she rolled onto her back and inhaled deeply. Reaching her arms upward, she spread her fingers wide as if touching unseen stars. It was delicious, this feeling of life growing inside of her. She had never come this far, and she was enjoying each new step. Lowering her arms gently, she let her hands rest on her rounded belly that formed a soft, blanketed hill. Rubbing her stomach affectionately, the baby, seemingly sensitive to Jane's touch, moved within her. Sweetly and lovingly Jane began to talk and to sing to her unborn child. It was a morning shared by mother and child, a child as real to her in the safety of her body as in the safety of her arms.

There were no sounds of shouting siblings or rapidly running feet. Mary, by God's good grace of firm conviction, had corralled the boys from the start and had emphasized the importance of calm for the health of their mother and their growing baby brother. Michael and Eric understood immediately and had become quite protective of their mother. Robert, though he loved his mother equally as much, found the new constraints a bit overwhelming at times. Mary, always quick to see and quicker to solve, found that a gentle push out of doors for a quick game of Wiffle ball did the trick. Mary was the pitcher, Blackie was the outfield, and Robert hit and ran the bases, again and again and again. This sufficiently tired both boy and dog.

The silence of the morning was interrupted as Jane heard a soft tapping at her door. Beckoning the unknown person in, Jane smiled as she saw Robert's face peeking through the cracked door. Quietly he entered and then tiptoed to the bedside. She knew how hard this was for him, and without hesitation she patted the empty spot beside her. Robert responded instantly and with a hop and a jump landed with a bounce on the bed. Catching his actions after the fact, he looked anxiously at Jane.

"Okay?" he asked with uncertainty.

"Just fine," Jane answered as she pulled him to her and hugged him. Snug in her arms, he was motionless and content to be so, for a bit. Enough was enough, as Robert pulled back gently from his mother but kept his small hands in hers. Looking at her intently, he had important issues to address.

"Are you hungry?" Robert asked.

"You know, I believe that I am," Jane responded as Robert nodded his head in mutual affirmation.

"Is Daniel hungry too?" Robert asked, pointing at Jane's belly. They had known for a month or so that Jane was having a boy, and as soon as they knew they had named him. Seeing that Robert wanted even more support in his desire for breakfast, Jane smiled and quickly confirmed.

"If I am hungry, I bet that Daniel is hungry too."

"Good," Robert acknowledged with noted relief, "'cause Ms. Mary says that I can have breakfast in bed with you before I *hafta* go to *school*." Helping Jane to sit up and aptly propping her back with pillows, Robert fortified his own spot with pillows and, sitting back comfortably, waited. They were not long in waiting as Mary soon appeared with a tray in her hands filled with aromatic delectables.

"How is Mother today?" Mary asked, giving a quick glance to Robert's left-out expression. "I already know how you are, you little devil." Keeping her attentions on Jane, she explained. "He was fakin' another tummy ache today tryin' to get outta goin' to school. As you can see, he has recovered." Jane laughed as Mary began covering Robert and as much of the surrounding area as possible with dishtowels in preparation.

"Mother and baby are feeling just wonderful," Jane finally found the opportunity to answer, "though I am feeling a bit guilty over being so spoiled."

It was Mary's turn to smile. "Then I'm doin' my job" was her simple response though Mary never looked at anything that she did in the Bell home as a job. She cooked and she cleaned with a commitment bound by care, not by obligation. They had all come together from different backgrounds and from different places and joining beneath one roof formed one family. It was a family connected by love, not lineage, and they each understood it and treasured it.

"Will I get spoiled when I have a baby?" Robert garbled, his mouth already filled with food. Mary and Jane looked at each other; no answer was offered. The explanation could wait for later, much later. Thankfully, Robert became interested in what he was eating.

Christmas was on its way. Jane could not remember when she had enjoyed another holiday season more. It was the first Christmas in many years when she had not worked, and she was fully engaged in the spirit and the wonder of anticipation. Her activities were somewhat limited. The shopping was relegated to Mary and David to ensure that Jane stayed off of her feet, but she was enjoying the wrapping of gifts, the decorating of the house though restricted, and even the writing of Christmas cards, a chore that David had gladly relinquished. Sitting on her stool in the kitchen, Jane relished helping with the Christmas cookies, and she and Robert were keeping a record as to who had eaten the most broken ones, broken by accident or intent. Eric had taken up playing the guitar and frequently serenaded the family with "Silent Night," the one Christmas carol that he could play without too much twanging. Michael was often out in the evenings as he had finally gotten the courage to try out for basketball and had made the team. His coach thought that he was a little short but soon found that Michael's speed and ball handling amply compensated for his size. It was a glorious season that kept the Bell family in a blissful spin of activity.

The Day finally arrived. As morning broke, just barely, a blizzard ensued inside as paper began flying and swirling around the Bell Christmas tree. New toys, gadgets, and games met with quick "ooohs" and "aaahs" as hands reached for more. The interminable wait had climaxed in a matter of minutes as all lay before them unwrapped and discovered. A silence settled as each of the Bell brood surveyed their stash. A yet-to-be-tended collection of baby toys and clothes was piled neatly next to the tree.

Jane and Mary sat side by side on the sofa, exhausted from preparation, from lack of sleep, and from watching Robert spinning around and around, an energy surge from the consumption of too many candy canes. David entered from the kitchen carrying a tray with two hot cups of cinnamon-sweetened tea for the two much deserving ladies of the house. Handing each their cup, David took a seat next to Jane and, putting his arm around her, handed her a small elegantly wrapped box. Robert, spying the sparkle of an unwrapped gift, quickly went to the source to be sure that he had not missed one.

"This one is just for Mom, Robert," David answered the unasked question, "from me." Jane, holding the gift in her hand, turned to David with tears in her eyes. "Tears already," he chided her lovingly, "you haven't even opened it yet." David had seen tears of late from Jane for just about any reason and, knowing that it was to be expected did as he always did, wiped them gently with his handkerchief that he now always kept in his pocket. Unwrapping the gift, Jane knew by the box that it was jewelry. Opening the lid slowly, she found inside a pendant heart of gold. Her face illuminated with wonder as she observed the diamonds that encrusted the top two crescents of the heart and then continued down both sides. The lines of diamonds stopped just short of reaching the point where the two sides met for instead of diamonds, four gemstones completed the shape at the bottom of the heart: two on each side, meeting to form the point.

"I had it made just for you see … " David explained proudly

pointing as Jane admired her gift, "that stone right there is Robert's birthstone and ... "

"Where?" Robert interrupted.

"Right there." David indicated as Jane had turned the pendant around for Robert to see. "And there is Eric's birthstone, and on the other side is Michael's birthstone." Jane had a full audience now as both Eric and Michael had joined in to look at the gift. "And this last stone," David finished, "is Daniel's birthstone." Keeping fast hold of her pendant, Jane turned and wrapping her arms around David, buried her head into his shoulder and cried. "I hope that you don't deliver too early or too late," David whispered. Eric and Michael didn't care for the mushy stuff, so they returned to their presents. Robert was confused.

"Doesn't Mom like her present, Miss Mary?"

With a slight sniffle Mary answered. "Your mom loves her present. She's just crying 'cause she's so happy."

Robert shook his head. "I only cry when I don't get what I want. Are you sure?"

It was Jane's turn to answer. Wiping her eyes and smiling she reached for Robert. "I'm sure, Robert, very sure."

January had settled in quiet and cold as the winter hibernation had begun. Their Maine town, like so many others, had frozen into a chilling timelessness as the festive December snow had now hardened, bracing for the long, harsh days ahead.

It was another evening that David and Jane had become accustomed to enjoying. The boys were in bed asleep as David and Jane sat comfortably chatting while the fire crackled warmly in the fireplace. Mary, seated in a chair nearby, listened passively and knitted. The clicking of her needles enhanced the atmosphere with a constant rhythm, like the ticking of a clock. Jane stirred in her seat and awkwardly began to rise.

"Why does everything on me seem to have gotten so big, but my bladder seems to have gotten so small?" Jane asked, laughing. David was on his feet instantly to assist his teetering wife. Watching Jane as she left the room, David then took his seat again and listened in quiet comfort to the click, click, clicking of the needles. It was one of the many things that he loved about Mary; conversation was never forced, and silence was never uncomfortable. Jane reappeared but stopped short of entering the room. Holding the doorway for support and looking pale, Jane appealed to David. "I am spotting." Freezing for but a second in shock, David was then instantly on his feet and at Jane's side. One thought swept David's mind; this had to be a false alarm, they were too close.

"I'll call the hospital. You two get goin'," Mary instructed firmly as she headed to the phone.

The ride to the hospital was a panic that seemed to last forever. Jane's bleeding rapidly increased. Trying to stay alert and calm, Jane could feel her efforts failing as she began to slip in and out of semiconsciousness. She could hear David yelling and yelling. He didn't need to yell. What was he yelling about?

The hospital was ready and waiting with full staff, even though it was almost midnight. Sylvia was there, having previously warned the entire staff of the hospital that she be notified immediately with any news of Jane regardless of the hour. The car squealed to a stop in front of emergency, and within seconds Jane was on a gurney being wheeled into the hospital. Sylvia was at her side but at the same time motioned for two staff to take care of David. Stained with Jane's blood, he looked ready to collapse from shock.

Time passed, the only constant. David found himself sitting in the staff lounge, the one nearest the intensive care unit where Jane was being treated. He was dressed in hospital scrubs. The kind nurses had removed his bloodstained clothes and redressed him as if he were a child. No calls were made. David knew nothing at this point, so what could he say? As he paced the room, his thoughts paced even faster. Stopping at the doorway, he looked for something that he couldn't define. *How is this helping?* he self-criticized. *Gather yourself. Jane needs you. Your family needs you. Stop thinking the worst.* Breathing deeply, he felt the maddening speed of his mind begin to slow, but the tears slid quickly down his cheeks. Angrily he wiped them away, but they were beyond his conscious control and no matter how many times he wiped them away, they returned unabated. *It just can't be,* he couldn't help himself from thinking; we are almost there.

It was dawn when Sylvia entered the staff lounge where David had been waiting. Her step was not as firm and her shoulders not as square. She was tired, so very tired. David rose from his seat and, facing his friend, waited for her words.

"Jane is going to be okay." She placed her hand on his shoulder. Making her gaze square with his, she continued. "We had to perform a complete hysterectomy. It was the only way that we could stop the bleeding, the only way that we could save her life." There was no response as David looked at her and waited. "David, did you hear me? Do you understand? Jane is going to be fine." Sylvia finished with concern. David nodded yes but remained silent with his gaze steady; he was waiting, still waiting. Sylvia's conviction faltered as her eyes dropped to the floor. She knew what he was waiting for.

"We lost him, David. We lost Daniel." Sylvia gasped as if the breath were being taken from her body. "We tried everything, everything … God Almighty … " She could say no more as her shoulders slumped and her hands flew to her face trying in desperation to somehow hold onto the strength that was now failing her. Wrapping his arms around his friend, he consoled her, knowing that no one could have done more.

David sat at her bedside. He had not moved from the spot since they had settled Jane into her own room. There were still quite a few machines and monitors in the room that constantly assessed Jane's condition, but she was out of any real danger, any real physical danger. She had not been fully awake yet, only drifting in and out of a sleepy state. Almost twenty-four hours had passed since the ordeal had begun, and there was much yet to come as Jane had not been told anything. A soft light infused the room, and David, looking at his sleeping wife, gently touched her face and let his fingers caress her hair. How warm she felt, how alive, thank God. Jane's eyes opened and stayed focused. Taking in where she was, she looked at David.

"What happened?" she asked groggily.

"Do you remember anything?" he asked softly.

Recollection began to settle the fog. Jane's eyes grew more open and alert. "Spotting...I was spotting." The alarm in her voice began to rise.

"You are in the hospital. You are okay." Jane's hand went with trepidation to rest on her belly; she knew at once.

"The baby, where's my baby?" Jane asked, searching David's face for the answer. She found it, but it was too horrible for belief. "Get my baby, David," she told him with a voice approaching hysteria. "I want my baby!" She was now screaming, and there was no need for David to call for help as the room instantly flooded with nurses. Sylvia promptly broke through and stood at Jane's bedside. "Sylvia, I want my baby. I want Daniel."

With flat command, Sylvia gave her instructions. "Everyone clear the room except for David." As the nurses left quietly, Sylvia turned once again to Jane. "I'll bring you Daniel."

As they waited, Jane was nonresponsive. Staring straight

ahead, she uttered not a word as David sat next to her, his hand never leaving hers. Sylvia entered the room with a small bundle wrapped in a newborn's blanket, the same as any other newborn. Placing the bundle in Jane's waiting arms, Sylvia stood back slightly. Tenderly cradling her baby in her left arm, Jane took her right hand and gently pulled back the blanket.

"He's beautiful." Jane smiled. "Look, David. Look at the little chestnut curls on the top of his head, just like yours." It was unbearable, but he did as his wife asked. Looking down at his lifeless child, he felt as if he were losing his mind, just as he feared that Jane was losing hers. Sylvia was silent, dissolving further into the back of the room. Lifting her baby, Jane placed his small face against hers. "He is just cold." Jane pathetically observed as she continued to cuddle his face against her own. "So terribly, terribly cold." The sobs came—hard, deep, soul-shaking sobs. David placed his arms around them, holding them tight. Love was not enough. Faith was not enough. Conviction was not enough. There was nothing, nothing that could stay the wave of utter despair that washed over them. What was so would always be so—unchangeable.

Jane was still recovering in the hospital, but she insisted that David go home; he had barely slept in two days. Mary had offered to stay with her as had Wilma, who had just arrived, but Jane said no. She just wanted to be alone. She could not bear one more word of condolence, sympathy, or spiritual platitude.

It was deep into the night. The hospital was relatively quiet, and Jane was asleep. He sat in the shadow of the room in silence, hoping to offer some small comfort in his presence. A word pierced his façade. She had woken.

"Why?"

Rising from the shadows, he came forward. Taking the seat next to her bed, he touched her hand. Repulsed, she pulled away. Jane turned the light on over her bed, and they could now see each other fully. He was unprepared for her expression. Anger and hatred had formed a shroud across her face, obscuring any evidence of the kindness or the tenderness of the woman he had come to know. He did not recognize her.

"Why?" she repeated without abatement and without clarification. He realized the intent of her question, but there was no clear answer that she could see or understand in her current state of mind.

"There is no 'why,'" he began tentatively, searching for words. "There is not always an explanation for what happens at least ... not, not right away. This is so hard." He lowered his head to his hands and swept his fingers through his hair. Raising his head again, he looked for some encouragement in her face; he found none. Frustration filled his voice as he addressed her. "Look, I don't have the answer. I don't know exactly why, but there is one thing that I do know." He grabbed her hand in desperation, refusing to let her pull away. "There is something good that comes from everything, even the most horrible things that happen. We learn something. We do something differently. We reach down and find something that we never knew that we had and we help somebody else with it. It's there, Jane. Look for it, look for it. The only purpose for Daniel's life was not the fact that he died. You know better, you know." Though he still held her hand in his, she had turned her face from him. He waited, hoping he had reached her. Turning back to face him, tears streamed down Jane's face.

"Do you know what it is to lose everything, everything?"

He looked at her intently and searchingly. "Have you? Have you lost everything?" She looked away for only a moment, and when she faced him again, her tears had dried and her eyes met his with scorching anger. There would be no tricks from him. No ten things to be thankful for, not this time. Her soul was deep in a pit, and she would not accept so much as a string to pull it back out.

"Life is everything," she responded without flinching. "His life was taken from me, and that was everything, not once, but twice. Twice I carried him in my body, and twice I held him lifeless in my arms. He was perfect—ten little fingers and ten little toes—perfect. You saw him, didn't you? You saw him when you took him away from me. You and your God of mercy, your God of compassion, you … you … you … " Jane began screaming and pointing as all reason left her mind. Nurses rushed into her empty room, and though the screams subsided, there was no calm.

Almost two months passed, and Jane's body began to heal. She returned to work, against ignored protests, and life continued but not life as it had been known to the Bell family. All tasks both at work and at home were performed efficiently and correctly by Jane, but there was no feeling, no emotion. Sylvia talked to her, Wilma talked to her, Mary talked to her, and even some close friends and nurses spoke with her. Jane listened to them politely and thanked them for their concern, but that was as far as it went. Any connections to her emotions or inner self were left untouched and unreachable.

It was Saturday, and a fun family evening had been planned; it was time to dye Easter eggs. Wilma, who was still visiting, Mary, and the rest of the family were in the kitchen busy with preparation. Jane was alone upstairs resting. Lying in bed, Jane heard a light knock of intention as the door opened immediately, and David entered the room. Looking at his wife he smiled encouragingly. He had not tried to reach Jane as the others had. Her detachment concerned him greatly, but he offered no intense lectures or conversations; the others had tried those and had so far failed. His only offering was unconditional love and attention and lots of it. Flowers, cards, dinners out, and affection; he tried anything and everything, and he would keep trying anything and everything even though it was not always warmly received.

"Jane," he addressed her softly as he slid next to her in bed. Putting his arm around her, he could feel her body tense. "We are getting ready to start dying the eggs. Are you coming down?" Turning her face to meet his, she looked at him with a mixed expression of disbelief and contempt.

"Is it really that easy for you to put a smile on your face and go on with your life as if nothing had happened?" Jane had been short tempered with him of late but never this confrontational.

"Is there a better option?" he asked with all sincerity.

Leaving him in bed, Jane rose and began pacing the floor restlessly. "For God's sake, David, you of all people," she scoffed, "you of all people have the right to be bitter and angry." She stopped and faced him as he sat upright. "Look at your life! Look at how you were raised and how you were treated! Look at everything that has happened to you! How can you not be bitter and angry?" Standing, David walked to his wife. Holding her arms firmly in his hands, he faced her. Locking his eyes with hers, he knew that it was time; enough was enough.

"Would my life somehow be better that way? Should I rant? Should I scream?" His voice began to rise and fill with unaccustomed anger. "Should I curse my parents, curse life, and curse God for all of the inequities in my life? Would it make my life happier? Has it made your life happier?" Jane had turned her face away, unable to bear the look on his face, though his grip on her remained firm. "No," he continued as his voice softened.

"Look at me, Jane." Releasing one hand, David gently turned Jane's face to meet his. "Bad things happen. They happen every day. You know this. You have seen them. You're a nurse. But good things happen too every day, and you have seen them too; miracles you have told me." Jane began sniffling and shaking her head no as if she were just a child.

"Not for me, David. Not for me. No miracles for me." David wrapped his wife in his arms tightly and kissed her.

"Yes, for you, Jane." David responded in confirmation. "That we are here together and that we love each other and that we are surrounded by so many that love us and care about us, that is a miracle that allows us to believe in the good and to let go of the bad." He whispered, "It's okay to grieve, sweetheart. I do, but in grieving, I won't let go of the good. Don't let go of the good, Jane; it's still there, but it's up to you to see it." When he released his hold, she slipped from him and again turned away. Hoping for the best, he turned to leave.

"Come down when you are ready," he said as he left the room. He heard no reply.

Jane lay back on her bed. He couldn't know what it was like, she thought to herself unyielding. It was not his body that had held life; it was hers. Still lying and staring aimlessly, she heard another knock at the door. With agitation in her voice, she instructed whoever it was to enter. Eric opened the door slowly and asked if he could come in. She beckoned him forward, and approaching the bed, he gingerly sat on the edge near Jane.

"How are you feeling, Mom?" Eric asked with care. Eric was the most sensitive of the three boys. Michael had immediately been drawn to and connected with David. They had become basketball buddies and frequently stayed after school together to practice. Robert connected with everybody, as long as he could ask a question. Eric was the caregiver of the three. He was always on hand when anyone needed help, and he remembered to ask about Jane's patients, often remember-ing them by name. Jane was constantly amazed by his natural compassion and felt that he would make a wonderful doctor. So as this unfamiliar pall had fallen over his mother, Eric had tried whenever and however he could to make her feel a little better.

"Fine" was Jane's curt response.

"Are you coming down to dye eggs?" Eric inquired hopefully.

"I'm not sure." Jane was again curt in her response.

"Can I say good-bye now then?" Eric asked, his voice infused with an emotion that Jane did not sense. Only aggra-vated by his question, she responded.

"You mean good night, Eric, not good-bye. You're not going anywhere," Jane chastised. Eric nodded his head yes.

"I am going somewhere. I made a bargain with God."

Jane sat upright. "What are you talking about?"

Eric began to sniffle but answered, "I promised God last night that he could trade me for Daniel. So I am going with God tonight, and when you wake up tomorrow morning you will have Daniel, and you will be happy again." The look of horror that crossed Jane's face startled the tears from Eric's eyes. He immediately began to console her. "It's okay, Mom, really. I'll be with my mom in heaven, and Daniel will be with you. We talked about my mom in heaven before, remember? It will be okay." Finishing, he gently reached for and held Jane's hand.

Jane was momentarily stunned. Suddenly Jane reached for and held Eric in an unyielding hug. Kissing his forehead, she cradled his head in her hands. "Eric," she began forcefully, "your mother is a blind idiot. Me, I mean me. This mother." She pointed to herself. Eric giggled but stopped promptly as Jane became quite serious. "Eric, you will have to break your bargain with God. You are exactly where you should be, and Daniel is exactly where he should be. I have questioned for too long and in the process almost lost what was mine to have and to love. Besides … " Jane began smiling as an image suddenly entered her mind. "I bet that your mom has her hands full taking care of Daniel, so do you mind if I keep taking care of you, Michael, and Robert?"

Eric smiled with evident relief but said, "As long as you are happy."

Jane smiled. "I am happy. I am very, very happy." And for the first time in months, she meant it, and she felt it. "Now, who's taking care of the egg dye?" Eric shuffled a bit with his words.

"Well," he began, "Grandma Wilma read that you can use onion skins to dye Easter eggs. So far the eggs are kinda smelly and brown."

"Oh no." Jane could only imagine. "Go right down and tell Grandma Wilma that Mom is coming right down and to wait. The eggs may yet be saved." Eric kissed his mom, jumped off of the bed, and rushed through the door. Rising quickly, Jane went to the mirror and, dabbing her eyes and adjusted her clothes. It was then that she sensed him.

"*Carpe diem*" were his only words in greeting.

"Seize the day," Jane translated vocally though her eyes remained averted from his. "Not enough. Seize every hour, every minute, and every second not in fear of what could be lost but in joy of what is already in hand; that is enough." Still refusing to look at him Jane quickly headed for the door, but as she reached it, she paused before opening it. She felt his hand on her shoulder.

"You found what you were looking for." He stated the fact with warmth in his voice. Too ashamed to turn and face him, she responded.

"Yes, and I am so sorry I…" Her golden-haired friend interrupted her before she could continue. Leaving his hand on her shoulder, he gently squeezed in understanding.

"It's okay now, Jane. You remembered. Good will grow where the rain has fallen."

"Yes, I remember, and I know it to be true," Jane answered her face still to the door. "God bless you." As the words left her lips, she opened the door and left to join her family.

CHAPTER 20

They made love early in the morning. It was an annual tradition. Not that they didn't make love throughout the year, but the morning of their wedding anniversary was special, a consecration of their love physically and emotionally.

"Does it ever get dull?" Jane asked coyly, goading him. Raising himself up on his side, he rested his slightly silver peppered but still curly brown head onto his hand and stared at her in mocked disbelief.

"Dull? Oh never dull," he responded in feigned comfort and then followed quickly. "Scarce comes to mind though." Jane pummeled him with her pillow. She knew better, and so did he. Surrender came quickly and willingly, and once again they rested with comfort in each other's arms. The first fragrance of freshly brewed coffee drifted into the room as an early mist.

"She has slowed down quite a bit, you know," David commented as he inhaled the well-accustomed aroma. He knew that if the coffee was on, Mary was already well at work cooking breakfast.

"I'd say that she has earned a slowdown, don't you? Slow or not, she's still up with dawn."

"Earned it?" David countered. "If she had only helped with Michael and Eric, she would have earned it. Adding Robert to the challenge made her a saint." They both laughed. Robert certainly was more than Eric and Michael put together. It was hard to believe that all three boys were out of high school with Michael already a college graduate and married, Eric in pre-med, and Robert with his future still a bit of a question, seemingly a victim of his own quizzical affectation.

"Are you ready?" David asked as their conversation had subsided and slipped into a relaxed silence. Jane smiled as she knew exactly what he meant. It was time to exchange gifts, and David looked forward to and planned for this proffering all year. Certainly there were other occasions for giving gifts like Christmas and birthdays, but this occasion belonged only to them, and he loved making it special. It had actually become a friendly competition each petitioning their gift as the best upon opening, though Jane hated to admit that David usually bested her. This year was going to be different.

"I am going to win this year you know," Jane admonished him sweetly.

"Unh, unh," David countered confidently, shaking his head no. "You're goin' down so you might as well go first." With a huff Jane hopped out of bed, but she was ready for the challenge. Rummaging in the closet, she found her hiding place and extracted David's gift. It was a small box that she handed to David.

"Looks awfully small to be a winner," he observed, looking at her slyly. Jane just shrugged. With great pleasure, she watched him open the box and observed his passive expression explode into astonishment.

"Wow" was his commentary as he read the piece of paper enclosed.

"Small, huh?" Jane chastised good-naturedly.

"Well, it's not often that you can fit a two-seated sea kayak into a box this size." He smiled, reaching for her. Falling into his arms, she laughed.

"That is the magic of a gift certificate, my darling. We can pick it up today. By the way ... " she added, "you will do the paddling while I recline as the lady in repose."

"I think not, my damsel in no distress," he countered, pulling her closer to him in embrace.

"Oh no, you don't." She tousled with him pulling back slightly. "Where is my gift?" Stealing one last kiss, he promptly jumped out of bed himself. Dramatically going to different spots in the room, pausing and then moving on, he finally arrived at his apparent hiding place. Pulling the box from its hidden resting place with great aplomb, he handed it to Jane. Looking at it, Jane could not help but laugh. It looked like a tie box.

"Really, David, a tie, how thoughtful," she teased as she began removing the wrapping paper.

"Go ahead and tease. It's just going to make you feel worse when you see what it is."

Lifting the lid, Jane pushed aside the tissue paper to reveal the contents. Puzzled at first, she lifted the leather-like portfolio and rotated it in her hands.

"Open it." David encouraged. Opening the bi-fold she began to read, and as she did her eyes widened in disbelief.

"A trip to Hawaii ... you bought us a trip to Hawaii?" David nodded, smiling broadly. "Hawaii! My God, where it's warm?" They both laughed at her observation for they both knew that escaping the Maine winter for a warmer location was the equivalent of ascending to the heavens, glorious no matter the duration. "But how did you ... skip that question ... when is it?" she asked, glancing back down at the papers. Finding the departure date she blinked hoping her vision was unclear. "December the twenty-sixth ... this December the twenty-sixth? David, I'm not prepared ... that's too soon ... I have work ... the kids ... the house." Her words came in fragments as a cascade of obstacles flooded her mind. Slipping back into bed, David faced his wife. In surprising full expectation, David flexed his hand forward as a traffic cop, authoritatively plugging the dam against the gushing of cannots.

"You are not working. That has already been arranged. I had someone on the inside." He winked. *That Sylvia,* Jane thought, *she knew and didn't say a word.* Not that her silence was a surprise. Sylvia had always been a loyalist to a worthy cause; past experience was proof of the fact. "As for the kids and the house, the kids are grown and on their own, and the house isn't going anywhere, but we are!" Accepting Jane's silence as acquiescence, David had one more victory to enjoy. "Now tell me. Go ahead."

Inserting the trip portfolio gently and intently back into the box, Jane placed it onto the side table. Turning to her husband, she slid her hands behind his neck. Guiding his lips to meet hers, she kissed him passionately, and as if the expression was still not sufficient, playfully she whispered into his ear.

"You won."

"More than the contest," he said in statement as he pulled her to him.

"What did you say about something being scarce?" she toyed.

"I didn't say anything." And they didn't say anything.

This anniversary was to be a little different. The big Victorian by the sea was decorated as usual in all of its seasonal grandeur. The process expanded in scope each year as each year without fail Aunt Cathy sent some new accent of Christmas pageantry. A life-sized Santa had appeared several days earlier and in keeping with Aunt Cathy's whimsy for the unusual, he was dressed for the beach. Perhaps even Santa needed to vacation someplace warm once in a while, though Jane felt that he still looked terribly cold standing in the foyer. In sympathy she had placed a scarf around his neck. Santa would also have to miss the anniversary party for it was taking place at Michael and Gwen's, his wife of six months, apartment in town. The wedding ceremony had taken place the past May. Both Michael and Gwen had been able to find jobs locally, allowing them to stay near family and friends; it had been a double blessing. This was to be their first hosted family gathering as a married couple, and the whole gang was to be there; they were both excited and anxious.

Jane, David, and Mary assembled in the foyer and dressed to leave. Hats, coats, scarves, and gloves were cast on in full anticipation of the elements in front of them. It had been an unusually cold November and the ice had already formed crystalline edges on the windows. Mary, eyeing the sunny Santa, shook her head in disapproval.

"He's indecent standing there in his bathin' suit and inner tube. Should be on his own bad boys list." Jane and David laughed as there was no dissuading her dislike of the newest decoration. Feeling that her words were still insufficient, she wagged her finger disapprovingly. "You mark my words. I'm still up earlier than the both of you, and one morning you'll find that poor fella in galoshes, slicker, and cap. Beach Santa, hah!" Her words were final, and with those words they left to face the night's chill.

The guests of honor and their companion were the last to arrive as the rest of the gang was already there waiting. Jane had been in the small apartment many times before. She had liked its warmth and its intimate rooms. It brought back memories of another time and another place, a pleasant reminder of her and David's early days of marriage and their first apartment together. The living room-dining room combination was merrily though sparsely decorated for the holidays. An artificial tabletop Christmas tree blinked merrily in front of the window and a few gaily wrapped presents gathered beneath it. Eyeing her planned destination, Mary quickly left Jane and David and headed for the kitchen, leaving them to begin their greetings.

Robert and Sylvia were sitting glued together on the sofa discussing one of their favorite subjects—football. Though they rooted for the same team, the fact would not have been evidenced by the tone of their conversation. Robert had squired Sylvia to the event, picking her up at the hospital. He had been five minutes late, and though Sylvia had expected it she still lectured him firmly on the importance of punctuality. Robert listened dutifully, as always and then asked if punctuality was more important than arriving or was arriving more important than punctuality. It was a long conversation for a short drive. He still, after all of these years, tried to best her, and after all of these years, she loved him more; a more welcome and loving challenge she could never have imagined. Rising from his seat quickly, Robert embraced his parents. Rising as well, Sylvia gave David a quick kiss to the cheek while grabbing Jane's hand with a warm squeeze.

"Okay," Robert was the first to speak, which was no surprise, "who won?" The anniversary gift competition was well known and its outcome always anticipated.

"Dad won, and I surrender willingly, but ... " Robert stopped his high five to his father in midmotion as he waited for the *but*. "Your father had the advantage of some additional inside help, which may ultimately result in a forfeit from coercion."

"A forfeit would be a shame as the gift would have to be forfeited as well," Sylvia countered without acknowledgment of guilt. Jane hugged her friend and laughed.

"Dad won without question, and he can win every time that he takes us to Hawaii!" Jane exclaimed happily. It was pretty well known to everyone except for Jane about the trip, but they still responded loudly in feigned surprise. Eric broke through the gathered huddle with his arm firmly wrapped around a young woman's waist, introducing his own guest to his parents.

"Mom, Dad, I want you to meet Trish. She wants to be a nurse, just like you, Mom. We met in anatomy class. We, we ... " Eric began to stutter a bit as the room went suddenly quiet. "I wanted her to meet all of you, okay?"

"Of course okay!" David answered for both himself and his wife as Jane nodded her head yes enthusiastically. "Has she met everyone else?" Trish smiled and acknowledged that she had but to no avail as an animated and repetitive reintroduction ensued accompanied by loud laughter. Mary appeared from the kitchen to inquire as to the fuss and to make an announcement. Having made the final finishes to the table, which was laden with food, Mary stood with her hands resting comfortably on her hips.

"Suppah is served" was the simple statement. Gwen walked to Mary and admired the table. She had tried to assuage Mary from taking over the kitchen but instead was swept aside and kindly instructed to enjoy her guests. Gwen was unoffended and outranked. As they gathered to admire the feast, Michael, looking every bit the man of his own house, clanged his glass to make the toast.

"As I stand here a happily married man of six months," Michael began to applause of appreciation, "I toast—we toast—Mom and Dad, David and Jane, a couple who have not labored through the years but have loved through the years. I can think of no better role model or testament to a successful and a loving marriage than them." Raising his glass, he finished. "May the years continue in kind and in kindness, and may we all be so blessed to follow in kind. Cheers." The clinking of glasses should have sounded the completion of the toast, but Eric was quick to continue in an unexpected finale.

"In the spirit of following in kind, Trish and I would like to make an announcement." Lips froze at the edge of their still unsipped glasses. Taking a deep breath, Eric continued. "Trish and I are engaged, and we plan to marry next summer." An understandable shock seemed to freeze the room. The family had only just met Trish for the first time that evening. How could they be engaged? How could no one have heard? Who was this girl, and what was Eric doing? This was not at all like him; not in the least. The silence persisted as the couple began to shuffle in discomfort. Robert broke the stalemate.

"Does this mean that we are in tuxes again next year?" Time renewed its movement as David was jolted into motion.

"Yes, that's exactly what it means!" David exulted as he shook Eric's hand wildly. Jane hugged her future daughter-in-law as well as the future groom. The atmosphere had indeed changed as congratulations, hugs, and kisses were showered on the obviously relieved couple. They didn't even know Trish's last name, but it little mattered; she had become family in an instant and getting to know her would come later. Mary had stood back waiting, and as the excitement settled she walked to Eric and kissed her boy's cheek. He would always be her boy; they were all three her boys, and she didn't mind sharing. Turning to Trish, she wrapped her in warm arms of welcome and acceptance. Wiping away the dampness that had gathered in the lines around her weathered eyes, Mary sniffled and then got back to business.

"Suppah's getting cold." The chatting crowd grabbed their plates and approached the well-laid feast invigorated by the bounty of good news. Sylvia, who was standing next to Robert, could not help a verbal poke at her favorite sparring partner.

"Well, Robert, it seems that you are the only unattached Bell left, and you know what that means." She baited with a thin grin on her face. His mouth already filled with food but thankfully closed, Robert swallowed quickly and then responded.

"Don't look at me, Aunt Sylvia," he countered sincerely. "After next summer I'm taking a tux break."

Sitting in the car, Jane nestled into her coat. The engine had just started, and the car was as cold as she was. It had been a wonderful evening. And Eric's news! He was making his own decisions and becoming quite the man on his own. She only wished that he could give them a little advanced insight before these types of momentous announcements. Perhaps, she chuckled to herself, he had picked up David's habit of sur- prise. God help Trish! Still, life would never be boring. David shifted the car into drive, and it began to putter stubbornly off. The first of the Christmas music tinkled on the radio.

"Some night, wasn't it?" David commented. Jane nodded but remained silent. The music continued to be the only sound in the car as the heater finally began to stave off the cold.

"You're awfully quiet," David observed, unable to read his wife's mood.

"Quiet and content," Jane answered lazily, "wonderfully content. Everyone is healthy. We are happy. The kids are happy and getting happier and more settled every day." Smiling and lapsing back into silence, Jane turned and stared at David's face, watching as he illuminated from the intermittent passing lights. Her smile faltered as a negative thought entered her mind. "Everything seems almost too good as if something bad should happen just to balance it all out."

David gave his wife a quick sideward glance. "Jane, something bad could happen at any moment. Do you want to waste your time trying to anticipate it?" Reaching for her hand, he squeezed it gently. "I say enjoy the good and deal with the bad when it comes. Enjoy the cake, Jane. Don't think about getting on the scale afterwards." Jane laughed; he had to join cake and the scale in the same sentence. Feeling a firm hand on her shoulder, Jane turned her head toward her shoulder.

"Stop worryin'," Mary added. "There's a lot to look forward to and much to be thankful for."

"Mary," Jane addressed their back-seat companion. "I thought that you were asleep."

"Only one eye, dear, and one ear ever."

A comfortable quiet again settled. Jane contented herself with catching a glimpse of the occasional homes already decorated with Christmas lights. They were not the only early birds who decorated. And still she watched David's face in quiet observation as the lights flickered and changed colors, the face that she had known and loved for so many years; his face, always his face.

David was fast asleep, but Jane was still wide awake and excited from the evening's events. Normally she would call her mother in the morning, but as it was only eleven p.m., she felt sure that her mother would be up. Fixing herself a quick cup of tea and grabbing the phone, Jane took a seat in the kitchen and dialed the number. A voice answered on the other end, but to Jane's surprise it was not her mother's voice but her father's.

"Dad, what are you doing still awake?" Jane asked as she knew that her dad was an early-to-bed, early-to-rise farmer.

"Well, your mom has been tossing and turning with the flu all day, and she just settled down and fell asleep." Jane admonished him for not having called her.

"No, no. Your mom made me promise not to call and to worry you on your anniversary. Now I know that normally you tell your mom all of the news and then I get it secondhand in your mom's exaggerated version. Do you think that just this once you could tell dear old Dad firsthand?" Jane laughed; it was true. News always seemed to travel to Wilma first and then trickled down in modified form to Filip. It was not as if Jane didn't talk to her dad, but it did seem as if it had been a long time since they had really talked. And so Jane began to tell her dad everything, starting with her gift to David and his gift to her. Filip had agreed immediately that David was the hands-down winner with his gift. He listened willingly about Jane and David's quiet luncheon together and everything that they ate; it all sounded good to him. Jane intentionally withheld the news of Eric's engagement for last. As the final bits of description left her lips about the dinner party at Michael and Gwen's apartment, she told him.

"Eric engaged?" he exclaimed in his gentle manner. She could almost see the expression on his face. "And he never mentioned a word about this girl before tonight?"

"Not a word, even to his brothers," Jane confirmed.

"Maybe he just wanted to be sure before he told everyone," Filip pondered.

"I'd call engaged pretty sure," Jane stated with conviction. Listening to her father's response, she could hear the smile in his voice.

"As I recall," Filip said, "your engagement to David was

quick and unexpected, and I would say that you two turned out quite well—very well."

"Dad, I agree with you wholeheartedly, and besides, I trust Eric's judgment."

"You are right there. He's a good boy. You and David have been good parents. I'm proud of you both, and so is your mom." Jane was quite enjoying her dad's words of compliment. "You know, honey," Filip continued as he chuckled in a deep and slightly devious tone, "I would love to hear your mother's version of all this. Let's not say anything about our conversation tonight. Just tell her everything as you normally would, and let's see what she gets out of it. What do you think?"

"Wicked, Dad, but fun; you have to promise me though that you'll call me after she tells you." Filip agreed, and they laughed.

"I know that you have had quite a few toasts today, but could you stand one more?" Filip asked.

"Dinner is not getting cold on the table and, even if it was, a toast from you, Dad, always." Smiling in remembrance, Filip began.

"Many gifts come to us. Like a Clue board game that a young girl so desperately wanted and then received from Santa one special Christmas. Bet you thought that I forgot?" Jane giggled. How she had wanted that game and how angry she used to get with her sister when Ann repeatedly stole the weapons. "Gifts come in all forms, and each time one is received, it seems the best one of all." Filip paused as they both seemed lost in their own memories. Only a moment passed as he quickly continued. "There is only one gift that is the best one of all, and that is the gift of love discovered and shared between one man and one woman. When the joining of that love creates a family, that love expands and reaches out, and unlike other tangible gifts it is never outgrown or cast aside; it only ripens and deepens with time. That gift was renewed for you and David today. Cherish it always and nurture it every day. Any day of your life that you can stand embraced by that kind of love, Jane, life is good. I raise my glass to you both."

Jane smiled through her tears; they were good tears. "I'm glad that Mom was sick, Dad … I mean … not really, but you know what I mean don't you, Dad?"

"Yes, honey," Filip responded with equal emotion in his voice, "I know what you mean."

CHAPTER 21

How many times had Jane traversed these floors, yet now everything seemed so different. Growing up had changed her perception, and as she stood in the bedroom of her childhood, how small it seemed even as it echoed in emptiness. Walking to the window, she rested her hands on the sill. How low the sill seemed to her now. And the tree, the same tree that had tapped at her window, sometimes in code she was convinced, and had nestled in its arms the baby birds of spring—where had it gone? Cut down years ago when her childhood had become a memory. Had she forgotten or had she just expected that it was always there? Staring, she saw nothing as her eyes and her mind were clouded and troubled. Just for a few moments she imagined as her mind relaxed into the comfort of her thoughts, she would gladly trade her heels for Mary Janes and slip blissfully into the days when everything really was as she remembered. Shaking her head, Jane left the window and walked to the door as she heard her name being called from downstairs. Closing the door behind her, the latch clicked firmly into place, seemingly locking out yesterday and forcing the movement forward into today.

Slowly Jane made her way down the stairway. Pausing often, she tried to burn as much as she could into her memory; the feel of the old woolen carpet under her feet, the sight of the robin's egg blue of the walls, the smoothness of the grooved walnut banister, and the vision of the stained-glass window inset in the wall at the landing. Stopping to look at the window, she admired the pattern, that of a large apple tree resplendent with bright green leaves and luscious red apples. How her father had loved it as it always reminded him of the promise of harvest. Concentrating, Jane did not want to forget anything. This house was her father; it was his dream and his father's dream. If she could just remember the look and the touch, then maybe she wouldn't have to say good-bye. She had said good-bye when her dad died; she didn't want to do it again when she left her home, his home.

As Jane entered the living room, she joined Wilma and Ann. The rooms of the old farmhouse were now empty except for the two fireplace rockers that had yet to be moved to Wilma's new house. The cheerful robin's egg blue walls could do little to lift the somber mood. Wilma's eyes were red from crying, and Ann's usually combative attitude had given way to defeat. "This stinks," Ann blurted out as her gaze panned the vacant rooms. Catching her mother's distraught expression, Ann quickly wrapped her arms around her mother and whispered in apology. "I'm sorry, Mom. I didn't mean to be hurtful. This was a family decision, and we all know that it was the best thing to do but, Mom"—Ann's breath caught as her own emotions gained expression—"is it okay if it still stinks?"

Wiping renewed tears from her eyes, Wilma reached for Ann's face and kissed her cheek. "It's okay, Ann. This does stink." After Filip's death two years earlier, Wilma had tried to run the farm. There was plenty of money to hire help and to continue the practical premise of operating the farm. But there was more than money and plowing needed, and Filip knew it and he had it—heart and spirit. Farming had been in his blood, in his instinct, and in his intuition. It was his gift. Not all can be taught, and like all true talent, it can be honed if present but never instilled if absent.

Filip had never wanted Wilma to keep the farm if anything happened to him. They had agreed that the farm would be sold when that day came. But when that unexpected day came, Wilma just could not do it, not without trying first. It would be like losing him again, and she couldn't bear it. And so she tried for almost two years. The farm performed as it could but not as it should. The fields produced and the buildings held, but something in the farm was dying. It needed the hands of those that had passion. Seeing Filip's life work slip little by little into decay was worse than losing it altogether. Wilma had called her family together, and they had discussed and decided on a necessary course of action, one they felt Filip would be pleased with.

The farm would not be sold in the traditional sense. Instead it was to become a teaching farm affiliated with the state university where the next generation of farmers could continue the traditions of tilling and harvesting the earth while learning new techniques for the farming of the future. It was an ambitious proposition, but after much negotiation and hard work an agreement was reached and all legal documentation completed. Wilma found comfort finally as Filip's dream was not dying; it was growing and expanding. Still on this day, the last day that their home would be home it was hard, so terribly hard. Still standing in the living room, Wilma found her eyes fixating on the doorway.

"You know, right after your dad died, there was so much

activity. You girls were here, and there was so much to be done and figured out that it never seemed quiet. And then when everything settled down and life somehow continued, that was the worst time, when it was quiet. In the evening when the sun would begin to set, I would sit here in the rocker, and I would wait. I would wait for him to come through that door just as he did every night when his work was done. How he used to fill that doorway. Do you both remember?" Ann and Jane nodded only, as words were just too painful. "And I'd wait and wait, but he didn't come, and I knew that he wouldn't, but I would still wait and watch. You never let go when you love somebody. Not when you say your final good-bye. Not when you close and lock the door."

Jane saw the tears begin to flow in her mother's eyes as Ann sobbed softly. Jane wished she could cry with them, but she felt a need to be strong. Putting her arms around them and drawing them close, she whispered words of encourage-ment and solace. Spotting her mother's familiar lapel pin, Jane touched it gently. "Mom, you have been wearing that pin for as long as I can remember, Uncle Joe's military wings."

Wilma touched the pin with warm acknowledgement. It was indeed true. She had worn the pin every day since the day that she had received it in the mail. It was included in the last correspondence that she had received from her brother, and it was a prized possession of mind and touch. There was little that she had from her own family, a few pictures and memories of course. It had been a family joke that the day that Wilma had landed her plane in the fields of the Krysochowski farm she was grounded permanently. Wilma agreed that she was and without regret. Though there had been a life before this place, this home and this family was her beginning and would always be her foundation.

Wishing to stay in the community, Wilma had purchased a small home closer to town for her transition after leaving the farm. It was close to Ann's house as well. An unlikely kinship had also developed over the past two years. Natasha Iverson, who had been widowed for almost five years, had mellowed enough for her and Wilma to have formed a bond of friendship. Still prone to extravagant dress, the vision of the two together was a picture of stark contrast, but in spirit it worked. Natasha laughed a bit more, and Wilma attempted a bit more polish in her attire. They joined in the commonality of loss and in it found companionship, helping each other in the tenuous movements ahead.

The small group remained in huddled comfort until Jane broke free. "Mom," Jane blurted out with alarm. "What about *Wilma's Wings?* What about your plane? What's going to happen to it?"

Wilma smiled for the first time that day. "The Smithsonian took it for their Aerospace museum," she responded proudly.

"Mom," Ann admonished immediately, "please don't tell me that you told them that kooky story about that rich guy that supposedly bought you the plane. It would embarrass even me."

Wilma's smile broadened. "True, it was a story, *but* it was a true story. I had the original bill of sale," she finished with obvious satisfaction. Both Ann and Jane froze in obvious surprise and shock.

"You never showed us!" they answered in sibling unison. "How could you have kept that from us all of this time?"

Wilma winked, looking almost like her old self. "Knowing can be boring, imagining is much more fun, and the story, well..."—she hugged her daughters—"that's what keeps it interesting." Taking in a deep breath, Wilma exhaled and then smiled. A few steps forward were finally in order. "You two have been in this house all morning. Go out and stretch your legs." When Ann and Jane shook their heads no vigorously, it promptly became apparent that Wilma was not accepting their protests. "Go, you two," she commanded as she shuffled her two daughters to the back door.

Exiting the kitchen, Ann and Jane found themselves stepping down the familiar back porch treads and then strolling into the yard. They began walking quietly in no particular direction, letting instinct and memory guide their path. Silence gave way to casual conversation. It was a pleasant passing as they caught up on family news and local happenings and gossip. The current day's events were strictly avoided as the fresh breeze of the outdoors kept the sadness at their backs. They were quite enjoying themselves when Ann abruptly stopped walking. "Jane." Ann turned to her sister with an air of enlightenment in her voice. "Do you know where we are?"

Jane had been quite unaware of their course, so she paused for the first time to take in their surroundings. The light of recognition caught her expression. Pointing, she stared in disbelief for it had been years since she had stood in this place. "I can see the grove of trees right over there and the bridge just beyond." Ann nodded in agreement as Jane continued. "You couldn't possibly think that … " Ann did not wait for her sister to finish as she broke into a sprint for the trees as quickly as her middle-aged legs could travel. Jane, pausing only a moment in hesitation, began running in earnest pursuit. They reached the bridge together and, stepping without thought into the brackish water, crossed the narrow expanse. Standing at the top of the small waterfall that in this case seemed so much higher then they remembered, they said a prayer and started down the slippery crag. Once at the bottom, they traveled but a few steps and stood before what they sought but in true belief thought that they would not find. Standing together with muddied feet and wet and stained pants, Ann and Jane stared in awe at the half dead willow tree of their childhood, the last-known resting place of Captain Dogel's infamous eye. Ann was the first to speak.

"It's still here after all of these years!" Ann exclaimed. "It doesn't look too good though." Jane agreed, though as they looked at the condition of the tree and then looked at the condition of each other in comparison, they couldn't help but laugh.

"Well," Jane answered their unspoken question, "we may be older, but we still look a sight better than that tree." It was true as the tree looked as if its best days were behind it as its limbs were few and the base of its trunk was littered with all manner of leaves, rubbish, and broken tree appendages. Jane was still in observant thought as Ann began poking around the base of the tree. Catching her sister's actions, Jane shook her head. "Ann, it can't possibly still be here, not after all of this time." Her protests belied her actions as she too began pushing aside debris in search. The pace increased beyond passive interest as branches and leaves were being thrown skyward in an all out effort to find it. One large branch had fallen and lay unmoving off to the side of the willow. Joining forces, Jane and Ann huffed and heaved and pulled at the large limb in an unrelenting force of mind and body. Finally the branch rolled, and the newly exposed ground seemed to reveal only a mush of decaying wood. Sweat and dirt streaked their faces, but they were unaware as their eyes remained focused in search through the new wreckage.

Ann was first to spot a small piece of wood with what appeared to be carving on it. An appearance was all that was needed as instantly both women fell to their knees, and with their hands began sifting through the earthen mess. Hands soon became caked with mud as did their clothes but they cared not for they were the obsessed participants of a quest from which they could not relent. Jane stopped for a moment as she leaned back on her knees to catch her breath. Looking at Ann for the first time with some semblance of reason, she pointed in shock at her sister's filth-ridden appearance. The shock melted quickly into hysteria as Jane began to laugh so hard that she literally choked. Ann did not stop her endeavor for a second, but her lips were still free to respond.

"Oh, so you think that I look bad, do you?" she countered snidely. "How do you think that you look?" Jane, taking in her sister's comments, took a good look at her own disheveled self; it only made her laugh harder.

"Funny, huh." Ann stopped digging. "Well, look at what I found." Opening her tightly clutched hand, Ann revealed the very dirty but very recognizable eye of Captain Dogel. They knelt in the mud dumbstruck. It was as if the most valuable jewel in the world had just been unearthed. Jane reached out her hand, and Ann gently placed the treasure in her palm. Rolling it between her palm and her fingers, Jane attempted to clean it, and when she felt that she had done her best, she opened her fingers to reveal their find.

"I can't believe it. Even with it here in my hand, I still can't believe it. After all of this time ... " Frozen in moments past they remained physically unmoved and fixated on the small stone before them. "What should we do with it now? I don't want to leave it here, do you, Ann?" Ann shook her head.

"Perhaps," Jane began with hesitation, "perhaps now is the time when we should finally return Captain Dogel's eye to the sea. Lisa would be proud of us at least."

"No," they answered in harmony.

"I know," Ann said happily. "You can take the captain's eye back to Maine and keep it in a jar on the windowsill in the kitchen. That way he will always have a great view of the sea. How about that?"

"Close enough," Jane agreed enthusiastically. "A fitting view rather than an unhappy ending for Captain Dogel's eye."

Rising from their knees at last, they stretched stiffly. Standing facing each other, they brushed themselves off in a hopeless attempt at regaining some propriety befitting their age; it was an impossible task.

"We look worse than we did on the pig feed days," Ann commented in contented disgust. Jane smiled. She didn't care as the treasure found had been more than worth it.

"We had better head back," Jane advised, taking one last look around. "I hope that you remember the way."

"We both do," Ann answered as she turned to begin the trek back home.

CHAPTER 22

They made love early in the morning. It was an annual tradition. Not that they didn't make love throughout the year, but the morning of their wedding anniversary was special, a consecration of their love physically and emotionally.

Leaning her head against David's shoulder, Jane inhaled slowly and softly with satisfaction. "It is so hard to believe that this is our thirty-fifth wedding anniversary."

"Yes. And that everything is still operational is even more amazing," David added. Jane gave David a well-deserved poke to his ticklish side. Countering a second attack, David instead grabbed his wife and pulled her to him. Resting back against the softness of the pillows, they nestled comfortably in each other's arms. The scent of freshly brewed coffee began to permeate the room as the morning sun stretched out and reached higher into the welcoming sky. Sniffing the traditional morning brew, an expression of remembrance crossed Jane's face.

"All of the modern conveniences." Jane began as she verbalized her thoughts. "We've worn out three automatic coffee pots fully equipped with timers, brew sensors, and all manner of filters, and none of them can make a cup of coffee that tastes as good as Mary's did."

Kissing his companion's furrowed forehead, David answered quickly. "What automatic anything makes anything with love? That was Mary's secret ingredient, and it cannot be duplicated by a machine." Jane nodded in complete agreement. Mary had been missed for almost five years. She had left them with so many gifts as not a day passed that there was not a reminder of her special touch, even something as simple as a cup of coffee.

"Okay, deep thinker, back to the moment at hand," David said. "So who's going first this year, you or me?"

"What do you mean, who's going first this year, you or me?" Jane answered. "You made the statement over a month ago that we were getting too old for this childish competition of gift giving for our anniversary, did you not?"

Smiling with just a hint of slyness to his expression, David attempted to soothe his wife by explaining. "Now, don't get angry. I just didn't want to put any additional pressure on you. You get very snippy when you lose. You have to be honest because it's true." Jane smiled and nodded her head yes just a little too submissively. "Besides," David continued to coo, "you have given me so much. You did not need to buy me a thing."

Kissing David's cheek affectionately, Jane smiled coyly. "You are so right, sweetheart. I did not buy a thing. That is, not one word of that 'we're getting too old' ploy, and I am going first this year because no matter your follow-up, I'm going to kick gift butt this year." Hopping out of bed and just missing a slight slap to her own butt, Jane promptly went to retrieve her sequestered gift for David.

Jane sat quietly. Staring at her reflection in the mirror, she touched with affection the single and simple strand of pearls that graced her neck. They spoke, without words, the story of love. That something so beautiful could come from the joining of two elements—a grain of sand and an oyster, a man and a woman. That its worth is not evident in an instant, rather it grows in luster and value over toil and time.

Joining his wife, David stood behind Jane and admired the vision that he saw. He did not see the fine lines that life offers to the face of those that travel further down its path. He did not see the errant strands of gray hair that stubbornly resisted the remedy of coloring. He did not see the rounding of physical shape that the changing of life and time with certainty brings. What he saw, in his mind and thus in his eye, was the same beautiful woman that he had married so many years before. Years that still seemed but a few days and at the same time seemed forever. Remaining silent, he kissed the top of Jane's head as she smiled.

"I love the pearls." Jane spoke first as her fingers continued to ply and admire the pearls. "I couldn't love them any more even though they were not the winning gift." David, still silent, reached into his pocket and pulled from it an object, a pocket watch, his anniversary gift from Jane. Holding it as precious treasure in his hand, gently he pressed the button on the side and the watch chimed softly to life, striking in a sweet sound and with rhythmic precision five times; it was indeed five hours past twelve.

"Your dad's pocket watch." He almost questioned rather than stated in fact as he stared at the watch in his hand in disbelief. "I remember the times that your father took this watch from his pocket and all that he had to do was push the button and the chime was enough to tell me that it was time to head home." They both laughed as they shared the memory. "After your dad died, I never knew what happened to the watch, and I didn't feel that I had the right to ask. That you would give this to me now...I never had anything from my..." David stopped as his voice choked with emotion. Jane, turning and rising from her seat, took her hands and wrapped them around David's as the watch stayed firmly in his grasp.

"Dad loved you as he loved me. When Mom gave me the watch, she knew as did I who Dad would have wanted to have it. You were the son of his heart. You know that, don't you?" Jane did not wait for an answer knowing that the question was really a confirmation of what they both knew. "Dad would be...is so happy that you have what was his and what was his father's." Smiling, Jane added, "It is old, but when I had it serviced, I was told that except for a few minor adjustments, it is in great shape. All ready for today and for the generations to come."

Shifting his hands to wrap around Jane's, David stared with intensity into his wife's eyes. "I said earlier that there was nothing that you needed to buy me; it was true. What you gave me is a legacy. This is something that I never had. I make a promise to you, to your dad, and to his dad that it will continue with our sons and their sons. This means so much to me. I don't know how to say thank you." Jane wrapped her arms around her husband and squeezed him tight. As she held him in warm embrace, an impish thought entered her mind. Whispering into David's ear, she suggested that there was a way that he could say thank you. Surprised, David asked how.

"Tell me that I won again," she pleaded pleasantly. "I have only heard it about two times in all of our thirty-five years of anniversaries."

"I can't," David responded simply.

"What do you mean you can't?" Jane admonished indignantly.

"I can't because you are not the only winner," he countered with sincerity. "We both won."

Pausing a moment, Jane processed his answer. It took but a few seconds before a wide smile broke across her momentarily puzzled face. "It is a first in the competition!" Jane commented jubilantly.

"Yes," David agreed, and with welcome surrender, he added, "and the accomplishment is all yours."

All of the windows of the house were burning brightly with electric candelabras. As David and Jane approached the front door, they could hear the thunder of approaching feet from inside before they even touched the doorbell, an additional announcement which proved unnecessary. The wood door promptly swung open, and there appeared the crowded faces of their five grandchildren peering through the glass of the still-closed storm door, some on foot and one nestled safely in caring arms.

"Come in outta the cold, Grandma," called a small voice as an equally small hand reached out through the now slightly opened storm door. Jane willingly reached for and joined her hand with her granddaughter Olivia's hand and then, grabbing David's hand, allowed them to be pulled inside. Standing in the foyer of Michael and Gwen's home, Jane and David were immediately surrounded by their extended brood—their grandchildren. They were all there for the grand celebration. Stephen aged eleven, Ryan aged nine, and Olivia aged six were the offspring of Michael and Gwen. Angela aged three and Jennifer aged one month were Eric and Trish's children. Robert and his wife of eight years, Elizabeth, stood just outside of the circle of grandchildren. They had been trying for several years to have children but had not yet been blessed and were becoming more discouraged as the years passed.

Slowly, amid hugs, kisses, and lots of chatter, the huddle

moved united toward the living room. It was a great joy that they could all be together for the occasion as Michael and Gwen were the only members of the family that had stayed in Maine. Eric and his family lived in Boston, where he was a practicing pediatrician at a hospital in the city. Robert and Elizabeth lived in the outskirts of New York City, where Elizabeth's family resided. Robert's passion for questions had served his chosen occupation well as Robert was an investigative reporter and writer for a city newspaper. Expanding his interest in writing, he was also hard at work on his first novel, a crime story based on his experiences. Both Eric and Robert seemed to thrive in their adopted big cities, but it was always home when they came back to the old Victorian by the sea.

As they finally entered the living room another guest rose to greet them. Sylvia approached her two favorite people briskly, kissing David as always on the cheek while giving a warm squeeze to Jane's hand. Still in her starched hospital attire, Sylvia had come directly from the medical center, willingly transported by Robert and Elizabeth. Though almost seventy-five years of age, she had yet to retire from her duties, a welcome relief to her staff as they could not imagine PM Northeastern Medical Center without her. Still, she could no longer maintain the long hours that she once demanded of herself, so she had agreed to a reduction in her hours, the balance left to her amply able and equally stern assistant. There were no complaints uttered as she usually used her new and unaccustomed free time to board a train headed for the outskirts of New York City. Robert teased her on her frequent visits that she had indeed mellowed. True or not, it was never admitted, and Robert was the only one to dare say it and get away with it.

The group continued in pleasant conversation until the clanging of a bell slowed their words and then left them completely in pause. The intensity of the pealing increased, leaving the children frozen in their places, uttering not a word. Sounding loudly and clearly and seeming just outside of the front door, the ringing suddenly stopped. Then as if by a burst of air cast by magical breath, the door swung open wide. Aunt Cathy stood in the doorway dressed in a long red velvet coat trimmed in white with an equally elaborate red velvet hat on her head that was encircled with fresh holly and berries. By her side her good friend and companion of many years, Albert S. Winston—S. for Samuel not Santa as Albert would confirm and Catherine contest—stood with a bulging red velvet bag tied with gold tassels.

"Happy holidays and happy anniversary!" Aunt Catherine called out robustly. "Let all be merry and well occupied! Dump the sack, Albert!" Dump he did with the help of many small hands. All manner of ornately wrapped gifts tumbled from the bag and onto the floor. There was an attempt made at order, which was quickly surrendered. Aunt Catherine happily watched as the children, foraging through the pile of gifts, matched their names and then shredded the paper to reveal their prizes.

Jane and David, stepping tenderly through the happy chaos, hugged Aunt Cathy in welcome. "Sorry to be late." Aunt Cathy reciprocated with warm hugs and kisses. "But you know me. I can never resist a grand entrance, right, Albert?" Albert nodded in understanding. He was like one of Aunt Cathy's teddy bears, cuddly and warm and complete with bow tie. As the children played with their gifts, the adults took the opportunity to talk and to catch up with each other's lives. It was a pleasant passing that lasted, with many appreciative thanks to Aunt Cathy and Albert, until dinner was served.

A buffet of delicious foods steamed on the dining room table. Little ones were helped first and then seated together in a happy circle. The taller members helped themselves to the feast and then enjoyed juggling eating, walking, and talking.

Groans gave way to eyes so much bigger than stomachs as dessert was presented, accepted, and eaten. These were moments welcomingly void of reason and sensibilities. Though the clock reminded many of bedtimes expected, the usual routine was cast aside to allow the enjoyment to continue.

"How about a story?" David encouraged to claps and cheers. "No one tells a story better than Aunt Cathy. She has told me quite a few and very few from books." Aunt Cathy winked and laughed; she needed no encouragement.

"I have the perfect story, but I will need the help of, let me see … two boys and two girls." Stephen, Ryan, Olivia, and a confused but willing Angela volunteered immediately. "Now this is the story," she began as the children nestled at her feet, "of a lost Christmas elf named Albert, no relation … " Aunt Cathy gave Albert a wink as the room chuckled. "Albert was a very hard-working elf. He painted the smiles on dolls, a very important job. But Albert had a bit of a naughty streak, and he, on occasion, did what he wanted to do rather than what he should do, which would land him on the naughty list. Can you imagine that? You good children are never on the naughty list, are you?" Stephen, Ryan, Olivia, and Angela shook their heads vehemently.

"Well, Albert, like all of the Christmas elves, has a lot of work to do this time of year, and they are never supposed to leave the North Pole without Santa's permission. What do you think that Albert did?" The children began answering the question at the same time. "That's right." Aunt Cathy acknowledged. "He left the North Pole without permission, and do you want to know why?" Her enamored audience remained silent. "Albert wanted to go trick or treating. They don't have trick or treating at the North Pole, and Albert wanted to see what it was all about. He is a very curious elf. You may have seen him. He was dressed like a ghost." Halloween was still very fresh in their minds, and they had certainly seen a lot of ghosts.

"So, Albert, in his ghost costume and with his bag, went house to house and filled his bag full of candy. He was having a grand time. Now he had made a promise to himself that instead of eating the candy himself, he would take it back to the North Pole and share it with his friends. But"—Aunt Cathy sighed with appropriate drama—"the naughtiness came out in little Albert again, and he ate every last piece of candy. When he realized what he had done, he was so ashamed and sick that he did not go back to the North Pole that night. In fact, he is still here somewhere hiding."

Ryan, his face filled with concern, wondered, "Where do think that he's hiding, Aunt Cathy?"

"Well, I'm told from very good sources that elves love to hide in pine trees just like the ones behind this very house." There was a small stampede to the back door. Straining and seeing nothing that looked like an elf dressed as a ghost hunched or hanging in the pines, the kids quickly returned to Aunt Cathy for the rest of the story.

"Now I told you in the beginning," Aunt Cathy continued, "that I needed your help, well really, poor little Albert needs your help. I was told by my same secret source that if Albert could just find some candy for his friends, then he could take it back to the North Pole, and he wouldn't be ashamed." Adding quickly, "He would still be in trouble, but he wouldn't be ashamed. Now do you think that you children could find—" No further explanation was needed as all four children ran to the kitchen on a candy treasure hunt. Gwen got a bag, and the found sweets were deposited: some not-too-old but disliked Halloween candy, some coveted bubble gum, a few apples, and some of last year's candy canes, still good. When they showed the bag and its contents to Aunt Cathy, she smiled and nodded her head in approval.

"Now tie the bag tight. And put it just outside the door. If it's gone in the morning, you will know that Albert took it, and that he is on his way back to the North Pole with many thanks to you children, I can tell you." The bag was fastened, and Stephen, Ryan, Olivia, and Angela gently placed the bag on the porch just outside of the door.

"Do you really think that Albert will find the candy?" a very worried Olivia asked.

"As much as Albert likes candy?" Aunt Cathy answered with conviction. "Oh, he will certainly find it."

The evening's events settled into restful conversation. Sylvia and Catherine along with Albert had left, and the children, finally exhausted beyond the will to stay up, were all in bed.

"It was a shame that Grandma Wilma and Aunt Ann couldn't have been with us," Michael reflected with regret. The plan had been for Wilma and Ann to attend the anniversary celebration together, but Wilma had become ill with a nasty cold. Though it was not serious, it prevented Wilma from traveling. Ann, not wanting to leave her mother home alone, had also decided to stay home to attend to Wilma.

"I am so glad that Ann decided to stay home with her," Jane continued. "Mom was so upset about being prevented from coming that she threatened to fly herself. Thank God that she doesn't have the plane anymore." They all laughed. Holding David's hand in hers, Jane contented herself with listening. She felt warm and secure. Her children and their wives were with them, and their grandchildren were safe upstairs in bed. Jane's eyes suddenly widened, and the smile on her face relaxed in recognition. No one noticed the transformation in Jane's expression as she was the only one who was aware of the change in the room. He was there with them now, Golden Boy, and in that instance of awareness Jane realized where she was, when it was, and what it was that she needed to do. There would be no tears she promised herself though her heart began to beat faster; there would be only the words that she so wanted to say. Eric was in the middle of a story about one of his patients when Jane interrupted.

"I'm sorry, Eric, but I need to say a few things," Jane began as Eric stopped talking. All eyes were immediately cast toward Jane with full attention. "First, I just want to say how much I...I mean how much we have enjoyed this evening. It was wonderful, just perfect really, I..." Stuttering and stumbling, she paused, wanting to continue yet uncertain, not knowing where to start. Desperately she looked at Golden Boy, who was standing relaxed in the corner of the room, unseen by everyone except Jane. As his eyes locked with hers, the confusion in her mind melted, and her once muted words gave voice to her heart. "This seems to be the perfect time, and there are few in life that we are privileged to realize, to tell you all how I feel about you, all of you." The air in the room was one of puzzlement as Jane let go of David's hand and stood.

"Mom, this sounds awfully heavy for an anniversary speech," Robert interjected as Jane turned in a circle, slowly including each person in the room in her vision.

"You have no idea," Jane answered with intended vagueness. David was mesmerized by his wife's unexpected actions, but not knowing exactly what he should do, he did nothing and stayed seated. Walking to Michael first, Jane knelt before him and reached for his hand as well as for Gwen's.

"I remember how lost you were when you first came to us; I worried about you the most. Then the surprise; you were the first to call me Mom. Do you remember?" Michael smiled and nodded. "Now here you sit, master of your own home...well, one of two masters." Jane squeezed Gwen's hand in deference as other voices in the room chuckled. "You are a loving husband and father and a much loved son and brother. You have given us, the both of you, three amazing grandchildren that your father and I have been blessed to watch grow. I am so proud of both of you. Life is such a gift, and you have been such a gift to my life … to all of our lives." Rising, Jane kissed both Michael and Gwen and then walked quietly to Eric and Trish. David watched with questions unspoken, confused by his wife's urgency and intensity. This anniversary was certainly different. Kneeling before Eric and Trish, she took their hands in hers.

"Eric, my little boy with the big heart, now the man with the bigger heart, and your Trish, an anniversary surprise as I recall, and a wonderful surprise she was and still is." Trish smiled at her mother-in-law as tears touched her eyes. "Two beautiful children and maybe more, but we won't talk about that now." Both Eric and Trish laughed as labor was too fresh in their minds to think about the prospect of another. Focusing her eyes solely on Eric, Jane continued, "Do you remember what you did after Daniel died?" The smile disappeared into shadow on Eric's face as he nodded; he would never forget. Looking at Eric's hand held in hers, Jane observed, "You gave a part of your heart that day to save me with a hand much smaller than this." Jane squeezed his hand gently. "God gave you the gift of the infinite. That you can give so much of your heart and still have ample to live and to love and to keep giving, that is the infinite. You have given it to me and to so many others. I love you for it and for so many things … for just you." The group sat in stunned silence, but Jane took no notice as she was not yet finished. Jane next went to Robert and Elizabeth and, as with the others, knelt before them and took their hands in hers.

"The little questioner." Jane smiled. Everyone in the room laughed, including Robert as nothing had changed from his youth. "You were like a light bulb that was constantly being turned off and on. You made us laugh then, and now you make us and a lot of other people think."

"And still laugh," Michael could not help adding. Taking both Robert's and Elizabeth's hands firmly in her own, Jane continued.

"You never knew my Babcia Grand." Robert nodded in agreement as Grand had died long before he and his brothers had come to live with Jane and David. "She told me something once, and I want to share it with you both now." Jane paused briefly to clarify her thoughts. "She said that what we receive may not be what was asked for or even wished for because often what we do receive is so much more than we could ever have imagined or dreamed. I know this to be true. Do you know why?" Jane stopped in question, watching the emotion of childless pain shroud their faces. She recognized it as she had seen it in her own reflection many times. "I know it to be true because not more than two years after Grand shared her words with me, God gave you, Eric, and Michael to us—a gift so much greater than we could ever have dreamed or imagined." Rising and hugging both Robert and Elizabeth, one last thought of comfort came into her mind, a thought given by a friend. Leaning and whispering, she offered the same words of hope that she had received long ago. "Good will grow where the rain has fallen."

Turning slowly from them, she knew that only one person remained that she had yet to address, and he would be the most difficult. Walking to David, she remained standing before him, taking his hands in hers. She spoke without regard to the questioning expression on his face. There was nothing to explain. There were only the words she so needed to say.

"To think that you were once a stranger to me, now I cannot imagine my life without you." Jane's voice finally began to choke with emotion. Holding back the tears, she refused to surrender to them, not until her task was complete. As David began to rise from his seat to comfort her, Jane tenderly put her hand up to stop him; it was not the time, not yet. Regaining some degree of composure, she continued, "Every happiness, every joy, and every moment of completeness in my life has come from an expression of love: the love from friends, the love from family, the love from you, my husband."

Stopping as if listening to words that only she could hear, Jane smiled and then looked into the eyes of the man that she had loved for over thirty-five years. "Dad told me once that the greatest love is the love shared between one man and one woman and any day that your life can be embraced by that kind of love; life is good, so very, very good. That day has been every day of our life together. Even with the tears and the sorrows, there always has and there always will be love." There were only two people in the room at that moment as Jane's and David's eyes were frozen upon each other. Jane spoke one last time with the simplicity and yet the importance of a last breath. "Thank you, David. Thank you for a life so very, very good." David was stunned beyond speech, yet Jane pulled her vision from David and looked over her shoulder seemingly toward Eric, but it was not Eric that she was seeing. "I did it," Jane said to her golden-haired companion as her eyes filled with tears. "I did it." David was on his feet in an instant, wrapping his arms around his now openly weeping wife.

"What did you do?" David asked as the rest of the family still remained glued to their seats. As the room emptied by one, Jane sniffed and then looked at David curiously.

"What did I do?" Jane responded. "I told my family how much that I love them and how proud I am of them. Whatever is wrong with that?" she finished feistily.

Robert was the first to break free from the frozen stance of the rest of the family. Hopping up from his seat, he hugged his mother. "You were awfully sentimental, Mom."

Kissing Robert on the cheek, Jane answered his concern. "It's just age and hormones. Just you wait. No one escapes!" The strange mood lifted, and the family returned to normal.

"Well," David commented with a firm arm still around Jane, "it's getting late, and I think that I should get your overly sentimental mother home. No champagne for you tonight," David stated as he left Jane's side to retrieve their coats.

"You older folks can head out, but we, the younger generation, are going to hang around a bit to talk about things that our parents shouldn't know about," Robert jested. "We'll see you both a little later, okay?" Both Eric and his family and Robert and Elizabeth were staying with Jane and David for the visit.

"Not a problem," Jane answered with ease. "Us 'old folks' need our sleep." Kisses, hugs, and thanks were handed out generously, and then Jane and David left to travel home in the cold night air.

Sitting in the car, Jane nestled into her coat. The engine had just started, and the car was as cold as she was. It had been a wonderful evening, an evening preserved in memory to be remembered and relived often. David shifted the car into drive, and it began to putter stubbornly off. The first of the Christmas music tinkled on the radio. A quiet comfort settled. Jane contented herself with catching a glimpse of the occasional home that was already decorated with Christmas lights. Still, she watched David's face in silent observation as the lights flickered and changed colors; the same face that she had known and loved all of these years, his face, always his face.

As an image that burns still brightly in the mind though no longer to the eye, so it was that Jane saw still his face. Through the darkness, the image of David's face shimmered brightly, and she saw it so. But as hard as Jane tried to hold onto the comfort that she saw, like all images absent, David's at last faded into the darkness. Opening her eyes at last, Jane found herself in familiar surroundings, the same as before as if this place and this moment, no matter where she was, seemed to be standing still in waiting.

The train station was the same, quaint, Victorian in structure, and graced with lilacs in bloom. Jane sat in numb silence, not knowing if what had happened had really happened. He was there, Golden Boy, sitting at the opposite end of the bench. Jane could not help smiling at him. What a journey they had shared. Turning her head to the right, she observed the same two trains resting on the same track, caboose to caboose, huffing and puffing restlessly. *What now?* she wondered.

"How do you feel?" her companion asked, compassion in his voice.

"I don't know," Jane answered honestly. "I feel happy and sad, contented and unsettled, focused and confused all at the same time."

Her friend nodded in understanding. "As I recall the last thing that you said to me was that you 'did it.' What did you do?"

Jane smiled as she remembered her words, her last words. "I did what I set out to do. I told the people that I loved most in the world, my family, how I felt about them and how much I loved them. But what did I really do, really? Did they really hear what I said, or was it all just a performance played out for my benefit?" Jane stared and waited, not knowing what to expect in answer.

Golden Boy slid easily down the bench as if on wings of air. Taking Jane's hand in his, he patted it gently. "Your words did not change the outcome, did they? You are here, and everything happened as it did and is happening as it should, right?" Jane agreed in despair. Indeed she was right back where it had all started, and nothing seemed changed. "The only difference is," he continued, smiling broadly, "that you have left behind words of love and comfort that they will always remember, words guided by the intimacy of intuition of what was to come it will be said. You have heard of this before from other people's experiences, haven't you, Jane?"

Jane's expression ignited with recognition. It was true. She had heard many times of words spoken and thoughts shared to the ears of loved ones yet to be left behind from the lips of those who then passed unexpectedly, as if somehow knowing what was to come. It was true that nothing had really changed, but for Jane everything had changed. They would remember her words and keep them always: her one last comfort, her one last gift. "I did do it, didn't I?" Jane said, smiling as she squeezed her companion's hand. Smiling in return, he nodded his head in agreement. Taking in a deep breath, Jane released the air from her lungs, and with it the painful anxiety that had lingered there. They would remember; they would always remember. Her heart and her soul felt light, and she lapsed into silence, enjoying the beauty and the fragrance of her surroundings for the first time. Passengers with the familiar unfamiliar faces began milling around the station, which caused Jane to become aware again of her current situation.

"Now what?" Jane pondered.

"Now," her guider answered, "I make you the same offer that I did before. You can take the same train back to your life before and relive all or just parts of it, or you can board the other train and journey forward."

"What is the journey forward?" Jane asked with uncertainty.

"The same journey that we all take, that we must take," he responded simply.

It wasn't so simple to decide as Jane's brow furrowed with consternation. She knew what was back, but she had no idea what was forward. Finally the wrinkles rested and smoothed as her soul guided her answer.

"To go back again would be like reliving a dream, a wonderful dream, but the dream of a life already lived nonetheless.

I think … " She paused as the answer was still difficult as her words would bring a finality that her thoughts could no longer escape. "I think that I need to wake up, to take my dreams, my life as I knew it, and tuck them as memories as they should be, as they are. I have done what I wanted to do. Now I need to do what I should do. I am ready."

Jane finished with the needed conviction. Without notice, one train left without sound, leaving one train waiting on the track. Rising from her seat, Jane prepared to board. Expecting her companion to join her, Jane paused in her progression as she became aware that he was still seated. It also became apparent that the strangers that had once roamed aimlessly now stood motionless around the bench, and they were no longer strangers; they were family.

Jane felt as if her eyes were playing tricks, but his voice was unmistakable. "Hello, sweetheart," Filip said as he came toward his daughter. He took but a few steps as Jane ran to him and threw herself into his open arms. He was as she remembered, tall and broad. Sobbing, she burrowed deeper into his embrace and inhaled deeply. Oh, it was him! The scent of his pipe and the richness of the earth that he toiled filled her senses and her heart. He was there with her; he was really there. Feeling a hand on her shoulder, Jane pulled back slightly from her father and turned her head. It was Grand, no longer frail and sickly but straight and regal. There were no words at all, no words needed as she grabbed her grandmother in a most unladylike fashion and held her tight in her arms. Jane didn't care as there was not a rule or a propriety that could have held her back. The rest of the family greeted Jane, some she knew and some she would come to know. It was overwhelming. Golden Boy finally made his way through the tight group and put his arm around Jane.

"You didn't think that I was going to let you take this trip all by yourself, did you?" he said warmly. Jane shook her head no and then wrapped her arms around her faithful guider in a loving embrace. Whispering into his ear, she finally found the words.

"This was more," Jane uttered through her tears, "so much more than good-bye."

"Mom," he whispered back, "life always is."

|LIVE

listen|imagine|view|experience

AUDIO BOOK DOWNLOAD INCLUDED WITH THIS BOOK!

In your hands you hold a complete digital entertainment package. In addition to the paper version, you receive a free download of the audio version of this book. Simply use the code listed below when visiting our website. Once downloaded to your computer, you can listen to the book through your computer's speakers, burn it to an audio CD or save the file to your portable music device (such as Apple's popular iPod) and listen on the go!

How to get your free audio book digital download:

1. Visit www.tatepublishing.com and click on the e|LIVE logo on the home page.
2. Enter the following coupon code:
   559b-0171-5744-47c8-cdac-dbe8-4e01-2b79
3. Download the audio book from your e|LIVE digital locker and begin enjoying your new digital entertainment package today!